HAUNTS &
HORRORS

HAUNTS & HORRORS

STRANGE & SUPERNATURAL FICTION BY M. P. SHIEL

COACHWHIP PUBLICATIONS

Landisville, Pennsylvania

Haunts & Horrors: Strange and Supernatural Fiction by M. P. Shiel
Copyright © 2012 Coachwhip Publications
No claim made on public domain material.

M. P. Shiel (1865-1947)

ISBN 1-61646-119-5
ISBN-13 978-1-61646-119-5

Cover Image: Viking Ship © Krystsina Birukova

CoachwhipBooks.com

CONTENTS

HUGUENIN'S WIFE

Huguenin, my friend—the man of Art and thrills and impulses,—the finished *boulevardier*, the *persifleur*—must, I concluded with certainty, be frenzied. So, at least, I reasoned when, after long years of silence, I received from him this letter:—

"'*Sdili*,' my friend; that is the name by which they now call this ancient Delos. Wherefore has it been written, 'so passeth the glory of the world.'

"Ah! but to me it is—as to *her* it was—still Delos, the Sacred Island, the birthplace of Apollo, son of Leto! On the summit of Cynthus I look from my dwelling, and within the wide reach of the Cyclades perceive even yet the fruity offerings arriving from Syria, from Sicily, from Egypt; I see the barks that bring the sacred envoys of Pan-Ionium to festival—I note the flutter of their hallowed garments—on the breeze once more floats to me their 'Songs of Deliverance.'

"The island now belongs almost entirely to me. I am, too, almost its sole inhabitant. It is, you know, only four miles long, and half as broad, and I have purchased every available foot of its surface. On the flat top of the granite Cynthus I live, and here, my friend, shall I die. Chains more inexorable and horrible than any which the limbs of Prometheus ever knew bind me to this crag.

"A friend! a friend! That is the thing after which my sick spirit pants. A *living man*: of the dead I have enough; of

living monsters, ah, too much! An aged servant or two, who
seem persistently to shun me—this is all I possess of human
fellowship. Would that I dared to ask you, an old companion, to come to the solace of a sinking man in this place of
desolation!"

The letter continued long in this strain of mingled rhapsody
and despair, containing, moreover, a lengthy disquisition on the
Pythagorean doctrine of the metempsychosis of the soul. Three
times did the words "living monsters" occur. Such a communication,
coming from *him*, did not fail to excite my utmost curiosity and pity.

From London to Delos is no inconsiderable journey; yet,
conquered during the course of a long vacation by an irresistible
impulse, and the fond memories of other days, I actually found
myself, on a starry night, disembarking on the sands that bound
the once famous harbour of the tiny Greek island. My arrival may
be dated by the fact that it fell out just two months before the very
extraordinary natural phenomena of which Delos was the scene
during the night of August 13th, 1880. I crossed the ring of flat
land which nearly encircles the islet, and began the ascent of the
central mountain. The slumberous air languished with the wild
breath of rose and jessamine and almond; the pipe of the cicala
and the gleam of the firefly were not wanting to add to the nar-
cotic charms of this land of dreams. In less than an hour I walked
into a tangled garden, and placed my hand on the shoulder of a
tall, stooping man, dressed in Attic attire, who walked solitary
under the trees.

With a fearful start he turned and faced me.

"Oh," he said, panting, and placing both his hands upon his
chest, "I was greatly surprised! My heart—"

He could utter no more. It was Huguenin, and yet not he. The
heavy beard rolling down his white woollen garments was, I could
see, still black as ever; but the masses of unkempt hair which
floated with every zephyr about his face and neck were bleached
to the whiteness of snow. He stared at me through the dull and
cavernous eyes of a man long dead.

We walked into the house together. The mere sight of the building was enough to convince me that in some mysterious way, to some morbid degree, the Past had fettered and darkened the intellect of my friend. The mansion was of the purely Hellenic type, but nothing less than inconceivable in extent—a wilderness rather than a habitation. I found myself in an ancient Greek house—only, a Greek house multiplied many times over into an endless, continuous congeries of Greek houses. It consisted of a single story, though here and there on the vast flat roof there rose a second layer of apartments. These latter were reached by ladders. We walked through a door—opening inwards—into a passage, which in turn led us to an oblong marble court-yard; this was the *aule*, surrounded by Corinthian pillars, and having in the centre an altar of stone to *Zeus Herkeios*. Around this court on every hand was ranged a series of halls, chambers, *thalamoi*, hung with rich velvets; and the whole mighty house—made up of a hundred and a hundred reproductions of such court-yards with their surrounding chambers—formed a trackless desert of rooms, through whose uniform labyrinths the most cunning would assuredly fail to find his way.

"This building," said Huguenin to me, some days after my arrival, "this building—every stone, plank, drapery of it—was the creation of my wife's wild and restless fancy."

I stared at him.

"You doubt that I have, or had, a wife? Come, then, with me; you shall—you shall—see her face."

He led the way through the dark and windowless house, lighted throughout the day and night by the dim purple radiance shed from many small, open lamps of earthenware filled with the fragrant *nardinum*, an oil pressed from the flower of the Arabian grass *nardus*.

I followed the emaciated figure of Huguenin through a great number of the gloomy chambers. As he moved slowly forward, visibly panting, I noticed that he kept his form bent downward, seeming to seek for something; and this something I soon found to be a scarlet thread, laid down to afford guidance for the feet through the mazes of the house, and running along the black floor. Suddenly he stopped before the door of one of the apartments called *amphithalamoi*, and, himself remaining without, motioned to me to enter.

I am not a man of what might be called "a tremulous diathesis," yet not without a tremor did I glance round the room. For a time I could discern nothing under the sombre glimmer radiated from a single *lampas* pendent from wrought brazen chains. But at length a great painting in oils, unframed, occupying nearly one whole side of the chamber, grew upon my sight. It was the picture of a woman. My heart throbbed with a most strange, deep excitement as I gazed upon her lineaments.

She stood erect, robed in a flowing, crimson, embroidered *peplos*, with head slightly thrown back, and one hand and arm pointing stiffly outward and upward. The countenance was not merely Grecian—ancient Grecian, as distinct from modern—but it was so in a highly exaggerated and unlifelike degree. Was the woman, I asked myself, more lovely than ever mortal was before— or more hideous? She was the one or the other, or both; but the riddle baffled me. The Lamia of Keats arose before me—that "shape of gorgeous hue, vermilion-spotted, golden, green and blue." A hardly-breathing surprise of eyes held me fixed as the image slowly took possession of my vision. Here, then, I muttered, was the Gorgon's head, whose hair was serpents and her eye a basilisk's; and as I so thought, I reflected, too, on the myth of how from the dripping blood of Medusa's head strange creatures sprang to life; and then, with a shuddering abhorrence, I remembered Huguenin's childish ravings about "monsters." I drew nearer, in order to analyse the impression almost of dread wrought upon me, and I quickly found—or thought I found—the key. It lay, surely, in the woman's eyes. They were the very eyes of the tiger: circular, green, large, with glittering yellow radii. I hurried from the room.

"You have seen her?" asked Huguenin, with a cunning, eager distortion of his ashen face.

"Yes, Huguenin, I have seen her. She is very beautiful."

"She painted it herself," he said in a whisper.

"Really!"

"She considered herself—she *was*—the greatest painter who has lived since Apelles."

"But now—where is she now?"

He brought his lips quite close to my ear.

"She is dead. You, at any rate, would call her so."

This ambiguity appeared to me only the more singular when I discovered that it was his habit, at stated intervals, to make regular and stealthy visits to distant parts of the dwelling. Our bed-chambers being contiguous, I could not fail, as time passed, to notice that he would rise in the dead of night, when he supposed me asleep, and gathering together the fragments of our last meal, depart rapidly and silently with them through the dim and vast house, led always in one particular direction by the scarlet thread of silk which ran along the floor.

I now set myself strenuously to the study of Huguenin. The nature of his physical malady, at least, was clear. He laboured under the singular affection to which physicians have given the name of Cheyne Stoke's Respiration, the disease manifesting itself at intervals by compelling him to lie back in a perfect agony of inhalation, and groan for air; the bones of his cheeks seemed on the point of appearing through their sere wrapping of mummy-skin; the *alæ* of his nose never rested from an extravagance of expansion and retraction. But even this ruin of a body might, I considered, be made partially whole, were it not that to lull the rage and fever of such a *mind* the world contained no anodyne. For one thing, a most curious belief in some unnamed fate hanging over the island on which he lived haunted him. Again and again he recalled to me all that in the long past had been written about Delos: the strange notion contained both in the Homeric and the Alexandrian hymns to the Delian Apollo that the island was *floating*; or that it was merely secured by chains; or that it had only been thrown up from the deeps as a temporary resting-place for Ortygia in her travail; or that it might *sink* before the spurning foot of the new-born god. He was never tired, through long hours, of pursuing, as if in soliloquy, a kind of somnolent, mystical

exegesis of such passages as we read together. "Do you know," he
said, "that the ancients really supposed the streams of Delos to
rise and fall with the rise and fall of the Nile? Could anything point
more clearly to a belief in the extraordinary nature of the island,
its far-reaching volcanic affinities, occult geologic eccentricities?"
Often would he repeat the punning hexameter line of the very ancient Sibylline prophecy—

ἔσται καὶ Σάμος ἄμμος ἐοειται Δηλος ἄδηλος ;

[*And Samos shall be sand,
and Delos (the far-seen) sink from sight*]

often, too, having repeated it, he would strike from the repining
chords of an Æolian lyre the air of a threnody which, as he told
me, his wife had composed to suit the verse; and when to the funeral wail of this dirge—so wild, so mournful, that I could never
hear it without a shudder—Huguenin added the melancholy note
of his now hollow and plaintive voice, the intensity of effect produced on me reached the intolerable degree, and I was glad of the
dubious and pallid and purple gloaming of the mansion, which
partially hid my face from him.

"Observe, however," he added one day, "the meaning of the
implied epithet 'far-seen' as applied to Delos: it means 'glorious,'
'illustrious'—far-seen to the spiritual rather than to the bodily eye,
for the island is not very mountainous. The words 'sink from sight'
must therefore be supposed to have the corresponding significance
of an extinction of this glory. And now judge whether or no this
prophecy has not been already fulfilled, when I tell you that this
sacrosanct land, which no dog's foot was once allowed to touch,
on which no man was permitted to be born or to die, bears at this
moment on its bosom a monster fouler than the brain of demon
ever conceived. A fearful literal and physical fulfilment of the
prophecy cannot, I consider, be far distant."

That all this esotericism was not native to Huguenin I was certain. His mind, I was convinced, had been ploughed into by some

tremendous energy, before ever this rank growth had choked it. I drew him on, little by little, to speak of his wife.

She was, he told me, of a very antique Athenian family, which by constant effort had conserved its purity of blood. It was while passing southward through Greece in a world-weary mood, some years before my visit, that he came one night to the village of Castri; and there, on the site of the ancient Delphi, in the centre of an angry crowd of Greeks and Turks, who threatened to rend her to pieces, he first saw Andromeda, his wife. "This incredible courage," he said, "this vast originality was hers, to take upon herself the part of a modern Hypatia—to venture on the task of the bringing back of the gods, in the midst of a fanatical people, at the latter end of a century like the present. The furious mob from which I rescued her was standing around her in front of the vestibule of a just completed temple to Apollo, whose worship she was then and there attempting to restore."

The love of the woman fastened on her preserver with passionate intensity. Huguenin felt himself constrained by the impulse of an irresistible Will. They were united, and came at her bidding to live in the grey abode of her creation at Delos. In this solitude, under this shadow, the man and the woman faced each other. As the months passed the husband found that he had married a seer of visions and a dreamer of dreams. And visions of what hue! and dreams of what madness! He confessed to me that he was greatly awed by her, and with this awe was blended a feeling which, if it was not fear, was akin to fear. That he loved her not at all he now knew, while the excess of her passion for him he grew to regard with the hate which men feel for the distilled elixir of the hemlock. Yet his mind inevitably took on the lurid hue of hers. He drank in unfailingly all her creeds. He followed her in the same way that a satellite follows a world. When for days together she hid herself from him and disappeared, he would wander desolate and full of search over the pathless house. Finding that she habitually yielded her body to the lotus delights of certain opiate seeds produced on the island, he found the courage to frown and warn, and ended by himself becoming a bond-slave to the drowsy *ganja* of India. So too with the most strange fascination she exercised over the animal world: he disliked it—he dreaded it; regarded it as excessive and unnatural; but he looked on only with the furtive, pale eye of suspicion, and said nothing. When she walked she was accompanied by a long magnetised *queue* of living things, felines in particular, and birds of large size. Dogs, on the contrary, shunned her, bristling. She had brought with her from the mainland a collection of these followers, of which Huguenin had never seen the half; they were imprisoned in unknown nooks of the building; ever and anon she would vanish from the house, to reappear with new companions. Her kindness to these dumb creatures should, I presume, have been amply sufficient to account for her power over them; but Huguenin's mind, already grown morbid, probed darkly after some other explanation. The primary *motif* of this unquietness doubtless lay in his wife's fanaticism on the subject of the Pythagorean theory of the transmigration of souls. On this theme Andromeda, it was clear, was violently deranged. She would stand, he declared, with outstretched arm, with eye wild-staring, with rigid body, and in a rapid, guttural recitative—like a rapt, delirious Pythoness—would prophesy of the eternal mutations prepared for the spirit of man. She would dwell, above all, with a kind of contempt, on the limitations of animal forms in the actual world, and would indignantly insist that the spirit of an extraordinary and original man, disembodied, *should and must* re-embody itself in a correspondingly extraordinary and original form. "And," she would often add, "such forms do really exist on the earth, but the God, willing to save the race from frenzy, hides them from the eyes of common men."

It was long, however, before I could induce Huguenin to speak of the final catastrophe of his singular wedded life. He related it in these words:—

"You now know that Andromeda was among the great painters of the world—you have seen her picture of herself. One day, after dilating, as was her wont, on the narrow limitation of forms, she said suddenly, 'But you, too, shall be of the initiated: come, come, you shall see *something*.' She went swiftly forward, beckoning, looking back repeatedly to smile on me a loving patronage, with the condescension of a priestess to a neophyte; I followed, till before a lately finished painting she stopped, pointing. I will not attempt—the attempt would be folly—to tell you what thing of horror and madness I saw before me on the canvas; nor can I explain in words the tempest of anger, of loathing and disgust, that stirred within me at the sight. Kindled by the blasphemy of her fancy, I raised my hand to strike her head; and to this hour I know not if I struck her. My hand, it is true, felt the sensation of contact with something soft and yielding; but the blow, if blow there were, was surely too slight to harm the frame of a creature far feebler than the human. Yet she fell; the film of coming death grew over her dull, upbraiding eyes; one last word only she spoke, pointing to the Uncleanness: 'In the flesh you may yet behold it!' and so, still pointing, pointing, she passed away.

"I bore her body, embalmed in the Greek manner by an expert of Corinth, to one of the smaller apartments on the roof of the house. I saw, as I turned to leave her in the gloom of the strait and lonely chamber, the mortal smile on her waxen face within the open coffin. Two weeks later I went again to visit her. My friend, she had vanished utterly—save that the bones remained; and from the vacant coffin, above the now fleshless skull, two eyes—living—the very eyes of Andromeda's soul, but full of a new-born, intenser light—the eyes, too, of the pictured horror whose whole form I now discerned in the darkness—gleamed out upon me. I slammed to the door, and fainted on the floor."

"The suggestion," I said, "which you seem to wish to convey is that of a transition of forms from the human to the animal; but, surely, the explanation that the monster, brought secretly by your wife into the house, imprisoned unawares by you with the dead, and maddened by hunger, fed on the uncovered body, is, if not less horrible, at least less improbable."

He looked doubtingly at me for a moment, and then replied: "There was no monster imprisoned with the dead. Be not rash with 'explanations.' You do not require me to tell you, what you must know, that there are many more things in earth—to say nothing of heaven—than were ever dreamt of in your philosophy."

But at least, I urged, he would see the necessity of flying from that place. He answered with the extraordinary avowal that it was no longer doubtful to him, from the effect which any neglect to minister to the creature's wants produced on his own bodily health, that his life was intimately bound up with the life of the being he stayed to maintain; that with the *second* murder of which he should be guilty—nay, with the very attempt to commit it, as, for example, by flight from the house—his own life would inevitably be forfeited.

I accordingly formed the resolution to work the deliverance of my friend in spite of himself. Two months had now passed; the end of my visit was drawing near; yet his maladies of brain and body were not alleviated. It tortured me to think of leaving him once more alone, a prey to the manias which distracted him.

That very day, while he slept his damp, unquiet, opiate slumbers, I started out on the track indicated by the scarlet thread. So far it led—and the rooms through which it passed were of such uniformity, and the path so serpentine, and the sameness of construction on every hand so unbroken—that I could not doubt but that, the clue once snapped at any point, the journey to the desired end could be accomplished only by the most improbable good fortune. I followed the thread to its termination: it stopped at the foot of a ladder-like stair, which I ascended. At the top of the stair, and close to it, I was faced by a narrow wall, in which was a closed wooden door; in the door a hole large enough to admit the hand. As I placed my foot on the topmost step, a long, low, plaintive whine, with a sickening likeness to a human wail, broke upon my ear.

I hurriedly descended the steps. Some little distance from them I broke the silken thread, and, gathering it up in my hand as I went, again broke it near the region of the house which we occupied.

"Hereby," I said, as I held the gathered portion to the flame of a lamp, "shall a soul be saved alive."

I watched him later on through half-closed lids, as he departed, haggard and shivering, on his nightly errand. My heart throbbed under an agony of disquiet while I awaited his long-delayed return.

He came swiftly and softly into my room, and shook me by the shoulder. On his face was a look of unusual calmness, of dignity and mystery.

"Wake up," he said. "I wish you—I am a sorry host, am I not?— I wish you to leave me to-night, at once; to leave the island—*now*."

"But tell me—" I gasped.

"Nay, nay; I will take no refusal. Trust me this once, and go. There is a danger here. Destiny is against me—an impudent destiny, careless even to conceal its hand. Go. One or two of the fisher-folk of the harbour will convey you over to Rhenea before the morning light, and you will be saved."

"But saved from what?"

"From what? I cannot tell you: from the destiny, whatever it be, which awaits me. Do you know—can you dream—that the thread on which my life depends is *snapped?*"

"But suppose I tell you—"

"You can tell me nothing. Ah . . . you hear that?"

He held up his hand and listened. It was a sudden shriek of the wind around the house.

"It is but the rising wind," I muttered, starting up.

"Ah, but that—that which followed. Did you not *feel* it?"

"Huguenin, I felt nothing."

He had clasped with both arms a marble pillar, against which his forehead rested, while with one foot he gently and mechanically patted the floor. In this posture, now utterly demoralised and craven, he remained for some minutes. The wail of the wind was heard at intervals. Suddenly he turned towards me, with a ghastly face and the scream of a frightened woman.

"Now—now at least—*you feel it!*"

I could no longer deny. It was as if the whole island had gently rocked to and fro on a pivot.

Thoroughly unnerved myself, trembling more with awe than with terror, I seized Huguenin's arm, and sought to draw him from the pillar, which, muttering low, he still embraced. He sullenly refused to stir; and I, resolved in any event to stay by him, sat near. The seismic agitation increased. But he seemed to take no further note of anything,—only, with the regularity of a clock's oscillations, the tripudiary automatic motion of his foot persisted. In this way an hour, two hours, passed. At the end of that time the rocking movement of the earth had become intense, rapid and continuous.

There came a moment when, overwhelmed by a new panic, I sprang to my feet and shook him.

"Headstrong man!" I cried, "have you then parted with every sense? Do you not smell—can you not feel—that the house is in flames?"

His eyes, which had grown dark and dull, blazed up instantly with a new madness.

"Then," he shouted, with the roar of a clarion,— "then she shall—I say she shall be saved! The cheetah—*the feathered chee-tah!*"

Before I could lay hold of the now foaming maniac, he had dashed past me into a corridor. I followed behind in hottest pursuit. The carpets and hangings, as yet but dully glowing, filled the passages with the smoke of Tophet. I hoped that Huguenin, weak of lung, would fall choked and exhausted. Some power seemed to lend him strength—he rushed onward like the wind; some sure, mysterious instinct seemed to guide him—not once did he falter or hesitate.

The long chase through the cracking house, burning now on every side, was over. The just intuitions of insanity had not failed the madman—he reached the goal for which he panted. I saw him hasten up the half-consumed ladder, whose foot was already in a lake of flame. He rushed to the smouldering wooden door of the tomb of Andromeda, and tore it wide open. And now from out the vault there burst—above the roaring of the fire, and the whistle of the tempest, and the thousandfold rattle of the earthquake—a shrill and raucous shriek, which turned my blood to ice; and I saw proceeding from the darkness a creature whose native loathsomeness human language has no vocabulary to describe. For if I say that it was a cheetah—of very large size—its eyes a yellow liquid conflagration—its fat and boneless body swathed in a thick panoply of dark grey feathers, vermilion-tipped—with a similitude of miniature wings on its back—with a wide, vast, downward-sweeping tail like the tail of a bird of paradise,—how by such words can I image forth all the retching nausea, all the bottomless hate and fear, with which I looked? The fire, it was evident, had already reached the body of the beast; already it flamed. I saw it fly, rather than spring, at Huguenin's head; the burial of its fangs in his flesh, the meeting of its teeth about his windpipe, I saw. He tottered—gurgling—tearing at the feathery horror—backward over the spot where a moment before the stair had stood; together they fell into the sea of flame beneath.

I ran in headlong haste from the house, discovering by good chance an egress. The night was clear, yet all the winds seemed to tumble in disenchained ecstasy about the islet. As I descended I noted the scathed and scorched aspect of the trees and of certain of the rocks; at one spot a multitude of deep, smooth, conical openings, edged with grey, glowing scoriae, riveted my attention. Still lower, I stood on a bluff promontory and looked sheer into the sea. The sight was sublime and appalling. The deep—without billow or foam or ripple—luminous far down with phosphorescences—rushed, like some lambent lamina yoked to the fiery steeds of Diomedes, with a steady, intense, almost dazzling impetuosity towards the island. Delos, indeed, seemed to *float*—to swim, painfully struggling, like a little doomed bird, against the all-engulfing element. I passed with the earliest light from this mystic shrine of ancient piety. Among the last sights that greeted my gaze was the still ascending reek of the blighted and accursed dwelling of Huguenin.

THE SPECTRE-SHIP

"Groans, and convulsions, and a discoloured face,
and blacks, and obsequies."—*Bacon*

I

"Odin sends out his Valkyrs to choose the slain," said the Viking Sigurd to his nephew, Gurth; "I go, and may not return: you know my will—see, Gurth, that you do it."

His hands were on the heads of two children of nine, he kissed them, and leapt to his *yolle*, in which two champions rowed him to his dragon-ship lying near. As the lug-sail bulged hugely to the breeze, and the long galley stepped, gay with gilt spar and purple flag, down the *fjord*, Sigurd, on the poop, turned from his steering-oar and waved a hand. The setting sun glittered on his rich war-gear, he looming big, a towering bulk, with the long tile-beard of Assyrian kings, a white wire showing here and there in the russet. He waved his hand—his eighty rovers roared the refrain of a sea-song—and a bend hid them from the bay.

The bay was at the inner end of the winding *fjord*, a greensward sloping gently up from the beach, crowned at the top with an edge of forest; and midway stood the low "burg," or manor-house, of the Viking's domain. To this turned Gurth, holding a hand of each of the children. So fast he walked that he dragged them; his grasp hurt them; exultation dancing in his heart and gloomy eye. He was master at last—perhaps for good—for "Odin sends out his Valkyrs," and Sigurd the Viking was but mortal man.

Gurth, at a time when most men were warriors, was not a war-
rior; one saw that in his face—a puffy face, dark as a Norman's,
seamed with deep lines, and hairless, with shifty eyes, and a broken nose. His back stooped deeply, and, standing by Sigurd, his
head just reached the Viking's shoulder.

He sat late that night in the wide hall, while around, on benches,
lolled the residue of Sigurd's retainers, drinking mead from horns,
and from the long hearths by the table sprang the fire- smoke to
the open louvres in the roof. Gurth, brooding, sat at the table-head,
fingering his embossed cup. Presently he sprang up, somewhat
fuddled, and there was silence. "Men," he said, "I am your over-
man now; if there be thrall, or churl, or champion here disputes
that, let him say it. But by the belt of Thor—!" he peered cunningly
round, but no one stirred. "Sigurd," he continued, "is gone a-Viking in Britland. *When* he may return, who knows? Meanwhile, we
here have scarcity of much—of corn, fabrics, gold. Sigurd was a
free-hand, a feaster, winking at sloth, so it were brave and bloody.
I am for gathering together and husbanding. No idleness on the
lands while I lord it here! Let every thrall do his sweating: everyone bring his share from land or sea. He who fails will know me
better. I call a cheer!"

Malignity and a painful anxiousness wrinkled the face of Gurth:
but, slowly, the men stood up and drank.

When a snore or two began to sound, he rose and glided across
the courtyard. Frigga's lamp now westering low in the heavens.
After passing three corridors, he tapped at a door, and was admitted into a chamber by old Gunhild, the *vala* of the burg. He sat
near her, peering into her face.

"Well, now," he said, "have you wrought the spell for me?" The
old dame, robed in white, nodded meaningly far within her wimple.

"And is the good hap of Frey, *vala*, or the mischief of Loki to
rule this life of mine?"

Gurth's soft hands were writhing clammily together, an agony
of interest gazing from his eyes upon the grave old face.

"Loki or Frey?" she said, looking away at the setting moon:
"both, if you must know."

"Ah . . . ! tell me."

"You will conquer the living."

His eyes closed.

"But beware of the dead."

"How! the *dead!*"

The *vala* pointed a bent finger to a corner, where, on two beds, lay the children, the hair of the girl, Gerda, spreading over the coverlet like a mat of gold, the arm of Hrolf, the son of Sigurd, lay under his head, the fist clenched.

"If harm come to *them*," said Gunhild, "All-father will see to it, I tell you."

Little Gerda was an orphan, the daughter of a neighbouring Jarl, a close comrade of Sigurd, who, dying, had committed her to Sigurd, together with his lands and burg; and the last injunction of the Viking to Gurth had had reference to the marriage of the children, as soon as they should attain something like maturity. It was a project dear to his soul, and a foreboding that this his expedition might be one of those unending sails that brave men take at the behest of Heaven, had lent stern emphasis to his command.

"If harm come to *them* . . ." said Gunhild.

"But, look here, *vala*," coaxed Gurth, spreading his hands, "I mean no harm to them! Harm, do you think? As for the boy, if his father comes not back, in a few Yules we send him Viking, where let him bide the chances of the sea-fight; and fine, we all say, is death in the fight. As for the girl, seven, eight, passing summers will find her fit and marriageable. And why should not I, myself—?"

"What?"

"Well—*vala*—marry her."

Gunhild looked calmly sidelong at his oily face.

"And so make quite sure of the Jarl's lands, Gurth?"

He chuckled. "A wish to get, and increase in store, is but natural to us all."

"Yet do *you*, Gurth," she answered, shaking her finger at him, "curb well your lust for wealth! for if I read right the signs—but fie! Gerda is for none of your marrying: there is grey already in your hair."

"When—when will Sigurd return?"

"You mean to ask," she said bitingly, "whether he will return at all."

"Well, put it so."

"But I cannot tell. Only I know this, that he is of those high and great warriors who *do* return, though the world oppose them. And I say to you, Gurth, do your will and prosper; but beware of wrong to *those*."

Gurth rose, bent his knee, and walked away, a greyness of morning now mingling with the dark.

II

In nine years no one any longer expected Sigurd: for the cruises of the Vikings were annual; and the bones of a hero absent nine years were well known to whiten on some shore, or roll with the tides of the ocean-flood.

Gurth, meanwhile, had "conquered the living." The rovers disliked him, but the trophies of their excursions they laid at his feet, that slight, dark man acquired an iron power over them. Ditlew, the Berserk, the jötun-furious, and least erect of all the spirits of the burg-guard, on returning from a voyage on the Throndheim coast, deeming himself ill-rewarded with booty, had deserted at dead of night, and sped fugitive, his horse burdened with stolen things; and Ditlew, a huge body ending in a broad-bearded coffee-pot, had reached a point where fear of pursuit no longer troubled him, when, springing from the dark of the forest, stood before him—Gurth. Ditlew did not suspect that Gurth was trembling with even chillier fears than he himself, although six thralls lurked near to protect him; and the sword-arm of the Berserk hung inert in the presence of this alert eye and all-divining brain. He returned submissively with Gurth, and from that night was like a cur, waiting upon the glance of his master. So, one by one, by force, by fraud, Gurth "conquered" them.

One, however, no device could tame: when young Hrolf, at seventeen, had been ordered to sail a-Viking, and dying to go, had refused Ditlew, at a glance from Gurth, dragged him to the bay: and not till the Norway coast was low on the horizon did they release him. At once Hrolf sprang from the poop. His return he announced by firing a shed on the crag which was the watch-tower for the signalmen posted to flash the approach of enemies by means of beacons, Gurth believing himself invaded, while Hrolf dried his scarlet and yellow Viking-clothes at the burning shed.

At eighteen no love of opposition could longer keep him from the sea-joy. Gerda, sprung gracile now like the trepid gazelle on the crag-top, did the clasp of his ring-mail coat, and with a mock curtsey put "Tyrfing," his grandfather's falchion, into his hand, while Hrolf stooped, and brushed with his lips the pink bloom of her cheek. She hardly noticed the caress then; but four days later, folding his clothes, he being then in mid-ocean, remembered, and blushed.

So Hrolf had drunk delight of battle, and come back brown; and the brine had thrashed him out a reddish beardlet. Gerda at the signal of his coming went fluttering down the *fjord*; and he, seeing her white dress, put off from his "schip," and met her without the usual kiss; and they walked to the burg together, while Gurth, seeing them come, said: "Not too hasty, my young birds! Your wings grow fast, but I have a grave thought to clip them."

Half a mile off, in the forest's depth, was a lakelet, and there through many an autumn afternoon Gerda had drifted in her skiff among the sedge of the shallows, hearing the chatter of the kitti-wakes, or of tern, gull, osprey. It was there that from behind a tree, two days, after his coming back, Hrolf stood watching the lake flooded with the after-glow of the set sun, and, floating in the midst of it, Gerda, all glorified, transfigured, her head sunk, her chest heaving in the sort of gentle trouble with which the ducks heaved on the lake's swell. Presently, by a glance almost intuitive, she saw Hrolf's red sleeve peep, and went pale—starting so, that the paddle slapped into the water. Hrolf, as if something momentous had happened, breathed to his tree: "Odin! she's dropped her oar!"

He ran out then, shouting, to the shore.

"Wait, I am coming."

"No!" she cried from far.

"What do you say?"

"Do not trouble."

"But what will you do?"

"It is all right."

"What is?"

"You will wet yourself."

"I? Not a bit."

"You will."

"I am coming."

He plunged down the rushy scaur, routing scaup and whimbrel, swam to the oar, and, like a water-dog, towed it to the boat. With commotion, apprehension, she beheld him come, and half stood, red and blanched.

"There, I said you would!"

"Would what?"

"Wet yourself."

"Well, of course—"

"You said you wouldn't."

"Ha! ha! But I am quite used to all that now."

"You are such a very old—Viking."

"I have killed my man."

"And you have a beard."

"And *you* are not the same, either."

"I? Why not?"

"You seem so different since I have come back."

"I am sorry for that, Hrolf, we were always such friends. Why different?"

"You look to me taller, and your eyes—how wonderfully blue your eyes are, Gerda!"

She bent them down, muttering something, looking upon the ebb and flow of her own bosom, in which the keenest pang shrieked for passion.

"And, look here"—he was close to her, his hand on the gunwale— "you did not—kiss me—when I came back."

"Who didn't?"

"You didn't."

"Why, Hrolf, are you sure?"

"Don't you suppose I'd remember?"

"You never asked, Hrolf."

"Well—but can I come in?"

"No—don't! Hrolf, you will upset—"

"Let me!"

"But you couldn't!"

"If you sit heavily over yonder, perhaps I could."

She went, and he made an effort, but at his long-legged mass the skiff cranked deeply. He gave it up.

"Stupid shell!" he said.

Gerda leant more heavily over the other side.

"Now, once more—try—" she said.

He tried again, and the next moment Gerda was in his arm in the water, his other hand clinging to the skiff's keel.

"Well, now—!" he gasped.

Her hair, wrapped about her head under a gold band, was hardly wet, and she could swim like a fish; but her eyes were closed, the woman in her being, or pretending to be, faint.

"Darling! Gerda!"—he was kissing her lifted lips— "You will be ill—"

Her arm tightened about him; her eyes opened and laughed, and closed anew at the renewed fury of his lips.

But Gurth, at the burg-door, seeing them approach bedraggled, strolled to meet them, and noticed their faces, the new meaning in their looks, the complicity, and bliss.

"How now?" he cried.

"Oh, nothing—go away," said Hrolf: "fell into the water."

Gurth said to himself: "Tonight."

Then, close by Gerda, he whispered:— "Tonight I want to speak to you privately. You must come to the water-butt outside the burg, about nine—you hear?"

The world swam in a dream to her, so that she hardly heard, but answered: "Yes."

At the burg she snatched her hand free, and ran to change; then, in haste, rushed into the sanctum of Gunhild, to fall at the *vala's* knees, burying away her face, trembling: and Gunhild, gifted in heart-sight, understood, and stroked the gold, and bent her cheek to the ruby ear, crooning the rune:—

"Now may All-father,
  Odin, the work-skilled,
  Tunefullest song-smith,
  Gallant sea-rover,
  Faultless true-guesser,
  Guileful entangler,
  Odin wind-whispering,
  Grant that it end well!"

III

"*Marry* me?" said Gerda.

"Ay, that," said Gurth.

It was nine near the water-butt.

She meant to laugh, but a sob burst from her lips.

Gurth held her wrist, his dark eyes alight.

"No tremblings! no faintings and flutterings! You are mine. I have nurtured you for this. Not a word! If you rebel—if you tremble—I cut off your hair, I pinch and nip your pretty graces, and grind you to my will like corn beneath the quern—you hear?"

"But who are you that you dare—"

"Silence! and him, too, remember—your young strutting cockerel—"

"*Him!* why, he can protect himself and me from a thousand such as you, Gurth Hermodsson!"

"Go!"—he flung her from him; "say a month from now to prepare yourself within! And, meanwhile, you will be watched, be sure. Now run and tell your *vala* that it is I who swear it by the Thor's thunder!"

And to the *vala* Gerda did run, to sob the tale into the sibyl's ears. At midnight Gunhild stood alone, mumbling spells over a fire in a platter, and before morning had matured a plan in her world-wise brain.

She had Hrolf into her room, to tell the news: whereat "Tyrfing" leapt, and Hrolf was all for war. But the *vala*, threatening and entreating, won him to a calmer mood.

"The will of Loki is set strongly against your ever having Gerda at all," she said; "everything is against you. Unless you have the manhood to curb that hot blood, you may give up hope and be done."

He sat and listened. Her plan was flight, which seemed to her the only way of averting tragedy from the house of the Sigurdssons. The craft of Gurth she knew, his luck and knack of gaining an end; and she roused all her old acuteness to a combat of wits with him, she very feeble now, and this her final fight.

So Hrolf and Gerda should be seen no more together; on the third day Hrolf should pretend a journey to a neighbouring burg; and in the night the two should wait at appointed spots on the crags, Hrolf having secretly returned. She knew that Gurth's spies watched them; but that night she would summon Gurth, and while they talked, Frid, one of her women, would bolt the door outside, so that Gurth would be her prisoner. Frid would then run and light a peat fire at the back of the burg-wall, a signal for the children to meet and ride away; for his spies, not finding Gurth, would not dare or care to follow. Without danger the two could then fare away to Jarl Svegdir's burg on the Ivan *fjord*, who would not be slow to grant them asylum; and, once wedded, their battle was more than half won.

On that third night, then—a gale blustering through the drizzly gloom—Gerda stood muffled, wet, on the crags north of the *fjord*, while Hrolf watched from the southern cliffs. The hour appointed for their meeting was about nine. But at ten no signal-fire had shot up.

Gurth was then walking up and down the hall, his hands behind his back, and every time he came to the door, he opened it slightly and looked out into the night. Men lolled silent about the room; the log-fires burned bright; and the eye of Ditlew, the Berserk, with the sleepy fidelity of a watch-dog, followed every step of Gurth in his ceaseless, feline pacing.

Toward eleven Hrolf said to himself: "Beard of Thor! but will it never come?" and Gerda, trembling, haggard with terror, groaned aloud: "Oh, some dreadful chance must have happened!"

At this hour Gurth, stopping before Ditlew, said: "You are sure young Hrolf is back?"

"Yes," Ditlew answered, "I saw him."

"And the girl?"

"Haeng, the house-churl, has had an eye upon her today."

"And where is Haeng?"

"I thought the lout was here."

"No, you see: he is not," Gurth said, with a sly smile. "Get up now, and have the six horses I spoke of this morning ready at the door. And just take red brand from the fire, and kindle me a flame at the back of the burg-wall yonder."

Ditlew stared.

"Do it," said Gurth, and continued his walk.

By that time Hrolf was saying to himself: "Has Gunhild, then, played us false?" when he saw the flare at the appointed spot, and crying, "good!—at last," galloped through the forest to the other side of the *fjord*, near the cliff-edge of which he leapt off, and found Gerda.

"Quick now," he panted, "the way through the forest—"

"Hrolf," she whispered, "I have such a fear—Why was the signal so late?"

As she began to weep, he took her in his arms to the horse, lifted her to the pillion, sprang, and cantered.

A man, meanwhile, had crept from a cleft behind them, and run to the burg—the house-churl Haeng; and he rushed in to whisper to Gurth: "They are off—through the forest!"

"To horse! to horse, you six!" Gurth cried, stamping, his eye flashing— "young Hrolf and my ward, Gerda—the way through the forest!"

Six fellows ran to the waiting horses, two snatching flambeaux from the sconces. These, as they entered the forest, heard the tramp of Hrolf's horse before them. But it was doubly weighted, and not the best of the burg: nor was the chase long. Presently Hrolf was lying on his back, bound, though "Tyrfing" had passed through Haeng, the house-churl, and had chasmed the shoulder of Ditlew, the Berserk.

Meantime, Gurth as soon as his six had galloped from the door, sped across the courtyard, but his for a moment stopped, hesitating, full of doubts, then ran, and stopped, and ran again. At last, when near the *vala's* chamber, he drew off his *rivlins* from his feet, and crept, on tip-toe, to her door, which was fastened on the outside; and with an utter stealthiness Gurth undid the bolts. Fright and the triumph of his cunning fought for mastery in his face, but fright was uppermost: for the *vala* had thought to imprison him, and he had imprisoned her, the holy of the gods. Having noiselessly undone the bolt, he crept backward, took his slippers, and pelted back across the courtyard.

Listening at the door three days before he had heard the *vala* detail her scheme to Hrolf, and several plans had then passed through his brain: he might arrest the children at once; he might have men posted at the appointed spots to seize them separately. But he had decided that the lad must be caught in the act of snatching his ward from his control, in order that the subsequent cruelties which he intended might find justification in the eyes of the burg-men. His delay of hours in kindling the fire for their meeting had been prompted by the mere wantonness of the terrier playing with its prey.

In the morning a woman, entering the *vala's* chamber, found her sitting with both hands stiffly clenched, a stare of surprise and pride in her eyes. She, the long-honoured, in her old age, had been slain by an indignity, and Gurth had walked on tip-toe lest ears already dead should mark him—as the wicked flee when no man pursues.

IV

Success made of Gurth Hermodsson something of a devil—success and the death of the *vala* Gunhild. He had never dreamed of such a thing! and the incident upset and perverted him, he

believing himself under the curse of heaven. For three weeks
Gerda and Hrolf, each wondering where the other was, were pris-
oners near each other in rooms of the burg. Gerda, dishevelled,
woebegone, refusing food. Twice, since the *vala's* burial, Gurth
had visited her, and she had sprung to a corner, like a cat at bay,
hopeless, but ready to tear, if touched. To his talk of marriage,
threats of force, the slight downward curve of her lip gave answer.

"If the boy were dead!" thought Gurth, but he did not see his
way, as yet, to murder, the burg-men, though subdued, being yet
men, brave, and some of them might find murder intolerable. But
the thought put into his head a triumphant idea, and the next day
Ditlew, by instruction, slipped into Gerda's room.

He spoke kindly; told of Hrolf; that he was close to her, con-
fined like her.

"But I come as a friend to warn you," said Ditlew: "I come secretly—
no one knows. There's near danger hanging over the youth's head."

"Danger!"

"Well, you know Gurth Hermodsson: he is a man must have
his way. He does not say anything, but I know well enough what
he will do, if you hold out against him."

"To Hrolf?"

"Aye. If the lad's in the way, he will be removed, I tell you. Perhaps this very night—in his sleep—"

She leapt then to him, caught him by his two sleeves, on her
knees "Ditlew! have you a cat's heart, good Ditlew? Have I ever
done you harm?"

"Ah, now you rave," he said, "what can *I* do?"

He undid her grasp and went away, leaving her on the floor. In
an hour she sent a message to Gurth, saying that she was prepared
to marry him on the morrow.

V

And on the morrow an altar on the greensward ran gory with
bullock's blood, and the new *vala* chanted before it, and Gurth at
last was master, beyond the tricks of chance, of the old Jarl's lands.

As if half-ashamed of the mummery, he had performed his part stammeringly, shyly awkward; but afterwards walked blithely to the burg, shrilling high a summoning horn. For Gerda he had taken a silken robe from the store-house, which she wore, to everything she acquiescing with spiritless abandonment, stipulating only that Hrolf should not be released that day, and on the next that she should be conveyed away to her father's burg, and he set free.

And beside Gurth, at the table-head, she sat through the afternoon, while freer and freer flowed the mead, and higher swelled the tumult of good cheer and forgetfulness of sorrow, till Gurth, mollified by his cup, turned for the first time to his marble bride, and said: "Take heart, fair face! No mischief is meant you! There breathes no more harmless a rascal than thy old Gurth to them who let him go his way in quietness."

And, as if in answer, a cheer came wafted from the bay. In a lull of the festal uproar it came, and everyone seemed to hear it. A silence fell. Gurth looked, questioning, round.

The next moment a churl came running to him to murmur:—"Sigurd Sigurdsson *is come* back, and half his champions with him."

The drinking-horn dropped, and the rascal toppled, collapsed, head-prone upon the table, shot in the breast. It might be said that he swooned—the world whirled from under his foot. But only for a minute.

He sprang, straight, sober. He beckoned to Ditlew. He whispered to Gerda, his eyes rolling round the room: "Go now with Ditlew; later I will come to you." He whispered to Ditlew: "Lock her fast in the same place, and look well to the lad, too, and keep the keys. Sigurd is come. Later, keep close to me. I may want you." Then, the Berserk and his charge having passed out, he lifted his voice: "Men! good news for you. Sigurd Sigurdsson is here. Let us bid him hearty welcome, I say. But as to this marriage of mine, I would myself first tell of it to Sigurd. See, then, that ye say nothing. Remember!"

He turned, followed by the men, and half-way on the sward he met Sigurd.

The Viking in ten years had grown old: his beard was white, his hair was white. But that heroic frame stood still erect. His heart was calm, and the majesty of the world-warrior victorious over chance, and destiny, and death, crowned the man, ennobling the glance of his brow to something like god-likeness.

"Ah, Gurth Hermodsson!" he said, blithely calm: "good sight to see."

His hand fell upon Gurth's shoulder.

"And good sight, you, to see," said Gurth— "and—strange."

"Well, Gurth, the world is the field of battle for us poor god-sons, and a man must even fight his best in it, and die. I have been away in Britland, joined to a host of Saxon-men, fighting with Scot, fighting with Pict, fighting here, fighting there. I saw the work was worth doing, and in God's name I went and did it. . . . But, man, the children!"

"The children?" said Gurth.

"Aye, man."

For thirty eternal seconds Gurth hesitated. When his lips next moved, he was a lost soul.

"The children are but lately married; are gone away together to the old Jarl's burg."

He knew that in a day, at most, that lie must be detected—if Sigurd lived a day.

"Well said!" cried Sigurd, and patted the shoulder beneath his hand. They entered the burg, the other men, interchanging greetings, trooped in. Sigurd and Gurth sat apart in colloquy.

"But this is a merry day with you," Sigurd said, nodding at the table.

"A holiday for the cullions here. But as to treasure, now: come back full?"

"Full, Gurth, and over-full; and a cargo, over and above, is in keeping for me at Lerwick in Hjaltland, where I last year left it." Gurth's eyes kindled.

"Who keeps it?"

"Old Ragnar, who jarls it now at Lerwick."

"But it should be sent for."

"Let it lie, man. I am weary, Gurth, of spoil and treasure, of sea-flash and sword-flash. Let it lie."

"I will go and get it."

"As you will."

"This very day."

"As you will, man."

Sigurd's eyes were looking far away, as men, after a long night of storm, watch for morning. The goad which was urging Gurth was the necessity to be far—at once—far from the burg! and to be known by all men to be far.

Before nightfall he had forty of the men on board the *Skidblednir*, a swift dragon, and below decks, alone with Ditlew, smuggled a phial containing a green liquid into the Berserk's hand.

"There is enough for two," he said; "if you fail, you had better drink the rest."

Ditlew and others rowed to shore, and the *Skidblednir* moved down the *fjord*.

Sigurd, at supper that night, felt a stomach-gripe, and broke into the sweat of death. He was supported to his old chamber, and there for hours, from those lips which never uttered groan, burst groan on groan. Towards morning a shriek went piercing through the place, like the strong hinny of a horse in pain. But the dawn brought balm.

Men knew not what to think: it was so sudden. None dreamed of foul play, for Gurth, who might have had motive, was away. His chosen rovers hung round his couch, full of low-spoken stories of his reign and age, his heroic rage, and social soul. He was the greatest of the Vikings, they said; the type of a good man.

On the third morning, Hrolf and Gerda stood with the rest over him, for the new-returned rovers had insisted upon their release. And now on a bier they bore him, and laid him out on a pyre of wood raised high on the poop of his long old dragon-ship, placing beside him his gold casque, his target and sword: and his great bulk, thus raised up, lay far conspicuous in its tunic of ruby silk. The morning stormily dribbled a cold sleet that trickled tearfully from the closed lids to the beard, and guttered in streams over the great lug-sail. Down the length of the *fjord* they towed her, and moored her to a stake on the shore of an open roadstead, where, all day long, shallow rows of rollers trooped in to the funeral, crooning their coronachs; and with every heave of her beak to meet their frothy swarming, the dragon with her poop-end struck the sand, and gently shook her dead. Toward nightfall the shore was alive with rovers; and just as the sun's sinking brim broke in glory through the grey day and set the sea-breath ablaze, some of the braves held flames to the under-curve of the stern; some loosed the moorings; others, pushing, launched her forth, her scarlet sail paunching to the squall, as she walked flaming down the flame that the sunset made. From the shore, with spiritless hand-waves they called him, in chorus, a last farewell.

Such, as we know, was the form in which the Norsemen were accustomed to commit to the sea the corpses of its kings.

But, in the flurry of the moment, the dragon had somehow been pushed off before the hold of the flames was well established: and she had hardly dashed into the region of rough green swell, when the wash of the waves began to tell upon her flame. It burned low, and further out she butted into a surge, to come out of it scorched, but seaworthy, and without a spark, the corpse still unsinged. The rovers, hardly now observing, could not discern from afar that the sunset flames which wrapped her were not the flames which ravage.

The old Gunhild, by some lucky stroke of divination, had said to Gurth: "You will conquer the living—but *beware of the dead.*"

From that part of the Norway coast to the Hjaltland Isles, there and back, was a run of six or seven days; so on the morning of the fifth day out, Gurth was returning loaded, the centre of a horizon of sea: The morning came darkly, convulsed with squalls, the wind blowing somewhat from the West of South, and the *Skidblednir*, close-hauled was steering East, labouring heavily, when at seven a man rushed below, and woke Gurth with the news that a ship, larger than the *Skidblednir*, perhaps some hostile pirate-keel, bearing upon them straight before the wind, had been sighted. Gurth, a poltroon, had his ship been empty, would still have shunned any possibility in the nature of blows; loaded as she was, he sprang from his couch, apprehension widening his eyes, crying: "Tell them to put out every oar and run before the wind."

In three minutes the *Skidblednir* was flying north-east from the foam of her own wide wake; in an hour the other ship, from which no oars had been put out, had disappeared; and Gurth then agreeing to resume his course, they breathed from the oars, and drew her again to the wind. But now they had somewhat lost count of their position.

At noon, through the dimness of the sunless day, they sighted that ship again bearing down upon them.

Away, then, northward: once more let the oars march regimental over the sea-room, and the gust load the loosened lug! With every swoop of the thirty blades, Gurth stooped his body forward, to help her haste, his heart whispering to the knave strange awes, his hands as chill as the hands of Sigurd.

At three they breathed afresh. But a great gale was then raging, and no soul on the *Skidblednir* had any longer any notion where they were, whither they went. A half-darkness, gloomy as doom, immured them. But at about the hour that the sun, had it been visible, would have been seen to sink, the bleakness lifted a little just south of them, and beneath that lifted curtain they dimly observed—the ship.

Away, then! . . . They needed no longer the urgings of Gurth to fly for life, for in every breast trembled a terror never felt before, nameless, vague. And now down rushed suddenly upon them the raven draperies of night—the last sight that met their eyes having been the spectre-ship.

They were near the Norway sea-board, did not know it, and drove straight upon one of the whirlpools that swirl in frothy fury along that coast. A roar grew gross upon them, and before long the *Skidblednir* bolted suddenly from the control of her oars, and spurted like a bird into a wide circular flight. Some were at once tossed away like feathers into the waters; the others, felled to the deck, clung to whatever they could; and, racing two cable-lengths behind them, came the ship which had chased them to this, invisible in the blackness—till a lamp, shattered in the forehold of the

Skidblednir by her flight, belched forth an opal of smoke and fire. This light revealed, high above them, a writhing and reeling horizon; below, a well, toward which, in lessening whirls they were flying round and round an incline of churning surge. And now streaks of flying fire, streaming aft from the *Skidblednir*, having fastened upon the other ship, she, too, bloomed up into tulip bloom: and to Gurth Hermodsson, glancing abroad from his tafferel, was manifested the grim form of Sigurd lying grand and arrogant on his pyre. At this sight, Hermodsson sent to the skies a cry high above that agony-cry of the gulf, and dropped. When the *Skidblednir* bounded bow downward into the abyss he was already dead.

"But," said Hrolf, a year afterwards, "what if Gurth Hermodsson some day turn up? He may be alive all the time: then I should no longer be your husband."

"That is true," answered Gerda gravely, "we must talk the matter over—when he comes."

TULSAH

[Translation of a scorched Hindoo MS.]

Most wonderful, I often think, must have been the dower of vitality originally vouchsafed me. The passage of one hundred and twenty years has not availed to bleach a single hair of these raven masses. My memory is still, as it was, almost more than that of men. Undimmed is my eye. Yet the end is surely near. A hundred and twenty was the age at which the great Boodh, prince of Oude, passed into unending muckut; at such age, too, died he whom they called my father, and, they say, *his* father also; and, for what I know—but such speculations are frivolous.

It is singular that none of my subjects ever heard of, or even suspected, the undoubted connection which exists between Boodh and my race. He was one of its sons, and one of its fathers. Here in the profundity and gloom of this subterrene, I now for the first time in modern days commit this tremendous secret to parchment.

I have spoken of my memory: yet on one side at least the tree is bare of blossom or leaf. All my first youth has passed from me as completely as though I never *had* a first youth. Many and many are the days which I have spent, unconscious of the universe, rapt in contemplation of this mystery. But no intensest effort could bring one ray of remembrance. I can recall, indeed, the circumstance of my awaking to self-knowledge; but as to all that preceded it, there is the blackness of darkness. In a chamber hollowed out of the face of the natural rock I opened my eyes. I lay on my back in a coffin of red stone. A reddish cloth, studded with jewels, enwrapped my body, but the convolutions extended far below my feet, as though the swaddling had been intended for one of much greater stature than I. The coffin itself was large enough to contain the body of a man. Long I lay, first in listless dream, then with the burgeoning consciousness of entity. I rose from the coffin; I cast off the cerements; I crawled from the chamber of rock. I looked at my limbs, the limbs of a well-grown boy, and saw that they were perfect, and withy, and beautifully brown. I could have exclaimed at all the marvel and delight. But the lion's voice broke upon my ear. I at once felt terror, understanding him an enemy. The sun was setting. I was in the midst of the jungle of the unfathomable forest.

I passed during the night through the million-fold life of the wild. I exulted when I eluded the mad elephant and the prowling tiger-cat by the sinuousness of my limbs; I looked without fear upon the ape and the untamed zebu; but when I saw the *serpent*—heinously leprous—then hatred and loathing thrilled me, and I climbed, breathless in panic, to the branches of a tree.

With the light of the morning I came, on the edge of the forest, to a stately town, full of aëry edifices, traceried light as vision; it lay in a valley enclosed by a circle of high blue mountains, down which brawled many a rill; the whole mirrored in an oval lake which nearly occupied the rest of the valley. It was at this sight that, so far as I can now remember, the conception of *Time* first arose in my brain: I went back æon upon æon, and connected this city with memories, penumbral but real, and old, it seemed, as the world. The town is situated in the centre of Hindostan, is exceedingly ancient, a kingdom by itself, unvisited.

An aged priest met me on the outskirts. He looked with a quick intentness upon my face, and spoke some words to me. I did not understand, nor could I answer him. He led me to the temple where he ministered, and for three years concealed me in its recesses from the eyes of all. At the end of this time he made me lead him to the chamber of rock, and commanded me to point out the coffin in which I had opened my eyes. This satisfied him fully: it was the

coffin of the maharajah of the city, who, he told me, had died a
year before my awaking. The maharajah was then very old; he had
acquired, it was said, the sum of human wisdom. His people had,
by his own explicit directions, instead of burning the body, laid it
to its rest in the sarcophagus, at the spot where conscious life, as
far as I could recollect, was first born within me. Adjeebah, the
Brahmin *gooroo* who had instructed me, announced me as the
son, hidden by him till then, of the dead rajah. None could doubt
it: to doubt would have been the insanity of unbelief: I was the
living likeness of the dead! A day came when I mounted the throne
of the palace as sovereign of Lovanah amid the acclamations of
the people.

Among the first things I learned was that all my ancestors had
been known and reverenced during life as men who had attained
the holy calm of yug; that a long tradition had handed it down that,
without exception, they had left the cares of durbar (or state) to
their ministers, in order to muse in the interior palace upon the
deep things of wisdom. The same instinct rose spontaneously and
irresistibly within me. I became a species of Yati, resolving to
search out knowledge and the nature of things, if so be I might
arrive at the comprehension of the ultimate mystery. The years fled
rapidly. Many languages I learned; the wisdom of the Hellenes;
the zoomorphism of the Egyptians; the heights of the pyramids of
Chufu and Shafra. In intense meditations passed my leaden days.
I read in the Hebrew scroll of that Melchisedec, King of Salem,
priest of the Most High God, without father, without mother,
having neither beginning of days nor end of life. I learned how
Boodh, too, who was of my kin, was delivered of his mother Maia
in a manner most marvelous. I was convulsed at the thrilling
secrets of the world; my tongue shuddered, my eye rolled, in
ecstasy on ecstasy. I tracked the vanity and sublimity of Man to
their hiding-place; I sought out the meanings of religions, whence
they come, whither they go.

I lighted, many years after my accession to the kingdom, upon
a document, deep among the mouldening archives, and yellow
with the accumulation of ages. Having read it, I swooned upon the

agate floor, and lay through the long day and night as dead. It was a narrative inscribed on biblion, and by it I learned the dark fate which befel the first of my race. He was called Obal, and went out from his home a century before ever that Abram, from whom the Hebrews sprang as the sands of the sea, had yet departed out of Haran. The object of his pilgrimage was to know wisdom, and learn the modes of men. He traveled onward till he reached Hur of the Chaldees, one of the first cities built by the hand of the mason and the smith. It was in Mesopotamia, which was called Naharaïm. Here dwelled the votaries of that Zabaism from which is derived the Parsee hierology. The doctrine has its origins deep in the roots of the universe. Loosely allied to it is phallic, and—very much more intimately—*serpent*, worship: for, inasmuch as the mist of constellations in the farthest heaven assumes the form of a *serpent* in its uneasy writhings, here have we a connection—profound enough, terrible enough—between Flame and the Serpent; and since Flame is torture, so is the Serpent the fit emblem of Hell. Hence the wisdom of the Hebrew serpent-myth of the temptation and fall of man; and hence, too, came it, that the Zabians, worshipping in the first instance the heavenly hosts of fire, were also worshippers of the snaky uncleanness. At Hur the heart of Obal was seduced by the specious beauty of Star and Moon: he became a devotee to the fire and the serpent. For many years he lived there a life of study and peace; not till he was a very old man did the consummation of Fate overtake him. In a forecourt of a temple of Ashtoreth he saw a maiden priestess whose loveliness kindled his sere heart. Her name was Tamar. She was vowed to chastity. How foul the crime to draw her from the service of the Goddess Obal knew. But he seems to have been a man of daring eye and headlong lust. He found occasion to speak with the maiden; the abomination of love became mutual between them; he wedded her. Had he not been a great man in Hur, he, with the apostate woman, would without doubt have been stoned to death. But they lived—so long, and so securely—that it seemed as though the heavens were oblivious of the sacrilege. At last Tamar died. Obal was full of years. On the night preceding her journey to the tomb, the patriarch slept by her side—

for the last time—on the couch of ivory where she stiffly lay. He slept. In the morning his eunuchs, coming to the chamber, found him dead. His face, his staring eyes, were black with imprisoned blood. Around his throat had coiled itself a serpent, red of colour, as though a flame perfused its veins. The body of Tamar was not seen.

I have said that I swooned upon the floor, and lay as dead. This was singular, for I had so far traveled upon the road of knowledge as to be aware of the ancientness and universality of superstition, manifesting itself always by a certain historical metabolism. The tendency of my mind was indeed toward the exact. While the Jookaja believes that nothing exists but knowledge, things being only the forms thereof; and the Medheemuck that both knowledge and things, are *sun*, or cipher, and the All itself but a visionary vesture half concealing the eternal Glare; I, admitting the seemliness of these syntheses of dogma, must say that my own mental trend was the other way, toward a full belief in matter, and the truthfulness of the senses. I was therefore more and more inclined to assert that no impression of life is explicable save by facts in their essence "natural." *And yet* this unauthenticated tale of the old and vanished world rent my soul, "like a veil," in twain. Let me not attempt to explain this mystery. Here is a secret too dark—too dark—for speech. The nations of the far West blab of a Deity who travails and travails and travails for ever—just as though the bursting brain of a man could realize that thought and live! The yellow Brahmin, on the other hand, shaves his head, and with light heart full of craft, discusses a lazy Brimmah, omniscient, but clothed in inertia as in a mantle. I will say nothing. It is a subject *full* of fear. In the one doctrine at least is safety: in the other—could it be realized— is the frenzy eternal. Let me not therefore be understood to maintain this other: for who would believe if I say that *memory* was the secret of the effect which the tale of Obal wrought upon me? Would I not sputter the babblings of a maniac, did I assert that—vaguely, but really—afar off, but with no dubiety—I remembered—from beginning to end—ah! but at *this* mystery let silence cover with her hand the mouth of rashness!

I now set myself diligently to the study of the race of kings who had reigned since the beginnings of the over Lovanah. The facts which confronted me were startling. It was then that I first learned that the Boodh, who, like Obal, had left his home mad with the passion for wisdom, was of us. Of fifty kings in the direct line I found that all had lived to ages far beyond the ordinary span of human life; that more than half had taken as wives, not Hindoos, but believers in the Zend-Avesta, followers of Zoroaster, *fire-wor-shippers*; that at least ten had deserted their kingdom, and wandered far over Asia—in obscurity, poor—hounded by the criminal lust of our race for the *cabala* of knowledge; that at least twenty-five—among them my own predecessor— had met their death by the stings of venomous serpents; that all of them had married; and that the death of not one of them had preceded in order of time the death of his consort.

It was when I had understood the sinister meaning of these things that, in the dim chamber which I had made my abode, I fell upon my face to the ground, and swore in my heart three oaths, to which I called every power of the Universe to witness; I would moderate, and, if necessary, quench, the zeal to know which inflamed me; I would never for any purpose wander abroad from the land, from the house in which I then found myself; no daughter of man would I ever espouse. This I swore, and thus did I resolve to break in my person the continuity of that destiny which hunted my race.

I called to my presence my *dewan* and two other ministers of state, and ordered them to publish abroad a proclamation offering a reward of ten rupees of silver to the slayer of every serpent within my dominion.

"Your father published the identical proclamation," answered the chief minister.

I started.

"And," said another, "its only visible result was an enormous increase in the number of serpents in the district."

"An increase," added the third, "which was above all conspicuous in the multiplication of an unknown species, distinguished by its very remarkable colour, and extreme rancour."

These announcements did not fail to have their full effect upon me. I had then arrived at the age of perhaps fifty. From thenceforth I shut myself from mankind with even greater persistency than ever, and to lull into quiescence my too restive brain, I now abandoned my body to the delight of the lotus pipe, and the peace of the sleepy *bhang*. As the Jain, tangled in a mesh of religious frivolities, never slaying a living thing, seeks by strong crying to Parswanath, and the practice of self-torment, to enter forcibly into *nirvana*; so I, by another and a broader gate, entered the *nirvana* of vision. Thirty years passed over me as a watch in the night, opaline with vague prismic hues. I was a confirmed hermit: in a year hardly two of my servants saw my face: the active memory of me passed from men. I still studied—sought—thought—but over the intensity of research was shed the appeasing glamour of the long, long, trance, the hyperborean dream.

I walked one night in an out-court of the palace, and admired that "crooked serpent" which trails in everlasting length athwart the heaven. It was the first time for many years that I had passed from the gloom of my chamber. I was alone. The sound of voices in a neighbouring field reached my ear. I walked pensive toward a gate, and chanced to see a concourse of people standing some little distance away. Long it was since I had mingled with my fellow: I walked quietly toward the crowd, and saw it grouped round a funeral-pile, on which lay stretched the body of a man. It was a *suttee*. In their midst stood a very young woman—most godlike tall—surpassing lovely—delirious with opiates; her body perfumed; her head sprinkled with sandal-powder; the wife of the dead man, who had devoted herself to the flames which were to consume him. Tulsah!—dame of my life—sovereign mistress of my destiny—Tulsah! then first, under the moon, did my eye light upon that serpentine form, that iridescent grace! I beheld how with wavy ease she ascended the pyre—the imponderable limbs of spirit composed themselves beside the shape of the dead—her eyes closed; from a corner of the resinous pile I saw the red flame dart upward, upward! Already I was aged—but strong too, and lithe: I dashed forward—with victorious energy I tore her from the lick of the tongues of the fire, and to the murmuring mob I cried aloud:

"Back, fools—I am the Maharajah!"

I know not what extremity of change now accomplished itself within me. My disenchained spirit danced and danced in the ecstasy of a new youth. True, I had vowed—I had vowed. But Tulsah had that dear quality of the eyes to which the Greek artists gave the name τὸ ὑγρόν, "liquidity." This impression they produced in their statues by a slight raising of the underlid. Man is folly itself. Let this one fact only be considered: those same Greeks believed that they alone of the nations possessed the thing they called *philosophia*—the love of the subtleties of wisdom; and even while they were thus believing, the Vedic Hymns had been sung; the Brahmin had codified the intricate activities of the Attributes Sut, Raj, and Tum; and the Boodh had denied that Brahma, Vishnu, and Mahadeva were emanations of the Spirit of God. Such is the inborn vanity and shallowness of man.

And I, too, was vain and shallow! My oath I flung to the winds. The passions of a youth, intensified a million-fold, pulsated within my bosom. My zenana, so long tenantless, at last received an inmate—and her name was Tulsah!

Little cared I for the prejudices—deep, religious, though they were—of my uncultured people, who declared that I had robbed her from the dead. I loved to recline through the sluggish hours by her side, and watch the ichor that swelled and swelled her veins. Surely her skin was not the skin of the Hindoos: but I cannot remember that I ever definitely learned her origin. I know only that Tulsah adored me. We passed our lives together in the twilight of a perfect and happy solitude; and never did I surfeit of her ethereal presence, or tire of gazing upon the strangely delicate streaks of reddish hue which mingled with her jet-black hair, or upon the torpidly- indolent and sinuous movements of her exquisitely soft, and supple, and undulating form.

In an evil hour one day, when, heavy with opiates, I lay in waking trance, by her side I revealed to her the history of the tragedy of the patriarch Obal.

She listened to the whole with agitation, with heaving bosom, and an intense alertness for which I could not account.

"He seduced her," she said after a long time, speaking bitingly, and gazing afar— "he seduced her from her devotion to the heavenly hosts—"

"Ay!—Tulsah!—he snatched her from her ministry upon the eternal flames—"

"And you—"

"I, my Tulsah? *I! I!*"

"Yes—you—*you* snatched me, a devotee to the flames, from the very flames themselves—"

I folded her panting to my lean bosom.

"Angel! angel!" I shrieked, "yet does the Power not live whose craft could prevail to change thy dear perfection into the viper's tooth!"

In such manner we spent our life. The years multiplied themselves and passed. Tulsah approached the borders of age. Her beauty waned—markedly waned. As she grew older the sinuosity of her muscular and osseous systems became, I must say it, too pronounced to be longer fascinating. A singular affection of the skin covered her body with a multitude of regularly-shaped small dull-red erythemata. Her eyes reddened, uttering a rheumy mucus. I looked for the whitening of her hair. My disappointment was bitter. The heavy surges which, once black, billowed like a torrent to her feet, and wide overflowed the floor like the surf of a sea of ink, gradually at first—then rapidly—took on the gorgeous, and the *farouche*, and the unhuman semblance of a mantle of vivid flame.

She died. With my own hand I swaddled her corpse, and helped to place it upon the pyre. Death among our Eastern nations is surely never a comely sight: yet it was with sorrow rather than with loathing that I looked for the last time upon the wan face of my Tulsah.

We were alone together in a court of the palace. The fulsome gloat of moon and stars shone over and about us. I held a torch to the pile: a sheet of flame shot up, crackling, around the beloved sacrifice.

To this day I know not how it was: either the fire consumed its victim with a rapidity inconceivable, or a suspension of consciousness, due to the anodynes which I had that day freely imbibed, deprived me of sight: but from the moment when I applied the torch to the moment when I again looked at the pile was an interval which seemed so short as to be inappreciable; and yet within it, in sharp disproof of my estimate of its length, both the pyre and its occupant had passed, utterly consumed, from before my eyes.

I stood amazed, gazing at the column of blue smoke which rolled up from the very small heap of ashes into the air: and now a new impression—born perhaps of my own fantasy—or born of the despotism of drugs—or born of the more dread despotism of reality—an impression this time of absolute terror—forced itself upon my mind. I beheld, or thought so—the blue of the ascending reek turn to the sanguine hue of Sardius; and now with a spasmodic jerk the whole high and solid pillar of the reddened smoke split itself into innumerable dismemberment; and I saw every wreath, and curl, and tortured tendril stand apart in definite isolation, and shape itself into a changing snaky form, till the whole vast nest, coalescing, writhed together in infinite implication, with hollow eye, and extruded fang.

Aghast at the illusion, I hurried from the spot. I entered the palace. Through a secret corridor I passed to the chamber where Tulsah and I had spent the years of our love. A light shed itself from a vessel of oil in the ceiling. I sank doddering to a seat, and covered my face. Hours went by, and still I sat. All the past was around me—she herself. How like a dream the whole mystery of her coming, her abiding, her going! Tulsah!—I groaned her name. I lifted up my voice weeping. "Where now remote in some green sanctity of ocean cave or azure fold of space broods thy ethereal presence?" I rose to throw my despairs upon the couch where she had been wont to lie, when, in the gloom, I saw—within the palsy of horror saw—coiled thick upon the bed, with gorge erect above a foul vast base of clotted wreaths, and palpitant through all its mucous swelth, the fat and lazar loathliness of a monstrous Snake, whose ruby eyes regarded me.

I ran from the palace! A secret portal led me to the borders of the forest. Here I came upon the traces of a highway, the windings of which I followed. The rising sun of the next day found me still fugitive—hasting in wildest panic—already many a mile from the towers of Lovanah.

I had thus broken the second of my vows, which bound me to my home. It was not till long afterwards that this thought occurred to me. But there remained the third: never, by my own seeking, to penetrate the ultimate secret of the world: and by this I have faithfully abided.

. . . . .

Ten years passed and left me, as they found me, vagabond over India. I journeyed from city to city, meditating on the manners of men, and begging my bread from the charitable. I have wandered in the streets of that Benares to which Boodh first retired from the world; I have stood beneath the great granite mosque of Jumna Musjid at Delhi; and through all the cities of the north I have passed.

But my pilgrimage was very far from purposeless. I sought with intense scrupulousness—as for hid treasures—after something. I hoped to find a retreat in which, with absolute security from the designs of destiny, I might lay me down, and die the natural death of the rest of men.

I came at last, in the vale of Cashmere, to a lonely Hindoo temple—one of the great vihâras—consisting of a long oblong chamber. The roof was supported by two rows of huge stone pillars connected by vaulted architraves, and at the farthest end, semicircular in shape, stood a colossus of the seated Boodh. The temple had been chiseled out of the base of the Himalaya.

Through a burning lamp hung from a pillar, the sanctuary seemed deserted. I entered, and passed up the broad central nave. At the extremity, near the statue, where the vihâra might be expected to end, I happened to find an open door. I walked through it, and descended a long stairway which brought me to a second temple; all was now the intensity of darkness; but happening to meet with another door-way, I descended still farther—down and down—until, in this way, I had traversed six stair-ways of equal descent. I must by this time have traveled a very considerable distance both into the interior of the mountain and the depths of the earth.

Yet another series of steps, and I came to a passage, at the end of which was a circular apartment: here was clearly the termination of this great excavation. From its roof hung a lamp which distilled a vermilion light. I could see from the appearance of the chamber that it had been unvisited perhaps for ages, and I was unable to conjecture by what means the lamp was kept alive, except it were by means of feeding pipes from the far outermost temple of all; but, at any rate, it showed me that the key-contrivance of the door of the chamber was *on the outside*. With the deliberate purpose of there ending my days, I passed into the apartment, and pulled the door toward me. I heard with joy the click of the fastening which sealed my fate.

In the room is a small stone table and a stool. I had brought with me parchment, and the materials for writing. This history, as far as it has now gone, has by these means been recorded. I shall leave it to moulder beside my bones. As the half-pleasurable pangs of hunger, and the languor of coming disease, invade my body, I may add yet a phrase or two.

. . . . .

I have now observed that this chamber is not of stone, as far at least as its interior lining is concerned. It is certainly extraordinary; but there can be no doubt that the flooring and ceiling are of wood, and that the circular sides are of old iron-plate paneled at regular intervals with narrow wooden laminæ. The faintness of the lamp's scarlet glow doubtless prevented me from noticing this singularity from the first.

. . . . .

I have brought with me a quantity of opium. On the lap of an ocean of rainbows will I embark when the great hour comes.

. . . . .

The opium works well in stanching the current of the blood, and in overdriving the spent heart to its final throbbings. It will thus quicken the action of the hunger. The past five or six hours I have spent in a coma full of luxuriousness.

. . . . .

Spare me! Spare me! frail man that I am! This chamber, in which—with my own hand—I have imprisoned myself, *is the neth-ermost hell itself!* Happening to rise from my seat, I saw—in the shadow thrown by the table—a sight! the skeleton of a man; having a burnt appearance; old as the mountain; dismembered now in the lower limbs, the ribs in fragments; but the cervical vertebræ still cohering, and around them—coiled—in perfect preservation, in hideous symmetry, the vertebræ of a great—No! not that word again! I dashed my body against the door of my prison; for a full hour of frenzy beat my life against its adamant: then fell to the ground.

. . . . .

As I lay on the floor, my senses having returned to me, I seemed to hear a very faint sound, proceeding apparently from beneath the casing of wood. I bent down my ear. It was a gentle crepitant sound, as though a rat gnawed the wood.

But this it could hardly have been which made me leap up with an alacrity so frantic. The action was involuntary; but I soon recognized its reason. On placing the palm of my hand upon the board-ing, a marked degree of *warmth* communicated itself to my skin. I have also touched the iron casing of the chamber all round, and find the same condition.

. . . . .

This apartment must be at a great depth in the bowels of the earth. Can it be that huge geologic forces, volcanic in character, are tumbling in Acherontic travail around me? The heat of the floor and walls slowly but steadily increases.

. . . . .

Seventy years ago I made a threefold vow. Forty years ago I broke the first, and wedded. Ten years ago I broke the second, and left my home. Three days ago I broke, thou seeing God, the third, when, within my own hand, I closed upon me this tomb of woe. For now—at last!—I know—with clear precision—the ultimate, the flaming, the maddening secret of being.

It is old: it has been heard from the beginning; but heard as an incredible tale. Upon no heart of man has its intolerable incubus ever rested as now it rests upon mine; no eyeball has its excess of light so scorched and blasted into ashes. And this I say in foolish and feeble words; that there is knowledge, and there may be things; but gibbering spectres of this One Thing only: *an Eye that glares and glares for ever!* And wise are they who call it Hammon, Brimmah, Zeu—Ya, and Ra, and Allah; but wiser they who say *Saranyû* (i.e. "Eninyes," Counteraction).

. . . . .

I will write even to the bitter and fiery end.

. . . . .

The scraping and gnawing sound has multiplied itself a million-fold, amid is now clamorous and constant. At every point beneath the flooring—along the length of every wooden panel—over all the wooden ceiling, it is heard. An army of creatures boring, *boring* their invincible way to reach me. . . .

. . . . .

The floor I can no longer touch with my feet; the table of stone itself grows hot; the iron casing of the chamber, even under the scarlet gleam of the lamp, now emits the redding glow of heated metal. . . .

. . . . .

Tulsah!—that name again!—the fiery furnace of intensest hell— ah bitter, *bitter* love! to the centre it blazes. And now—ah now— from a thousand apertures—around, above, beneath—a thousand small and crimson serpent-heads extrude! convulsive—O bile of God!—in ecstasy— they expel and retract their salamandrine necks! Crimson, crimson, is their name! But what a Babel of hissing! Once, in sleep, did I not see her tongue loll black and long—And now— wage, wage of lawless love!—now—O Majesty—they come—that flaming fault in worms—now—ten thousand forked and jagged— [three words of doubtful meaning follow].

VAILA

E caddi come l'uome cui sonno piglia.—Dante.

A good many years ago, a young man, student in Paris, I was informally associated with the great Corot, and eye-witnessed by his side several of those cases of mind-malady, in the analysis of which he was a past master. I remember one little girl of the Marais, who, till the age of nine, in no way seemed to differ from her playmates. But one night, lying a-bed, she whispered into her mother's ear: "Maman, can you not hear the *sound of the world?*" It appears that her recently-begun study of geography had taught her that the earth flies, with an enormous velocity, on an orbit about the sun; and that *sound of the world* to which she referred was a faint (quite subjective) musical humming, like a shell-murmur, heard in the silence of night, and attributed by her fancy to the song of this high motion. Within six months the excess of lunacy possessed her.

I mentioned the incident to my friend, Haco Harfager, then occupying with me the solitude of an old place in S. Germain, shut in by a shrubbery and high wall from the street. He listened with singular interest, and for a day seemed wrapped in gloom.

Another case which I detailed produced a profound impression upon my friend. A young man, a toy-maker of S. Antoine, suffering from chronic congenital phthisis, attained in the ordinary way his twenty-fifth year. He was frugal, industrious, self-involved. On

a winter's evening, returning to his lonely garret, he happened to
purchase one of those vehemently factious sheets which circulate
by night, like things of darkness, over the Boulevards. This simple
act was the herald of his doom. He lay a-bed, and perused the
feuille. He had never been a reader; knew little of the greater world,
and the deep hum of its travail. But the next night he bought another leaf.

Gradually he acquired interest in politics, the large movements,
the roar of life. And this interest grew absorbing. Till late into the
night, and every night, he lay poring over the furious mendacity,
the turbulent wind, the printed passion. He would awake tired,
spitting blood, but intense in spirit—and straightway purchased
a morning leaf. His being lent itself to a retrograde evolution. The
more his teeth gnashed, the less they ate. He became sloven,
irregular at work, turning on his bed through the day. Rags overtook him. As the greater interest, and the vaster tumult, possessed
his frail soul, so every lesser interest, tumult, died to him. There
came an early day when he no longer cared for his own life; and
another day, when his maniac fingers rent the hairs from his head.

As to this man, the great Corot said to me:

"Really, one does not know whether to laugh or weep over such
a business. Observe, for one thing, how diversely men are made!
There are minds precisely so sensitive as a cupful of melted silver;
every breath will roughen and darken them: and what of the si-
moon, tornado? And that is not a metaphor but a simile. For such,
this earth—I had almost said this universe—is clearly no fit habitation, but a Machine of Death, a baleful Vast. *Too* horrible to many
is the running shriek of Being—they *cannot* bear the world. Let
each look well to his own little whisk of life, say I, and leave the
big fiery Automaton alone. Here in this poor toy-maker you have a
case of the ear: it is only the neurosis, Oxyecoia. Splendid was that
Greek myth of the Harpies: by *them* was this man snatched—or,
say, caught by a limb in the wheels of the universe, and so perished. It is quite a grand exit, you know—translation in a chariot
of flame. Only remember that the member first involved was *the
pinna*: he bent *ear* to the howl of Europe, and ended by himself

howling. Can a straw ride composedly on the primeval whirlwinds? Between chaos and our shoes wobbles, I tell you, the thinnest film! I knew a man who had this peculiarity of aural hyperæsthesia: that every sound brought him minute information of the matter causing the sound; that is to say, he had an ear bearing to the normal ear the relation which the spectroscope bears to the telescope. A rod, for instance, of mixed copper and iron impinging, in his hearing, upon a rod of mixed tin and lead, conveyed to him not merely the proportion of each metal in each rod, but some strange knowledge of the essential meaning and spirit, as it were, of copper, of iron, of tin, and of lead. Of course, he went mad; but, beforehand, told me this singular thing: that precisely such a sense as his was, according to his *certain* intuition, employed by the Supreme Being in his permeation of space to apprehend the nature and movements of mind and matter. And he went on to add that *Sin*— what we call *sin*—is only the movement of matter or mind into such places, or in such a way, as to give offence or pain to this delicate diplacusis (so I must call it) of the Creator; so that the 'Law' of Revelation became, in his eyes, edicts promulgated by their Maker merely in self-protection from aural pain; and divine punishment for, say murder, nothing more than retaliation for unease caused to the divine aural consciousness by the matter in a particular dirk or bullet lodged, at a particular moment, in a non-intended place! Him, too, I say, did the Harpies whisk aloft."

My recital of these cases to my friend, Harfager, I have mentioned. I was surprised, not so much at his acute interest—for he was interested in all knowledge—as at the obvious pains which he took to conceal that interest. He hurriedly turned the leaves of a volume, but could not hide his panting nostrils.

From first days when we happened to attend the same seminary in Stockholm, a tacit intimacy had sprung between us. I loved him greatly; that he so loved me I knew. But it was an intimacy not accompanied by many of the usual interchanges of close friendships. Harfager was the shyest, most isolated, insulated, of beings. Though our joint *ménage* (brought about by a chance meeting at a midnight *séance* in Paris) had now lasted some months, I knew

nothing of his plans, motives. Through the day we pursued our
intense readings together, he rapt quite back into the past, I equally
engrossed upon the present; late at night we reclined on couches
within the vast cave of an old fireplace Louis Onze, and smoked to
the dying flame in a silence of wormwood and terebinth. Occasionally a *soirée* or lecture might draw me from the house; except once,
I never understood that Harfager left it. I was, on that occasion,
returning home at a point of the Rue St. Honoré where a rush of
continuous traffic rattled over the old coarse pavements retained
there, when I came suddenly upon him. In this tumult he stood
abstracted on the trottoir in a listening attitude, and for a moment
seemed not to recognise me when I touched him.

Even as a boy I had discerned in my friend the genuine Noble,
the inveterate patrician. One saw that in him. Not at all that his
personality gave an impression of any species of loftiness, opu-
lence; on the contrary. He did, however, give an impression of
incalculable *ancientness*. He suggested the last moment of an æon.
No nobleman have I seen who so bore in his wan aspect the assur-
ance of the inevitable aristocrat, the essential prince, whose pale
blossom is of yesterday, and will perish to-morrow, but whose root
fills the ages. This much I knew of Harfager; also that on one or
other of the bleak islands of his patrimony north of Zetland lived
his mother and a paternal aunt; that he was somewhat deaf; but
liable to transports of pain or delight at variously-combined musical sounds, the creak of a door, the note of a bird. More I cannot
say that I then knew.

He was rather below the middle height, and gave some promise of stoutness. His nose rose highly aquiline from that species of
forehead called by phrenologists "the musical," that is to say,
flanked by temples which incline *outward* to the cheek-bones,
making breadth for the base of the brain; while the direction of
the heavy-lidded, faded-blue eyes, and of the eyebrows, was a
downward *droop* from the nose of their outer extremities. He wore
a thin chin-beard. But the astonishing feature of his face were the
ears: they were nearly circular, very small, and flat, being devoid
of that outer volution known as the *helix*. The two tiny discs of

cartilage had always the effect of making me think of the little ancient round shields, without rims, called *clipeus* and *peltè*. I came to understand that this was a peculiarity which had subsisted among the members of his race for some centuries. Over the whole white face of my friend was stamped a look of woeful inability, utter gravity of sorrow. One said "Sardanapalus," frail last of the great line of Nimrod.

After a year I found it necessary to mention to Harfager my intention of leaving Paris. We reclined by night in our accustomed nooks within the fireplace. To my announcement he answered with a merely polite "Indeed!" and continued to gloat upon the flame; but after an hour turned upon me, and said:

"Well, it seems to be a hard and selfish world."

Truisms uttered with just such an air of new discovery I had occasionally heard from him; but the earnest gaze of eyes, and plaint of voice, and despondency of shaken head, with which he now spoke shocked me to surprise.

"*À propos* of what?" I asked.

"My friend, do not leave me!"

He spread his arms. His utterance choked.

I learned that he was the object of a devilish malice; that he was the prey of a hellish temptation. That a lure, a becking hand, a lurking lust, which it was the effort of his life to eschew (and to which he was especially liable in solitude), continually enticed him; and that thus it had been almost from the day when, at time age of five, he had been sent by his father from his desolate home in the sea.

And whose was this malice?

He told me his mother's and aunt's.

And what was this temptation?

He said it was the temptation to return—to fly with the very frenzy of longing—back to that dim home.

I asked with what motives, and in what particulars, the malice of his mother and aunt manifested itself. He replied that there was, he believed, no specific motive, but only a determined malevolence, involuntary and fated; and that the respect in which it manifested itself was to be found in the multiplied prayers and commands with which, for years, they had importuned him to seek again the far hold of his ancestors.

All this I could in no way comprehend, and plainly said as much. In what consisted this horrible magnetism, and equally horrible peril, of his home? To this question Harfager did not reply, but rose from his seat, disappeared behind the drawn curtains of the hearth, and left the room. He presently returned with a quarto tome bound in hide. It proved to be Hugh Gascoigne's *Chronicle of Norse Families*, executed in English black-letter. The passage to which he pointed I read as follows:

> "Nowe, of thise two brethrene, tholder (the elder), Harold, beying of seemely personage and prowesse, did goe pilgrimage into Danemarke, wher from he repayred againward hoom to Hjaltlande (Zetland), and wyth hym fette (fetched) the amiabil Thronda for hyss wyf, which was a doughter of the sank (blood) royall of danemark. And his yonger brothir, Sweyne, that was sad and debonayre, but far surmounted the other in cunnying, receyued him with all good chere. Butte eftsones (soon after) fel sweyne sick for alle his lust that he hadde of Thronda his brothir's wyfe. And whiles the worthy Harold, with the grenehede (green-ness) and folye of yowthe, ministred a bisy cure aboute the bedde wher Sweyne lay sick, lo, Sweyne fastened on him a violent stroke with a swerde, and with no lenger taryinge enclosed his hands in bondes, and cast him in the botme of a depe holde. And by cause Harold wold not benumb (de-prive) hymself of the gouernance of Thronda his wif, Sweyne cutte off boeth his ere[s], and putte out one of his iyes, and after diverse sike tormentes was preste (ready) to slee (slay) hym. But on a daye, the valiant Harold, breking hys bondes, and embracinge his aduersary, did by the sleight of wrast-lyng ouerthrowe him, and escaped. Nat-with-standyng, he foltred whan he came to the Somburgh Hed not ferre (far) fro the Castell, and al-be-it that he was swifte-foote, couth

ne farder renne (run) by reson that he was faynte with the
longe plag[u]es of hyss brothir. And whiles he ther lay in a
sound (swoon) did Sweyne come sle (sly) and softe up on
hym, and whan he had striken him with a darte, caste him
fro Samburgh Hede in to the See.

"Nat longe hereafterward did the lady Thronda (tho she
knew nat the manere of her lordes deth, ne, veryly, yf he
was dead or on live) receyve Sweyne in to gree (favour), and
with grete gaudying and blowinge of beamous (trumpets)
did gon to his bed. And right soo they two wente thennes
(thence) to soiourn in ferre partes.

"Now, it befel that Sweyne was mynded by a dreme to
let bild him a grete maunsion in Hialtland for the hoom-
cominge of the ladye Thronda; where for he called to hym a
cunninge Maistre-worckman, and sente him hye (in haste)
to englond to gather thrals for the bilding of this lusty
Houss, but hym-self soiourned wyth his ladye at Rome.
Thenne came his worckman to london, but passinge thennes
to Hialtland, was drent (drowned) he, and his feers (mates),
and his shippe, alle and some. And after two yeres, which
was the tyme assygned, Sweyne harfager sente lettres to
Hialtlande to vnderstonde how his grete Houss did, for he
knew not the drenchynge of the Architecte; and eftsones he
receiued answer that the Houss *did wel*, and was bildinge
on the Ile of Vaila; but that ne was the Ile wher-on Sweyne
had appoynted the bilding to be; and he was aferd, and nere
fel doun ded for drede, by cause that, in the lettres, he saw
before him the mannere of wrytyng of his brothir Harold.
And he sayed in this fourme: 'Surely Harolde is on lyue
(alive), elles (else) ben thise a lettres writ with gostlye
hande.' And he was wo many dayes, seeing that this was a
dedely stroke. Ther-after, he took him-selfe back to Hjaltland to know how the matere was, and ther the old Castell
on Somburgh Hede was brek doun to the erthe. Thenn
Sweyne was wode-worthe, and cryed, 'Jhesu mercy, where
is al the grete Hous of my faders becomen? allas! thys

wycked day of desteynye.' And one of the peple tolde him
that a hoost of worckmen fro fer partes hadde brek it doun.
And he sayd: 'who hath bidde them?' but that couth none
answer. Thenne he sayd agayn; 'nis (is not) my brothir
harold on-lyue? for I haue biholde his writinge'; and that,
to, colde none answer. Soo he wente to Vaila, and saw there
a grete Houss stonde, and whan he looked on hyt, he
saye[d]: 'this, sooth, was y-bild by my brothir Harolde, be
he ded, or bee he on-lyue.' And ther he dwelte, and his ladye,
and his sones and hys sones sones vntyl nowe. For that the
Houss is rewthelesse (ruthless) and withoute pite; where-
for tis seyed that up on al who dwel there faleth a wycked
madness and a lecherous agonie; and that by waye of the
eres doe they drinck the cuppe of the furie of the erelesse
Harolde, til the tyme of the Houss bee ended."

I read the narrative half-aloud, and smiled.

"This, Harfager," I said, "is very tolerable romance on the part
of the good Gascoigne; but has the look of indifferent history."

"It is, nevertheless, genuine *history*," he replied.

"You believe that?"

"The house still stands solidly on Vaila."

"The brothers Sweyn and Harold were literary for their age, I
think?"

"No member of my race," he replied, with, a suspicion of hau-
teur, "has been illiterate."

"But, at least, you do not believe that mediæval ghosts super-
intend the building of their family mansions?"

"Gascoigne nowhere says that; for to be stabbed is not neces-
sarily to die; nor, if he did say it, would it be true to assert that I
have any knowledge on the subject."

"And what, Harfager, is the nature of that 'wicked madness,'
that 'lecherous agonie,' of which Gascoigne speaks?"

"Do you ask me?" He spread his arms. "What do I know? I know
nothing! I was banished from the place at the age of five. Yet
the cry of it still reverberates in my soul. And have I not *told*

you of agonies—even within myself—of inherited longing and loathing. . ."

But, at any rate, I answered, my journey to Heidelberg was just
then indispensable. I would compromise by making absence short,
and rejoin him quickly, if he would wait a few weeks for me. His
moody silence I took to mean consent, and soon afterward left him.

But I was unavoidably detained; and when I returned to our
old quarters, found them empty. Harfager had vanished.

It was only after twelve years that a letter was forwarded me—
a rather wild letter, an excessively long one—in the well-remem-
bered hand of my friend. It was dated at Vaila. From the character
of the writing I conjectured that it had been penned *with furious
haste*, so that I was all the more astonished at the very trivial nature of the voluminous contents. On the first half page he spoke of
our old friendship, and asked if, in memory of that, I would see his
mother who was dying; the rest of the epistle, sheet upon sheet,
consisted of a tedious analysis of his mother's genealogical tree,
the apparent aim being to prove that she was a genuine Harfager,
and a cousin of his father. He then went on to comment on the
extreme prolificness of his race, asserting that since the fourteenth
century, over four millions of its members had lived and died in
various parts of the world; three only of them, he believed, being
now left. That determined, the letter ended.

Influenced by this communication, I traveled northward;
reached Caithness; passed the stormy Orkneys; reached Lerwick;
and from Unst, the most bleak and northerly of the Zetlands,
contrived, by dint of bribes to pit the weather-worthiness of a lug-
sailed 'sixern' (said to be identical with the 'lang-schips' of the
Vikings) against a flowing sea and a darkly-brooding heaven. The
voyage, I was warned, was, at such a time, of some risk. It was the
Cimmerian December of those interboreal latitudes. The weather
here, they said, though never cold, is hardly ever other than
tempestuous. A dense and dank sea-born haze now lay, in spite of
vapid breezes, high along the waters enclosing the boat in a vague
domed cavern of doleful twilight and sullen swell. The region
of the considerable islands was past, and there was a spectral

something in the unreal aspect of silent sea and sunless dismal-
ness of sky which produced upon my nerves the impression of a
voyage *out* of nature, a cruise *beyond* the world. Occasionally, however, we careered past one of those solitary 'skerries,' or sea-stacks,
whose craggy sea-walls, cannonaded and disintegrated by the
inter-shock of the tidal wave and the torrent currents of the Ger-
man Ocean, wore, even at some distance, an appearance of frightful ruin and havoc. Three only of these I saw, for before the dim
day had well run half its course, sudden blackness of night was
upon us, and with it one of those tempests, of which the winter of
this semi-polar sea is, throughout, an ever-varying succession.
During the haggard and dolorous crepuscule of the next brief day,
the rain did not cease; but before darkness had quite supervened,
my helmsman, who talked continuously to a mate of seal-maid-
ens, and water-horses, and *grülies*, paused to point to a mound of
gloomier grey in the weather-bow, which was, he assured me, Vaila.

Vaila, he added, was the centre of quite a system of those *rösts*
(dangerous eddies) and cross-currents, which the action of the tidal
wave hurls hurrying with complicated and corroding swirl among
the islands; in the neighbourhood of Vaila, said the mariner, they
hurtled with more than usual precipitancy, owing to the palisade
of lofty sea-crags which barbicaned the place about; approach was,
therefore, at all times difficult, and by night fool-hardy. With a
running sea, however, we came sufficiently near to discern the
mane of surf which bristled high along the beetling coast-wall. Its
shock, according to the man's account, had oft-times more than
all the efficiency of a bombing of real artillery, slinging tons of
rock to heights of several hundred feet upon the main island.

When the sun next feebly climbed above the horizon to totter
with marred visage through a wan low segment of funereal murk,
we had closely approached the coast; and it was then for the first
time that the impression of some *spinning* motion in the island
(born no doubt of the circular movement of the water) was produced upon me. We effected a landing at a small *voe*, or sea-arm,
on the western side; the eastern, though the point of my aim, being, on account of the swell, out of the question for that purpose.

Here I found in two feal-thatched *skeoes* (or sheds), which crouched beneath the shelter of a far over-hanging hill, five or six poor peasant-seamen, whose livelihood no doubt consisted in periodically trading for the necessaries of the great house on the east. Beside these there were no dwellers on Vaila; but with one of them for guide, I soon began the ascent and transit of the island. Through the night in the boat I had been strangely aware of an oppressive booming in the ears, for which even the roar of the sea round all the coast seemed quite insufficient to account. This now, as we advanced, became fearfully intensified, and with it, once more, the unaccountable conviction within me of *spinning* motions to which I have referred. Vaila I discovered to be a land of hill and precipice, made of fine granite and flaggy gneiss; at about the centre, however, we came upon a high table-land sloping gradually from west to east, and covered by a series of lochs, which sullenly and continuously flowed one into the other. To this chain of sombre, black-gleaming water I could see no terminating shore, and by dint of shouting to my companion, and bending close ear to his answering shout, I came to know that there *was* no such shore: I say *shout*, for nothing less could have prevailed over the steady bellowing as of ten thousand bisons, which now resounded on every hand. A certain tremblement, too, of the earth became distinct. In vain did the eye seek in its dreary purview a single trace of tree or shrub; for, as a matter of course, no kind of vegetation, save peat, could brave, even for a day, that perennial agony of the tempest which makes of this turbid and benighted zone its arena. Darkness, an hour after noon, commenced to overshadow us; and it was shortly afterward that my guide, pointing down a precipitous defile near the eastern coast, hurriedly set forth upon the way he had come. I frantically howled a question after him as he went; but at this point the human voice had ceased to be in the faintest degree audible.

Down this defile, with a sinking of the heart, and a most singular feeling of giddiness, I passed. Having reached the end, I emerged upon a wide ledge which shuddered to the immediate onsets of the sea. But all this portion of the island was, in addition, subject to a sharp continuous ague evidently not due to the heavy ordnance of the ocean. Hugging a point of cliff for steadiness from the wind, I looked forth upon a spectacle of weirdly morne, of dismal wildness. The opening lines of *Hecuba*, or some drear district of the *Inferno*, seemed realized before me. Three black 'skerries,' encompassed by a fantastic series of stacks, crooked as a witch's fore-finger, and giving herbergage to shrill routs of osprey and scart, to seal and walrus, lay at some fathoms' distance; and from its race and rage among them, the sea, in arrogance of white, tumultuous, but inaudible wrath, ramped terrible as an army with banners toward the land. Leaving my place, I staggered some distance to the left: and now, all at once, a vast amphitheatre opened before me, and there burst upon my gaze a panorama of such heart-appalling sublimity, as imagination could never have conceived, nor can now utterly recall.

"A vast amphitheatre" I have said; yet it was rather the shape of a round-Gothic (or Norman) doorway which I beheld. Let the reader picture such a door-frame, nearly a mile in breadth, laid flat upon the ground, the curved portion farthest from the sea; and round it let a perfectly smooth and even wall of rock tower in perpendicular regularity to an altitude not unworthy the vulture's eyrie; and now, down the depth of this Gothic shape, and *over all its extent*, let bawling oceans dash themselves triumphing in spendthrift cataclysm of emerald and hoary fury,—and the stupor of awe with which I looked, and then the shrinking *fear*, and then the instinct of instant flight, will find easy comprehension.

This was the thrilling disemboguement of the lochs of Vaila.

And within the arch of this Gothic cataract, volumed in the world of its smoky torment and far-excursive spray, stood a palace of brass . . . circular in shape . . . huge in dimension.

The last gleam of the ineffectual day had now almost passed, but I could yet discern, in spite of the perpetual rain-fall which bleakly nimbused it as in a halo of tears, that the building was low in proportion to the vastness of its circumference; that it was roofed with a shallow dome; and that about it ran two serried rows of shuttered Norman windows, the upper row being of smaller size than the lower. Certain indications led me to assume that the house had been built upon a vast natural bed of rock which lay, circular and detached, within the arch of the cataract; but this did not quite emerge above the flood, for the whole ground-area upon which I looked dashed a deep and incense-reeking river to the beachless sea; so that passage would have been impossible, were it not that, from a point near me, a massive bridge, thick with algæ, rose above the tide, and led to the mansion. Descending from my ledge, I passed along it, now drenched in spray. As I came nearer, I could see that the house, too, was to half its height more thickly bearded than an old hull with barnacles and every variety of brilliant sea-weed; and—what was very surprising that from many points near the top of the brazen wall huge iron chains, slimily barbarous with the trailing tresses of ages, reached out in symmetrical divergent rays to points on the ground hidden by the flood: the fabric had thus the look of a many-anchored ark; but without pausing for minute observation, I pushed forward, and dashing through the smooth circular waterfall which poured all round from the eaves, by one of its many small projecting porches, entered the dwelling.

Darkness now was around me—and sound. I seemed to stand in the very throat of some yelling planet. An infinite sadness descended upon me; I was near to the abandonment of tears. "Here," I said, "is Khoreb, and the limits of weeping; not elsewhere is the valley of sighing." The tumult resembled the continuous volleying of many thousands of cannon, mingled with strange crashing and bursting uproars. I passed forward through a succession of halls, and was wondering as to my further course, when a hideous figure, bearing a lamp, stalked rapidly towards me. I shrank aghast. It seemed the skeleton of a tall man, wrapped in a winding-sheet. The glitter of a tiny eye, however, and a sere film of skin over part of the face, quickly reassured me. Of ears, he showed no sign. He was, I afterwards learned, Aith; and the singularity of his appearance was partially explained by his pretence—whether true or false—that he had once suffered *burning*, almost to the cinder-stage, but had miraculously recovered. With an expression of malignity, and strange excited gestures, he led the way to a chamber on the upper stage, where having struck light to a vesta, he pointed to a spread table and left me.

For a long time I sat in solitude. The earthquake of the mansion was intense; but all sense seemed swallowed up and confounded in the one impression of sound. Water, water, was the world—nightmare on my chest, a horror in my ears, an intolerable tingling on my nerves. The feeling of being infinitely drowned and ruined in the all-obliterating deluge—the impulse to gasp for breath—overwhelmed me. I rose and paced; but suddenly stopped, angry, I scarce knew why, with myself. I had, in fact, found myself walking with a certain *hurry*, not usual with me, not natural to me. The feeling of giddiness, too, had abnormally increased. I forced myself to stand and take note of the hall. It was of great size, and damp with mists, so that the tattered, but rich, mediæval furniture seemed lost in its extent: its center was occupied by a broad low marble tomb bearing the name of a Harfager of the fifteenth century; its walls were old brown panels of oak. Having drearily observed these things, I waited on with an intolerable consciousness of loneliness; but a little after midnight the tapestry parted, and Harfager with hurried stride, approached me.

In twelve years my friend had grown old. He showed, it is true, a tendency to corpulence; yet, to a knowing eye, he was, in reality, tabid, ill-nourished. And his neck protruded from his body; and his lower back had quite the forward curve of age; and his hair floated about his face and shoulders in a disarray of awful whiteness. A chin-beard hung grey to his chest. His attire was a simple robe of bauge, which, as he went, waved aflaunt from his bare and hirsute shins, and he was shod in those soft slippers called *rivlins*.

To my surprise, he spoke. When I passionately shouted that I could gather no fragment of sound from his moving lips, he clapped both palms to his ears, and thereupon renewed a vehement siege to mine: but again without result. And now, with a seemingly angry fling of the hand, he caught up the taper, and swiftly strode from the chamber.

There was something singularly unnatural in his manner—something which irresistibly reminded me of the skeleton, Aith:

an excess of zeal, a fever, a rage, a *loudness*, an eagerness of walk, a wild extravagance of gesture. His hand constantly dashed the hair-whiffs from his face. Though his countenance was of the saffron of death, the eyes were turgid and red with blood—heavy-lidded eyes, fixed in a downward and sideward intentness of gaze. He presently returned with a folio of ivory and a stylus of graphite hanging from a cord about his garment.

He rapidly wrote a petition that I would, if not too tired, take part with him in the funeral obsequies of his mother. I shouted assent.

Once more he clapped palms to ears; then wrote: "Do not shout: no whisper in any part of the building is inaudible to me."

I remembered that, in early life, he had seemed slightly *deaf*.

We passed together through many apartments, he shading the taper with his hand. This was necessary; for, as I quickly discovered, in no part of the shivering fabric was the air in a state of rest, but seemed for ever commoved by a curious agitation, a faint windiness, like the echo of a storm, which communicated a gentle universal trouble to the tapestries. Everywhere I was confronted with the same past richness, present raggedness of decay. In many of the chambers were old marble tombs; one was a museum piled with bronzes, urns; but broken, imbedded in fungoids, dripping wide with moisture. It was as if the mansion, in ardour of travail, sweated. An odour of decomposition was heavy on the swaying air. With difficulty I followed Harfager through the labyrinth of his headlong passage. Once only he stopped short, and with face madly wild above the glare of the light, heaved up his hand, and uttered a single word. From the shaping of the lips, I conjectured the word, "Hark!"

Presently we entered a very long black hall wherein, on chairs beside a bed near the centre, rested a deep coffin, flanked by a row of tall candlesticks of ebony. It had, I noticed, this singularity, that the foot-piece was absent, so that the soles of the corpse were visible as we approached. I beheld, too, three upright rods secured to the coffin-side, each fitted at its summit with a small silver bell of the kind called *morrice* pendent from a flexible steel spring. At the head of the bed, Aith, with an appearance of irascibility, stamped to and fro within a small area. Harfager, having rapidly traversed the apartment to the coffin, deposited the taper upon a stone table near, and stood poring with crazy intentness upon the body. I too, looking, stood. Death so rigorous, Gorgon, I had not seen. The coffin seemed full of tangled grey hair. The lady was, it was clear, of great age, osseous, scimitar-nosed. Her head shook with solemn continuity to the vibration of the house. From each ear trickled a black streamlet; the mouth was ridged with froth. I observed that over the corpse had been set three thin laminæ of polished wood, resembling in position, and shape, the bridge of a violin. Their sides fitted into groves in the coffin-sides, and their top was of a shape to exactly fit the inclination of the two coffin-lids when closed. One of these laminæ passed over the knees of the dead lady; another bridged the abdomen; the third the region of the neck. In each of them was a small circular hole. Across each of the three holes passed vertically a tense cord from the morrice-bell nearest to it; the three holes being thus divided by the three cords into six vertical semicircles. Before I could conjecture the significance of this arrangement, Harfager closed the folding coffin-lid, which in the centre had tiny intervals for the passage of the cords. He then turned the key in the lock, and uttered a word, which I took to be, "Come."

At his summons, Aith, approaching, took hold of the handle at the head; and from the dark recesses of the hall a lady, in black, moved forward. She was very tall, pallid, and of noble aspect. From the curvature of the nose, and her circular ears, I conjectured the lady Swertha, aunt of Harfager. Her eyes were red, but if with weeping I could not determine.

Harfager and I, taking each a handle near the coffin-foot, and the lady bearing before us one of the candlesticks, the procession began. As we came to the doorway, I noticed standing in a corner yet two coffins, inscribed with the names of Harfager and his aunt. We passed at length down a wide-curving stairway to the lower stage; and descending thence still lower by narrow brazen steps, came to a portal of metal, at which the lady, depositing the candlestick, left us.

The chamber of death into which we now bore the coffin had for its outer wall the brazen outer wall of the whole house at a point where this approached nearest the cataract, and must have been deep washed by the infuriate caldron without. The earthquake here was, indeed, intense. On every side the vast extent of surface was piled with coffins, rotted or rotting, ranged upon tiers of wooden shelves. The floor, I was surprised to see, was of brass. From the wide scampering that ensued on our entrance, the place was, it was clear, the abode of hordes of water-rats. As it was inconceivable that these could have corroded a way through sixteen brazen feet, I assumed that some fruitful pair must have found in the house, on its building, an ark from the waters; though even this hypothesis seemed wild. Harfager, however, afterwards confided to me his suspicion, that they had, for some purpose, been *placed* there by the original architect.

Upon a stone bench in the middle we deposited our burden, whereupon Aith made haste to depart. Harfager then rapidly and repeatedly walked from end to end of the long sepulchre, examining with many an eager stoop and peer, and upward strain, the shelves and their props. Could he, I was led to wonder, have any doubts as to their security? Damp, indeed, and decay pervaded all. A piece of woodwork which I handled softened into powder between my fingers.

He presently beckoned to me, and with yet one halt and uttered "Hark!" from him, we traversed the house to my chamber. Here, left alone, I paced long about, fretted with a strange vagueness of anger; then, weary, tumbled to a horror of sleep.

In the far interior of the mansion even the bleared day of this land of heaviness never rose upon our settled gloom. I was able however, to regulate my *levées* by a clock which stood in my chamber. With Harfager, in a startlingly short time, I renewed more than all our former intimacy. That I should say *more*, is itself startling, considering that an interval of twelve years stretched between us. But so, in fact, it was; and this was proved by the circumstances that we grew to take, and to pardon, freedoms of expression and manner which, as two persons of more than usual reserve, we had

once never dreamed of permitting to ourselves in reference to each
other. Down corridors that vanished either way in darkness and
length of perspective remoteness we linked ourselves in perambu-
lations of purposeless urgency. Once he wrote that my step was
excruciatingly deliberate. I replied that it was just such a step as
fitted my then mood. He wrote: "You have developed an aptitude
to *fret*." I was profoundly offended, and replied: "There are at least
more fingers than one in the universe which *that* ring will wed."

Something of the secret of the unhuman sensitiveness of his
hearing I quickly surmised. I, too, to my dismay, began, as time
passed, to catch hints of loudly-uttered words. The reason might
be found, I suggested, in an increased excitability of the auditory
nerve, which, if the cataract were absent, the roar of the ocean,
and bombast of the incessant tempest about us, would by themselves be sufficient to cause; in which case, his own aural interior
must, I said, be inflamed to an exquisite pitch of hyperpyrexial
fever. The affection I named to him as the Paracusis Willisii. He
frowned dissent, but I, undeterred, callously proceeded to recite
the case, occurring within my own experience, of a very deaf lady
who could hear the fall of a pin in a rapidly-moving railway-train.[1]
To this he only replied: "Of ignorant persons I am accustomed to
consider the mere scientist as the most profoundly ignorant."

Yet that he should affect darkness as to the highly morbid condition of his hearing I regarded as simply far-fetched. Himself,
indeed, confided to me his own, Aith's, and his aunt's proneness
to violent paroxysms of *vertigo*. I was startled; for I had myself
shortly before been twice roused from sleep by sensations of reeling and nausea, and a conviction that the chamber furiously spun
with me in a direction from right to left. The impression passed
away, and I attributed it, perhaps hastily (though on well-known

---

[1] Such cases are known, or at least easily comprehensible,
to every medical man. The concussion on the deaf nerves is said
to be the cause of the acquired sensitiveness. Nor is there any
limit to such sensitiveness when the concussion is abnormally
increased.

pathological grounds), to some disturbance in the nerve-endings of the "labyrinth," or inner ear. In Harfager, however, the conviction of wheeling motions in the house, in the world, attained so horrible a degree of certainty, that its effects sometimes resembled those of lunacy or energumenal possession. Never, he said, was the sensation of giddiness wholly absent; seldom the feeling that he stared with stretched-out arms over the verge of abysmal voids which wildly wooed his half-consenting foot. Once, as we went, he was hurled, as by unseen powers, to the ground; and there for an hour sprawled, cold in a flow of sweat, with distraught bedazzlement and amaze in eyes that watched the racing house. He was constantly racked, moreover, with the consciousness of sounds so very peculiar in their nature, that I could account for them upon no other hypothesis than that of *tinnitus* highly exaggerated. Through the heaped-up roar, there sometimes visited him, he said, the high lucid warbling of some Orphic bird, from the pitch of whose impassioned madrigals he had the inner consciousness that it came from a far country, was of the whiteness of snow, and crested with a comb of mauve. Else he was aware of accumulated human voices, remotely articulate, contending in volubility, and finally melting into chaotic musical tones. Or, anon, he was stunned by an infinite and imminent crashing, like the huge crackling of a universe of glass about his ears. He said, too, that he could often see, rather than hear, the parti-coloured whorls of a mazy sphere-music deep, deep, within the black dark of the cataract's roar. These impressions, which I ardently protested *must* be purely entotic, had sometimes upon him a pleasing effect, and long would he stand and listen with raised hand to their seduction; others again inflamed him to the verge of angry madness. I guessed that they were the origin of those irascibly uttered "Harks!" which at intervals of about an hour did not fail to break from him. In this I was wrong: and it was with a thrill of dismay that I shortly came to know the truth.

For, as once we passed together by an iron door on the lower stage, he stopped, and for several minutes stood, listening with an expression most keen and cunning. Presently the cry "Hark!"

escaped him; and he then turned to me, and wrote upon the tab-
let: "You did not hear?" I had heard nothing but the monotonous
roar. He shouted into my ear in accents now audible to me as an
echo heard far off in dreams: "You shall see."

He lifted the candlestick; produced from the pocket of his garment a key; unlocked the door. We entered a chamber, circular,
very loftily domed in proportion to its extent, and apparently
empty, save that a pair of ladder-steps leaned against its wall. Its
flooring was of marble, and in its centre gloomed a pool, resembling the impluvium of Roman atriums, but round in shape; a pool
evidently deep, full of an unctuous miasmal water. I was greatly
startled by its present aspect; for as the light burned upon its jet-
black surface, I could see that this had been quite recently *disturbed*, in a manner for which the shivering of the house could not
account, inasmuch as *ripples* of slimy ink sullenly rounded from
the centre toward its marble brink. I glanced at Harfager for explanation. He signed to me to wait, and for about an hour, with
arms in their accustomed fold behind his back, perambulated. At
the end of that time he stopped, and standing together by the margin, we gazed into the water. Suddenly his clutch tightened upon
my arm, and I saw, not without a thrill of horror, a tiny ball, doubtless of lead, but smeared blood-red by some chymical pigment, fall
from the direction of the roof and disappear into the centre of the
black depths. It hissed, on contact with the water, a thin puff of
vapour.

"In the name of all that is sinister!" I cried, "what thing is this
you show me?"

Again he made me a busy and confident sign to wait; snatched
then the ladder-steps toward the pool; handed me the taper. I,
mounting, held high the flame, and saw hanging from the misty
centre of the dome a form—a sphere of tarnished old copper,
lengthened out into balloon-shape by a down-looking neck, at the
end of which I thought I could discern a tiny orifice. Painted across
the bulge was barely visible in faded red characters the hieroglyph:

"harfager-hous: 1389-188"

Something—I know not what—of *eldritch* in the combined aspect of spotted globe, and gloomy pool, and contrivance of hourly hissing ball, gave expedition to my feet as I slipped down the ladder.

"But the meaning?"

"Did you see the writing?"

"Yes. The meaning?"

He wrote: "By comparing Gascoigne with Thrunster, I find that the mansion was *built* about 1389."

"But the final figures?"

"After the last 8," he replied, "there is another figure, nearly, but not quite, obliterated by a tarnish-spot."

"What figure?"

"It cannot be read, but may be surmised. The year 1888 is now all but passed. It can only be the figure 9."

"You are *horribly* depraved in mind!" I cried, flaring into anger. "You assume—you dare to *state*—in a manner which no mind trained to base its conclusions upon fact could hear with patience."

"And you, on the other hand, are simply absurd," he wrote. "You are not, I presume, ignorant of the common formula of Archimedes by which, the diameter of a sphere being known, its volume may be determined. Now, the diameter of the sphere in the dome there I have ascertained to be four and a half feet; and the diameter of the leaden balls about the third of an inch. Supposing then that 1389 was the year in which the sphere was full of balls, you may readily calculate that not many fellows of the four million and odd which have since dropped at the rate of one an hour are now left within it. It could not, in fact, have contained many more. The fall of balls *cannot* persist another year. The figure 9 is therefore forced upon us."

"But you assume, Harfager," I cried, "most wildly you assume! Believe me, my friend, this is the very wantonness of wickedness! By what algebra of despair do you know that the last date *must* be such, was intended to be such, as to correspond with the stoppage of the horologe? And, even if so, what is the significance of the whole. It has—it can have—*no significance!* Was the contriver of this dwelling, of all the gnomes, think you, a being pulsing with omniscience?"

"Do you seek to madden me?" he shouted. Then furiously writing: "I know—I swear that I know—nothing of its significance! But is it not evident to you that the work is a stupendous hour-glass, intended to record the hours not of a day, but of a cycle? and of a cycle of five hundred years?"

"But the whole thing," I passionately cried, "is a baleful phantasm of our brains! an evil impossibility! How is the fall of the balls regulated? Ah, my friend, you wander—your mind is debauched in this bacchanal of tumult."

"I have not ascertained," he replied, "by what internal mechanism, or viscous medium, or spiral coil, dependent no doubt for its action upon the vibration of the house, the balls are retarded in their fall; that is a matter well within the cunning of the mediæval artisan, the inventor of the watch; but this at least is clear, that one element of their retardation is the minuteness of the aperture through which they have to pass; that this element, by known, though recondite, statical laws, will cease to operate when no more than three balls remain; and that, consequently, the last three will fall at nearly the same moment."

"In God's name!" I exclaimed, careless what folly I poured out, "but your mother is *dead*, Harfager! You dare not deny that there remain but you and the lady Swertha!"

A contemptuous glance was all the reply he then vouchsafed me.

But he confided to me a day or two later that the leaden balls were a constant bane to his ears; that from hour to hour his life was a keen waiting for their fall; that even from his brief slumbers he infallibly startled into wakefulness at each descent; that, in whatever part of the mansion he happened to be, they failed not to find him out with a clamorous and insistent *loudness*; and that every drop wrung him with a twinge of physical anguish in the inner ear. I was therefore appalled at his declaration that these droppings had now become to him as the life of life; had acquired an intimacy so close with the hue of his mind, that their cessation might even mean for him the shattering of reason. Convulsed, he

stood then, face wrapped in arms, leaning against a pillar. The
paroxysm past, I asked him if it was out of the question that he
should once and for all cast off the fascination of the horologe,
and fly with me from the place. He wrote in mysterious reply: "A
*three*fold cord is not easily broken." I started. How threefold? He
wrote with bitterest smile: "To be enamoured of pain—to pine
after aching—to dote upon Marah—is not that a wicked madness?"
I was overwhelmed. Unconsciously he had quoted Gascoigne: a
wicked madness! a lecherous agonie! "You have seen the face of
my aunt," he proceeded; "your eyes were dim if you did not there
behold an impious calm, the glee of a blasphemous patience, a grin
behind her daring smile." He then spoke of a prospect, at the infinite terror of which his whole nature trembled, yet which sometimes laughed in his heart in the aspect of a maniac *hope*. It was
the prospect of any considerable increase in the volume of sound
about him. At *that*, he said, the brain must totter. On the night of
my arrival the noise of my booted tread, and, since then, my occasionally raised voice, had caused him acute unease. To a sensibility such as this, I understood him further to say, the luxury of torture involved in a large sound-increase in his environment was an
allurement from which no human strength could turn; and when I
expressed my powerlessness even to conceive such an increase,
much less the means by which it could be effected, he produced
from the archives of the house some annals, kept by the successive
heads of his race. From these it appeared that the tempests which
continually harried the lonely latitude of Vaila did not fail to give
place, at periodic intervals of some years, to one sovereign
ouragan—one Sirius among the suns—one *ultimate* lyssa of ele-
mental atrocity. At such periods the rains descended—and the
floods came—even as in the first world-deluge; those *rösts*, or eddies, which at all times encompassed Vaila, spurning then the
bands of lateral space, shrieked themselves aloft into a multitudi-
nous death-dance of water-spouts, and like snaky Deinotheria, or
say towering monolithic in a stonehenge of columned and
cyclopean awe, thronged about the little land, upon which, with
converging *débâcle*, they discharged their momentous waters; and

the lochs to which the cataract was due thus redoubled their volume, and fell with redoubled tumult. It was, said Harfager, like a
miracle that for twenty years no such great event had transacted
itself at Vaila.

And what, I asked, was the third strand of that threefold cord
of which he had spoken?

He took me to a circular hall, which, he told me, he had ascertained to be the geometrical centre of the circular mansion. It was
a very great hall—so great as I think I never saw—so great that the
amount of segment illumined at any one time by the taper seemed
nearly flat. And nearly the whole of its space from floor to roof
was occupied by a pillar of brass, the space between wall and cylinder being only such as to admit of a stretched-out arm.

"This cylinder, which seems to be solid," wrote Harfager, "as-
cends to the dome and passes beyond it; it descends hence to the
floor of the lower stage, and passes through that; it descends thence
to the brazen flooring of the vaults, and *passes through that* into
the rock of the ground. Under each floor it spreads out laterally
into a vast capital, helping to support the floor. What is the pre-
cise quality of the impression which I have made upon your mind
by this description?"

"I do not know!" I answered, turning from him; "propound me
none of your questions, Harfager. I feel a giddiness . . ."

"Nevertheless you shall answer me," he proceeded; "consider
the *strangeness* of that brazen lowest floor, which I have discovered to be some ten feet thick, and whose under-surface, I have
reason to believe, is somewhat above the level of the ground; remember that the fabric is at no point *fastened* to the cylinder; think
of the chains that ray out from the outer walls, seeming to anchor
the house to the ground. Tell me, what impression have I *now*
made?"

"And is it for this you wait?" I cried— "for *this?* Yet there may
have been no malevolent intention! You jump at conclusions! Any
human dwelling, if solidly based upon earth, would be at all times
liable to overthrow on such a land, in such a situation, as this,
by some superlative tempest! What if it were the intention of the

architect that in such eventuality the chains should break, and the house, by yielding, be saved?"

"You have no lack of charity at least," he replied; and we returned to the book we then read together.

He had not wholly lost the old habit of study, but could no longer constrain himself to sit to read. With a volume, often tossed down and resumed, he walked to and fro within the radius of the lamp-light; or I, unconscious of my voice, read to him. By a strange whim of his mood, the few books which now lay within the limits of his patience had all for their motive something of the *picaresque*, or the foppishly speculative: Quevedo's *Tacaño*; or the mundane system of Tycho Brahe; above all, George Hakewill's *Power and Providence of God*. One day, however, as I read, he interrupted me with the sentence, seemingly *à propos* of nothing: "What I *cannot* understand is that you, a scientist, should believe that the physical life ceases with the cessation of the breath"—and from that moment the tone of our reading changed. He led me to the crypts of the library in the lowest part of the building, and hour after hour, with a certain *furore* of triumph, overwhelmed me with volumes evidencing the longevity of man after "death." A sentence of Haller had rooted itself in his mind; he repeated, insisted upon it: "*sapientia denique consilia dat quibus longævitas obtineri queat, nitro, opio, purgationibus subinde repetitis . . .*"; and as opium was the elixir of long-drawn life, so death itself, he said, was that opium, whose more potent nepenthe lullabied the body to a peace not all-insentient, far within the gates of the gardens of dream. From the *Dhammapada* of the Bhuddist canon, to Zwinger's *Theatrum*, to Bacon's *Historia Vitæ et Mortis*, he ranged to find me heaped-up certainty of his faith. What, he asked, was my opinion of Baron Verulam's account of the dead man who was heard to utter words of prayer; or of the leaping bowels of the dead *condamné*? On my expressing incredulity, he seemed surprised, and reminded me of the writhings of dead serpents, of the *visible* beating of a frog's heart many hours after "death." "She is not dead," he quoted, "but *sleepeth*." The whim of Bacon and Paracelsus that the principle of life resides in a subtle spirit or fluid

which pervades the organism he coerced into elaborate proof
that such a spirit must, from its very nature, be incapable of any
sudden annihilation, so long as the organs which it permeates remain connected and integral. I asked what limit he then set to the
persistence of sensibility in the physical organism. He replied that
when slow decay had so far advanced that the nerves could no
longer be called nerves, or their cell-origins cell-origins, or the
brain a brain—or when by artificial means the brain had for any
length of time been disconnected at the cervical region from the
body—*then* was the king of terrors king indeed, and the body was
as though it had not been. With an indiscretion strange to me before my residence at Vaila, I blurted the question whether all this
Aberglaube could have any reference, in his mind, to the body of
his mother. For a while he stood thoughtful, then wrote: "Had I
not reason to believe that my own and my aunt's life in some way
hinged upon the final cessation of hers, I should still have taken
precautions to ascertain the progress of the destroyer upon her
mortal frame; as it is, I shall not lack even the minutest information." He then explained that the rodents which swarmed in the
sepulchre would, in the course of time, do their full work upon
her; but would be unable to penetrate to the region of the throat
without first gnawing their way through the three cords stretched
across the holes of the laminæ within the coffin, and thus, one by
one, liberating the three morrisco bells to a tinkling agitation.

The winter solstice had passed; another year opened. I slept a
deep sleep by night when Harfager entered my chamber, and shook
me. His face was ghastly in the taper-light. A transformation within
a few hours had occurred upon him. He was not the same. He resembled some poor wight into whose unexpecting eyes—at midnight—have glared the sudden eye-balls of Terrour.

He informed me that he was aware of singular intermittent
straining and creaking sounds, which gave him the sensation of
hanging in aerial spaces by a thread which must shortly snap to
his weight. He asked if, for God's sake, I would accompany him to
the sepulchre. We passed together through the house, he craven,
shivering, his step for the first time laggard. In the chamber of the

dead he stole to and fro examining the shelves, furtively intent. His eyes were sunken, his face drawn like death. From the footless coffin of the dowager trembling on its bench of stone, I saw an old water-rat creep. As Harfager passed beneath one of the shortest of the shelves which bore a single coffin, it suddenly fell from a height with its burthen into fragments at his feet. He screamed the cry of a frightened creature, and tottered to my support. I bore him back to the upper house.

He sat with hidden face in the corner of a small room doddering, overcome, as it were, with the extremity of age. He no longer marked with his usual "Hark!" the fall of the leaden drops. To my remonstrances he answered only with the words, So soon! so soon! Whenever I sought I found him there. His manhood had collapsed in an ague of trepidancy. I do not think that during this time he slept.

On the second night, as I approached him, he sprang suddenly straight with the furious outcry: "The first bell tinkles!"

And he had hardly larynxed the wild words when, from some great distance, a faint wail, which at its origin must have been a most piercing shriek, reached my now feverishly sensitive ears. Harfager at the sound clapped hands to ears, and dashed insensate from his place, I following in hot pursuit through the black breadth of the mansion. We ran until we reached a mound chamber, containing a candelabrum, and arrased in faded red. In an alcove at the furthest circumference was a bed. On the floor lay in swoon the lady Swertha. Her dark-grey hair in disarray wrapped her like an angry sea, and many tufts of it lay scattered wide, torn from the roots. About her throat were livid prints of strangling fingers. We bore her to the bed, and, having discovered some tincture in a cabinet, I administered it between her fixed teeth. In the rapt and dreaming face I saw that death was not, and, as I found something appalling in her aspect, shortly afterwards left her to Harfager.

When I next saw him his manner had assumed a species of change which I can only describe as hideous. It resembled the officious self-importance seen in a person of weak intellect, incapable of affairs, who goads himself with the exhortation, "to

business! the time is short—I must even bestir myself!" His walk
sickened me with a suggestion of *ataxie locomotrice*. I asked him
as to the lady, as to the meaning of the marks of violence on her
body. Bending ear to his deep and unctuous heard, "A stealthy attempt has been made upon her by the skeleton, Aith."

My unfeigned astonishment at this announcement he seemed
not to share. To my questions, repeatedly pressed upon him, as to
the reason for retaining such a domestic in the house, as to the
origin of his service, he could give no lucid answer. Aith, he informed me, had been admitted into the mansion during the period
of his own long absence in youth. He knew little of him beyond the
fact that he was of extraordinary physical strength. *Whence* he had
come, or how, no living being except Swertha had knowledge; and
she, it seems, feared, or at least persistently declined, to admit him
into the mystery. He added that, as a matter of fact, the lady, from
the day of his return to Vaila, had for some reason imposed upon
herself a silence upon all subjects, which he had never once known
her to break except by an occasional note.

With a curious, irrelevant *impressement*, with an intensely
voluntary, ataxic strenuousness, always with the air of a drunken
man constraining himself to ordered action, Harfager now set himself to the ostentatious adjustment of a host of insignificant matters. He collected chronicles and arranged them in order of date.
He tied and ticketed bundles of documents. He insisted upon my
help in turning the faces of portraits to the wall. He was, however,
now constantly interrupted by paroxysms of vertigo; six times in a
single day he was hurled to the ground. Blood occasionally gushed
from his ears. He complained to me in a voice of piteous wail of
the clear luting of a silver *piccolo*, which did not cease to invite
him. As he bent sweating upon his momentous futilities, his hands
fluttered like shaken reeds. I noted the movements of his muttering and whimpering lips, the rheum of his far-sunken eyes. The
decrepitude of dotage had overtaken his youth.

On a day he cast it utterly off, and was young again. He entered
my chamber, roused me from sleep; I saw the mad *gaudium* in his
eyes, heard the wild hiss of his cry in my ear:

"Up! It is sublime. The *storm!*"

Ah! I had known it—in the spinning nightmare of my sleep. I felt it in the tormented air of the chamber. It had come, then. I saw it lurid by the lamplight on the hell of Harfager's distorted visage.

I glanced at the face of the clock. It was nine—in the morning. A sardonic glee burst at once into being within me. I sprang from the couch. Harfager, with the naked stalk of some maniac old prophet, had already rapt himself away. I set out in pursuit. A clear deepening was manifest in the quivering of the edifice; sometimes for a second it paused still, as if, breathlessly, to listen. Occasionally there visited me, as it were, the faint dirge of some far-off lamentation and voice in Ramah; but if this was subjective, or the screaming of the storm, I could not say. Else I heard the distinct note of an organ's peal. The air of the mansion was agitated by a vaguely puffy unease. About noon I sighted Harfager, lamp in hand, running along a corridor. His feet were bare. As we met he looked at me, but hardly with recognition, and passed by; stopped, however, returned, and howled into my ear the question: "Would you *see?*" He beckoned before me. I followed to a very small window in the outer wall closed with a slab of iron. As he lifted a latch the metal flew inward with instant impetuosity and swung him far, while a blast of the storm, braying and booming through the aperture with buccal and reboant bravura, caught and pinned me against an angle of the wall. Down the corridor a long crashing *bouleversement* of pictures and furniture ensued. I nevertheless contrived to push my way, crawling on the belly, to the opening. Hence the sea should have been visible. My senses, however, were met by nothing but a reeling vision of tumbled blackness, and a general impression of the letter O. The sun of Vaila had gone out. In a moment of opportunity our united efforts prevailed to close the slab.

"Come"—he had obtained fresh light, and beckoned before me— "let us see how the dead fare in the midst of the great desolation and *dies iræ!*" Running, we had hardly reached the middle of the stairway, when I was thrilled by the consciousness of a momentous shock, the bass of a dull and far-reverberating thud, which nothing

conceivable save the huge simultaneous thumping to the ground
of the whole piled mass of the coffins of the sepulchre could have
occasioned. I turned to Harfager, and for an instant beheld him,
panic flying in his scuttling feet, headlong on the way he had come,
with stopped ears and wide mouth. Then, indeed, fear overtook
me—a tremor in the midst of the exultant daring of my heart—a
thought that *now* at least I must desert him in his extremity, now
work out my own salvation. Yet it was with a most strange hesitancy that I turned to seek him for the last time—a hesitancy which
I fully felt to be selfish and diseased. I wandered through the midnight house in search of light, and having happened upon a lamp,
proceeded to hunt for Harfager. Several hours passed in this way.
It became clear from the state of the atmosphere that the violence
about me was being abnormally intensified. Sounds as of distant
screams—unreal, like the screamings of spirits—broke now upon
my ear. As the time of evening drew on, I began to detect in the
vastly augmented baritone of the cataract something new—a shrill-
ness—the whistle of an ecstasy—a malice—the menace of a rabies
blind and deaf. It must have been at about the hour of six that I
found Harfager. He sat in an obscure apartment with bowed head,
hands on knees. His face was covered with hair, and blood from
the ears. The right sleeve of his garment had been rent away in
some renewed attempt, as I imagined, to manipulate a window;
the slightly-bruised arm hung lank from the shoulder. For some
time I stood and watched the mouthing of his mumblings. Now
that I had found him I said nothing of departure. Presently he
looked sharply up with the cry "Hark!"—then with imperious impatience, "Hark! Hark!"—then with rapturous shout, "The second
bell!" And *again*, in instant sequence upon his cry, there sounded
a wail, vague but unmistakably real, through the house. Harfager
at the moment dropped reeling with vertigo; but I, snatching a
lamp, hasted forth, trembling, but eager. For some time the high
wailing continued, either actually, or by reflex action of my ear. As
I ran toward the lady's apartment, I saw, separated from it by the
breadth of a corridor, the open door of an armoury, into which I
passed, and seized a battle-axe; and, thus armed, was about to enter

to her aid, when Aith, with blazing eye, rushed from her chamber
by a further door. I raised my weapon, and, shouting, flew forward
to fell him; but by some chance the lamp dropped from me, and
before I knew aught, the axe leapt from my grasp, myself hurled
far backward. There was, however, sufficiency of light from the
chamber to show that the skeleton had dashed into a door of the
armoury: that near me, by which I had procured the axe, I instantly
slammed and locked; and hasting to the other, similarly secured
it. Aith was thus a prisoner. I then entered the lady's room. She
lay half-way across the bed in the alcove, and to my bent ear loudly
croaked the *râles* of death. A glance at the mangled throat convinced me that her last hours were surely come. I placed her su-
pine upon the bed; curtained her utterly from sight within the loosened festoons of the hangings of black, and inhumanly turned from
the fearfulness of her sight. On an *escritoire* near I saw a note,
intended apparently for Harfager: "I mean to defy, and fly. Think
not from fear—but for the glow of the Defiance itself. *Can* you
come?" Taking a flame from the candelabrum, I hastily left her to
solitude, and the ultimate throes of her agony.

I had passed some distance backward when I was startled by a
singular sound—a clash— resembling in *timbre* the clash of a tam-
bourine, I heard it rather loudly, and that I should now hear it at
all, proceeding as it did from a distance, implied the employment
of some prodigious energy. I waited, and in two minutes it again
broke, and thenceforth at like regular intervals. It had somehow
an effect of pain upon me. The conviction grew gradually that Aith
had unhung two of the old brazen shields from their pegs; and that,
holding them by their handles, and smiting them viciously together,
he thus expressed the frenzy which had now overtaken him. I found
my way back to Harfager, in whom the very nerve of anguish now
seemed to stamp and stalk about the chamber. He bent his head;
shook it like a hail-tormented horse; with his deprecating hand
brushed and barred from his hearing each recurrent clash of the
brazen shields.

"Ah, when—when—when—" he hoarsely groaned into my ear,
"will that rattle of hell choke in her throat? I will myself, I tell you—

with my own hand!—Oh God . . ." Since the morning his auditory
inflammation (as, indeed, my own also) seemed to have heightened in steady proportion with the roaring and screaming chaos
round; and the *râles* of the lady hideously filled for him the mea-
sured intervals of the grisly cymbaling of Aith. He presently hurled
twinkling fingers into the air, and with wide arms rushed swiftly
into the darkness.

And again I sought him, and long again in vain. As the hours
passed, and the slow Tartarean day deepened toward its baleful
midnight, the cry of the now redoubled cataract, mixed with the
throng and majesty of the now climactic tempest, assumed too
definite and intentional a *shriek* to be longer tolerable to any mortal reason. My own mind escaped my governance, and went its way.
Here, in the hot-bed of fever, I was fevered; among the children of
wrath, was strong with the strength, and weak with the feebleness
of delirium. I wandered from chamber to chamber, precipitate,
bemused, giddy on the up-buoyance of a joy. "As a man upon whom
sleep seizes," so had I fallen. Even yet, as I approached the region
of the armoury, the noisy ecstasies of Aith did not fail to clash
faintly upon my ear. Harfager I did not see, for he too, doubtless,
roamed a headlong Ahasuerus in the round world of the house. At
about midnight, however, observing light shine from a door on the
lower stage, I entered and found him there. It was the chamber of
the dropping horologe. He half-sat, swaying self-hugged, on the
ladder-steps, and stared at the blackness of the pool. The last
flicker of the riot of the day seemed dying in his eyes. He cast no
glance as I approached. His hands, his bare right arm, were red
with new-shed blood; but of this, too, he appeared unconscious.
His mouth gaped wide to his pantings. As I looked, he leapt suddenly high, smiting hands, with the yell, "The last bell tinkles!"
and galloped forth, a-rave. He therefore did not see (though he
may have understood by hearing) the spectacle which, with cow-
ering awe, I immediately thereupon beheld: for from the horologe
there slipped with hiss of vapour a ball into the torpid pool: and
while the clock once ticked, another! and while the clock yet ticked,
another! and the vapour of the first had not *utterly* passed, when

the vapour of the third, intermingling, floated with it into grey
tenuity aloft. Understanding that the sands of the house were run,
I, too, flinging maniac arms, rushed from the spot. I was, however, suddenly stopped in my career by the instinct of some stupendous doom emptying its vials upon the mansion; and was
quickly made aware, by the musketry of a shrill crackling from
aloft, and the imminent downpour of a world of waters, that a
water-spout had, wholly or partly, hurled the catastrophe of its
broken floods upon us, and crashed ruining through the dome of
the building. At that moment I beheld Harfager running toward
me, hands buried in hair. As he flew past, I seized him. "Harfager!
save yourself!" I cried— "the very fountains, man,—by the living
God, Harfager"—I hissed it into his inmost ear— "*the very fountains of the Great Deep . . .!*" Stupid, he glared at me, and passed
on his way. I, whisking myself into a room, slammed the door. Here
for some time, with smiting knees, I waited; but the impatience of
my frenzy urged me, and I again stepped forth. The corridors were
everywhere thigh-deep with water. Rags of the storm, irrageous
by way of the orifice in the shattered dome, now blustered with
hoiden wantonness through the house. My light was at once extinguished; and immediately I was startled by the presence of *another* light—most ghostly, gloomy, bluish—most soft, yet wild,
phosphorescent—which now perfused the whole building. For this
I could in no way account. But as I stood in wonder, a gust of greater
vehemence romped through the house, and I was instantly conscious of the harsh *snap* of something near me. There was a
minute's breathless pause—and then—quick, quick—ever quicker—
came the throb, and the snap, and the pop, in vastly wide circular
succession, of the anchoring chains of the mansion before the ur-
gent shoulder of the hurricane. And *again* a second of eternal
calm—and then—deliberately—its hour came—the ponderous palace *moved*. My flesh writhed like the glutinous flesh of a serpent.
Slowly moved, and stopped:—then was a sweep—and a swirl—and
a pause! then a swirl—and a sweep—and a pause!—then steady in-
dustry of labour on the monstrous brazen axis, as the husband-
man plods by the plough; then increase of zest, assuetude of a

fledgeling to the wing—then intensity—then the last light ecstasy
of flight. And now, once again, as staggering and plunging I spun,
the thought of escape for a moment visited me: but this time I shook
an impious fist. "No, but God, no, no," I cried, "I will no more wander hence, my God! I will even perish with Harfager! Here let me
waltzing pass, in this Ball of the Vortices, Anarchie of the Thun-
ders! Did not the great Corot call it translation in a chariot of flame?
But this is gaudier than that! redder than that! This is jaunting on
the scoriac tempests and reeling bullions of hell! It is baptism in a
sun!" Recollection gropes in a dimmer gloaming as to all that followed. I struggled up the stairway now flowing a steep river, and
for a long time ran staggering and plunging, full of wild words,
about, amid the downfall of ceilings and the wide ruin of tumbling
walls. The air was thick with splashes, the whole roof now, save
three rafters, snatched by the wind away. In that blue sepulchral
moonlight, the tapestries flapped and trailed wildly out after the
flying house like the streaming hair of some ranting fakeer stung
gyratory by the gadflies and tarantulas of distraction. The flooring
gradually assumed a slant like the deck of a sailing ship, its covering waters flowing all to accumulation in one direction. At one
point, where the largest of the porticoes projected, the mansion
began at every revolution to bump with horrid shiverings against
some obstruction. It bumped, and while the lips said one-two-
three, it three times bumped again. It was the levity of hugeness!
it was the mænadism of mass! Swift—ever swifter, swifter—in ague
of urgency, it reeled and raced, every portico a sail to the storm,
vexing and wracking its tremendous frame to fragments. I, chanc-
ing by the door of a room littered with the *débris* of a fallen wall,
saw through that wan and livid light Harfager sitting on a tomb. A
large drum was beside him, upon which, club grasped in bloody
hand, he feebly and persistently beat. The velocity of the leaning
house had now attained the *sleeping* stage, that ultimate energy of
the spinning-top. Harfager sat, head sunk to chest; suddenly he
dashed the hairy wrappings from his face; sprang; stretched horizontal arms; and began to spin—dizzily!—in the same direction as
the mansion!—nor less sleep-embathed!—with floating hair, and

quivering cheeks, and the starting eye-balls of horror, and tongue that lolled like a panting wolf's from his bawling degenerate mouth. From such a sight I turned with the retching of loathing, and taking to my heels, staggering and plunging, presently found myself on the lower stage opposite a porch. An outer door crashed to my feet, and the breath of the storm smote freshly upon me. An *élan*, part of madness, more of heavenly sanity, spurred in my brain. I rushed through the doorway, and was tossed far into the limbo without.

The river at once swept me deep-drowned toward the sea. Even here, a momentary shrill din like the splitting asunder of a world reached my ears. It had hardly passed, when my body collided in its course upon one of the basalt piers, thick-cushioned by sea-weed, of the not all-demolished bridge. Nor had I utterly lost consciousness. A clutch freed my head from the surge, and I finally drew and heaved myself to the level of a timber. Hence to the ledge of rock by which I had come, the bridge was intact. I rowed myself feebly on the belly beneath the poundings of the wind. The rain was a steep rushing, like a shimmering of silk, through the air. Observing the same wild glow about me which had blushed through the broken dome into the mansion, I glanced backward—and saw that the dwelling of the Harfagers was a memory of the past; then upward—and lo, the whole northern sky, to the zenith, burned one tumbled and fickly-undulating ocean of gaudy flames. It was the *aurora borealis* which, throeing at every aspen instant into rays and columns, cones and obelisks, of vivid vermil and violet and rose, was fairly whiffed and flustered by the storm into a vast silken oriflamme of tresses and swathes and breezes of glamour; whilst, low-bridging the horizon, the flushed beams of the polar light assembled into a changeless boreal corona of bedazzling candor. At the augustness of this great phenomenon I was affected to blessed tears. And with them, the dream broke!—the infatuation passed!— a hand skimmed back from my brain the blind films and media of delusion; and sobbing on my knees, I jerked to heaven the arms of grateful oblation for my surpassing Rephidim, and marvel of deliverance from all the temptation—and the tribulation—and the tragedy—of Vaila.

X´LUCHA

"He goeth after her . . . and knoweth not . . ."

[*From a Diary*]

Three days ago! by heaven, it seems an age. But I am shaken—
my reason is debauched. A while since, I fell into a momentary
coma precisely resembling an attack of *petit mal*. "Tombs, and
worms, and epitaphs"—that is my dream. At my age, with my phy-
sique, to walk staggery, like a man stricken! But all that will pass:
I must collect myself—my reason is debauched. Three days ago! it
seems an age! I sat on the floor before an old cista full of letters. I
lighted upon a packet of Cosmo's. Why, I had forgotten them! they
are turning sere! Truly, I can no more call myself a young man. I
sat reading, listlessly, rapt back by memory. To muse is to be lost!
of *that* evil habit I must wring the neck, or look to perish. Once
more I threaded the mazy sphere-harmony of the minuet, reeled
in the waltz, long pomps of candelabra, the noonday of the bacchanal, about me. Cosmo was the very tsar and maharajah of the
Sybarites! the Priap of the *détraqués!* In every unexpected alcove
of the Roman Villa was a couch, raised high, with necessary foot-
stool, flanked and canopied with *mirrors* of clarified gold. Consumption fastened upon him; reclining at last at table, he could,
till warmed, scarce lift the wine! his eyes were like two fat glow-
worms, coiled together! they seemed haloed with vaporous
emanations of phosphorus! Desperate, one could see, was the secret struggle with the Devourer. But to the end the princely smile

persisted calm; to the end—to the last day—he continued among that comic crew unchallenged choragus of all the rites, I will not say of Paphos, but of Chemos! and Baal-Peor! Warmed, he did not refuse the revel, the dance, the darkened chamber. It was utterly black, rayless; approached by a secret passage; in shape circular; the air hot, haunted always by odours of balms, bdellium, hints of dulcimer and flute; and radiated round with a hundred thick-strewn ottomans of Morocco. Here Lucy Hill stabbed to the heart Caccofogo, mistaking the scar of his back for the scar of Soriac. In a bath of malachite the Princess Egla, waking late one morning, found Cosmo lying stiffly dead, the water covering him wholly.

"But in God's name, Mérimée!" (so he wrote), "to think of Xélucha dead! Xélucha! Can a moon-beam, then, perish of suppurations? Can the rainbow be eaten by worms? Ha! ha! ha! laugh with me, my friend: *'elle dérangera l'Enfer'*! She will introduce the *pas de tarantule* into Tophet! Xélucha, the feminine Xélucha recalling the splendid harlots of history! Weep with me—*manat rara meas lacrima per genas!* expert as Thargelia; cultured as Aspatia; purple as Semiramis. She comprehended the human tabernacle, my friend, its secret springs and tempers, more intimately than any savant of Salamanca who breathes. *Tarare*—but Xélucha is not dead! Vitality is not mortal; you cannot wrap flame in a shroud. Xélucha! where then is she? Translated, perhaps—rapt to a constellation like the daughter of Leda. She journeyed to Hindostan, accompanied by the train and appurtenance of a Begum, threatening descent upon the Emperor of Tartary. I spoke of the desolation of the West; she kissed me, and promised return. Mentioned you, too, Mérimée— 'her Conqueror'— 'Mérimée, Destroyer of Woman.' A breath from the conservatory rioted among the ambery whiffs of her forelocks, sending it singly a-wave over that thulite tint you know. Costumed cap-à-pie, she had, my friend, the dainty little completeness of a daisy mirrored bright in the eye of the browsing ox. A simile of Milton had for years, she said, inflamed the lust of her Eye: 'The barren plains of Sericana, where Chineses drive with sails and wind their cany wagons light.' I, and the Sabæans, she assured me, wrongly considered Flame the whole

of being; the other half of things being Aristotle's quintessential
light. In the Ourania Hierarchia and the Faust-book you meet a
completeness: burning Seraph, Cherûb full of eyes. Xélucha combined them. She would reconquer the Orient for Dionysius, and
return. I heard of her blazing at Delhi; drawn in a chariot by lions.
Then this rumour—probably false. Indeed, it comes from a source
somewhat turgid. Like Odin, Arthur, and the rest, Xélucha—will
reappear."

Soon subsequently, Cosmo lay down in his balneum of malachite, and slept, having drawn over him the water as a coverlet. I,
in England, heard little of Xélucha: first that she was alive, then
dead, then alighted at old Tadmor in the Wilderness, Palmyra now.
Nor did I greatly care, Xélucha having long since turned to apples
of Sodom in my mouth. Till I sat by the cista of letters and re-read
Cosmo, she had for some years passed from my active memories.

The habit is now confirmed in me of spending the greater part
of the day in sleep, while by night I wander far and wide through
the city under the sedative influence of a tincture which has become necessary to my life. Such an existence of shadow is not without charm; nor, I think, could many minds be steadily subjected
to its conditions without elevation, deepened awe. To travel alone
with the Primordial cannot but be solemn. The moon is of the hue
of the glow-worm; and Night of the sepulchre. Nux bore not less
Thanatos than Hupnos, and the bitter tears of Isis redundulate to
a flood. At three, if a cab rolls by, the sound has the augustness of
thunder. Once, at two, near a corner, I came upon a priest, seated,
dead, leering, his legs bent. One arm, supported on a knee, pointed
with rigid accusing forefinger obliquely upward. By exact observation, I found that he indicated Betelgeux, the star "a" which
shoulders the wet sword of Orion. He was hideously swollen, having perished of dropsy. Thus in all Supremes is a grotesquerie;
and one of the sons of Night is—Buffo.

In a London square deserted, I should imagine, even in the day,
I was aware of the metallic, silvery-clinking approach of little shoes.
It was three in a heavy morning of winter, a day after my rediscov-
ery of Cosmo. I had stood by the railing, regarding the clouds sail

as under the sea-legged pilotage of a moon wrapped in cloaks of inclemency. Turning, I saw a little lady, very gloriously dressed. She had walked straight to me. Her head was bare, and crisped with the amber stream which rolled lax to a globe, kneaded thick with jewels, at her nape. In the redundance of her décolleté development, she resembled Parvati, mound-hipped love-goddess of the luscious fancy of the Brahmin.

She addressed to me the question:

"What are you doing there, darling?"

Her loveliness stirred me, and Night is *bon camarade*. I replied:

"Sunning myself by means of the moon."

"All that is borrowed lustre," she returned, "you have got it from old Drummond's *Flowers of Sion*."

Looking back, I cannot remember that this reply astonished me, though it should—of course—have done so. I said:

"On my soul, no; but you?"

"You might guess whence *I* come!"

"You are dazzling. You come from Paz."

"Oh, farther than that, my son! Say a subscription ball in Soho."

"Yes? . . . and alone? in the cold? on foot . . .?"

"Why, I am old, and a philosopher. I can pick you out riding Andromeda yonder from the ridden Ram. They are in error, M'sieur, who suppose an atmosphere on the broad side of the moon. I have reason to believe that on Mars dwells a race whose lids are transparent like glass; so that the eyes are visible during sleep; and every varying dream moves imaged forth to the beholder in tiny panorama on the limpid iris. You cannot imagine me a mere *fille!* To be escorted is to admit yourself a woman, and that is improper in Nowhere. Young Eos drives an *équipage à quatre*, but Artemis 'walks' alone. Get out of my borrowed light in the name of Diogenes! I am going home."

"Far?"

"Near Piccadilly."

"But a cab?"

"No cabs for *me*, thank you. The distance is a mere nothing. Come."

We walked forward. My companion at once put an interval
between us, quoting from the Spanish Curate that the open is an
enemy to love. The Talmudists, she twice insisted, rightly held
the hand the sacredest part of the person, and at that point also
contact was for the moment interdict. Her walk was extremely
rapid. I followed. Not a cat was anywhere visible. We reached at
length the door of a mansion in St. James's. There was no light. It
seemed tenantless, the windows all uncurtained, pasted across,
some of them, with the words, To Let. My companion, however,
flitted up the steps, and, beckoning, passed inward. I, following,
slammed the door, and was in darkness. I heard her ascend, and
presently a region of glimmer above revealed a stairway of marble,
curving broadly up. On the floor where I stood was no carpet, nor
furniture: the dust was very thick. I had begun to mount when, to
my surprise, she stood by my side, returned; and whispered:

"To the very top, darling."

She soared nimbly up, anticipating me. Higher, I could no
longer doubt that the house was empty but for us. All was a vacuum
full of dust and echoes. But at the top, light streamed from a door,
and I entered a good-sized oval saloon, at about the centre of the
house. I was completely dazzled by the sudden resplendence of the
apartment. In the midst was a spread table, square, opulent with
gold plate, fruit dishes; three ponderous chandeliers of electric
light above; and I noticed also (what was very *bizarre*) one little
candlestick of common tin containing an old soiled curve of tal-
low, on the table. The impression of the whole chamber was one of
gorgeousness not less than Assyrian. An ivory couch at the far end
was made sun-like by a head- piece of chalcedony forming a sea
for the sport of emerald ichthyotauri. Copper hangings, paneled
with mirrors in iasperated crystal, corresponded with a dome of
flame and copper; yet this latter, I now remember, produced upon
my glance an impression of actual grime. My companion reclined
on a small Sigma couch, raised high to the table-level in the Semitic
manner, visible to her saffron slippers of satin. She pointed me a
seat opposite. The incongruity of its presence in the middle of this
arrogance of pomp so tickled me, that no power could have kept

me from a smile: it was a grimy chair, mean, all wood, nor was I long in discovering one leg somewhat shorter than its fellows.

She indicated wine in a black glass bottle, and a tumbler, but herself made no pretence of drinking or eating. She lay on hip and elbow, *petite*, resplendent, and looked gravely upward. I, however, drank.

"You are tired," I said, "one sees that."

"It is precious little that *you* see!" she returned, dreamy, hardly glancing.

"How! your mood is changed, then? You are morose."

"You never, I think, saw a Norse passage-grave?"

"And abrupt."

"Never?"

"A passage-grave? No."

"It is worth a journey! They are circular or oblong chambers of stone, covered by great earth-mounds, with a 'passage' of slabs connecting them with the outer air. All round the chamber the dead sit with head resting upon the bent knees, and consult together in silence."

"Drink wine with me, and be less Tartarean."

"You certainly seem to be a fool," she replied with perfect sardonic iciness. "Is it not, then, highly romantic? They belong, you know, to the Neolithic age. As the teeth fall, one by one, from the lipless mouths—they are caught by the lap. When the lap thins— they roll to the floor of stone. Thereafter, every tooth that drops all round the chamber sharply breaks the silence."

"Ha! ha! ha!"

"Yes. It is like a century-slow, circularly-successive dripping of slime in some cavern of the far subterrene."

"Ha! ha! This wine seems heady! They express themselves in a dialect largely dental."

"The Ape, on the other hand, in a language wholly guttural."

A town-clock tolled four. Our talk was holed with silences, and heavy-paced. The wine's yeasty exhalation reached my brain. I saw her through mist, dilating large, uncertain, shrinking again to dainty compactness. But amorousness had died within me.

"Do you know," she asked, "what has been discovered in one of the Danish *Kjökkenmöddings* by a little boy? It was ghastly. The skeleton of a huge fish with human—"

"You are most unhappy."

"Be silent."

"You are full of care."

"I think you a great fool."

"You are racked with misery."

"You are a child. You have not even an instinct of the meaning of the word."

"How! Am I not a man? I, too, miserable, careful?"

"You are not, really, *anything*—until you can create."

"Create what?"

"Matter."

"That is foppish. Matter cannot be created, nor destroyed."

"Truly, then, you must be a creature of unusually weak intellect. I see that now. Matter does not exist, then, there is no such thing, really—it is an appearance, a spectrum—every writer not imbecile from Plato to Fichte has, voluntary or involuntary, proved that for good. To create it is to produce an impression of its reality upon the senses of others; to destroy it is to wipe a wet rag across a scribbled slate."

"Perhaps. I do not care. Since no one can do it."

"No one? You are mere embryo—"

"Who then?"

"*Anyone*, whose power of Will is equivalent to the gravitating force of a star of the First Magnitude."

"Ha! ha! ha! By heaven, you choose to be facetious. Are there then wills of such equivalence?"

"There have been three, the founders of religions. There was a fourth: a cobbler of Herculaneum, whose mere volition induced the cataclysm of Vesuvius in '79, in direct opposition to the gravity of Sirius. There are more fames than *you* have ever sung, you know. The greater number of disembodied spirits, too, I feel certain—"

"By heaven, I cannot but think you full of sorrow! Poor wight! come, drink with me. The wine is thick and boon. Is it not Setian?

It makes you sway and swell before me, I swear, like a purple cloud
of evening—"

"But you are mere clayey ponderance!—I did not know that!—
you are no companion! your little interest revolves round the lowest centres."

"Come—forget your agonies—"

"What, think you, is the portion of the buried body first sought
by the worm?"

"The eyes! the eyes!"

"You are *hideously* wrong—you are so *utterly* at sea—"

"My God!"

She had bent forward with such rage of contradiction as to approach me closely. A loose gown of amber silk, wide-sleeved, had
replaced her ball attire, though at what opportunity I could not
guess; wondering, I noticed it as she now placed her palms far forth
upon the table. A sudden wafture as of spice and orange-flowers,
mingled with the abhorrent faint odour of mortality over-ready for
the tomb, greeted my sense. A chill crept upon my flesh.

"You are so *hopelessly* at fault—"

"For God's sake—"

"You are so *miserably* deluded! Not the eyes *at all!*"

"Then, in Heaven's name, what?"

Five tolled from a clock.

"*The Uvula!* the soft drop of mucous flesh, you know, suspended
from the palate above the glottis. They eat through the face-cloth
and cheek, or crawl by the lips through a broken tooth, filling the
mouth. They make straight for it. It is the *deliciæ* of the vault."

At her horror of interest I grew sick, at her odour, and her
words. Some unspeakable sense of insignificance, of debility, held
me dumb.

"You say I am full of sorrows. You say I am racked with woe;
that I gnash with anguish. Well, you are a mere child in intellect.
You use words without realization of meaning like those minds in
what Leibnitz calls 'symbolical consciousness.' But suppose it were
so—"

"It is so."

"You know nothing."

"I see you twist and grind. Your eyes are very pale. I thought they were hazel. They are of the faint bluishness of phosphorus shimmerings seen in darkness."

"That proves nothing."

"But the 'white' of the sclerotic is dyed to yellow. And you look inward. Why do you look so palely inward, so woe-worn, upon your soul? Why can you speak of nothing but the sepulchre, and its rottenness? Your eyes seem to me wan with centuries of vigil, with mysteries and millenniums of pain."

"Pain! but you know so *little* of it! you are wind and words! of its philosophy and *rationale* nothing!"

"Who knows?"

"I will give you a hint. It is the sub-consciousness in conscious creatures of Eternity, and of eternal loss. The least prick of a pin not Pæan and Æsculapius and the powers of heaven and hell can utterly heal. Of an everlasting loss of pristine wholeness the conscious body is sub-conscious, and 'pain' is its sigh at the tragedy. So with all pain—greater, the greater the loss. The hugest of losses is, of course, the loss of Time. If you lose that, any of it, you plunge at once into the transcendentalisms, the infinitudes, of Loss; if you lose *all of it*—"

"But you so wildly exaggerate! Ha! ha! You rant, I tell you, of commonplaces with the woe—"

"Hell is where a clear, untrammelled Spirit is sub-conscious of lost Time; where it boils and writhes with envy of the living world; *hating* it for ever, and all the sons of Life!"

"But curb yourself! Drink—I implore—I *implore*—for God's sake—but *once*—"

"To *hasten* to the snare—*that* is woe! to drive your ship upon the *lighthouse* rock—that is Marah! To wake, and feel it irrevocably true that you went after her—*and the dead were there*—and her guests were in the depths of hell—*and you did not know it!*— though you *might* have. Look out upon the houses of the city this dawning day: not one, I tell you, but in it haunts some soul— walking up and down the old theatre of its little Day—goading

imagination by a thousand childish tricks, vraisemblances—elabo-
rately duping itself into the momentary fantasy *that it still lives,*
that the chance of life is not for ever and for ever lost—yet riving
all the time with under-memories of the wasted Summer, the lapsed
brief light between the two eternal glooms—riving I say and shriek
to you!—riving, *Mérimée, you destroying fiend—*"

She had sprung—*tall* now, she seemed to me—between couch
and table.

"Mérimée!" I screamed, "—*my* name, harlot, in your maniac
mouth! By God, woman, you terrify me to death!"

I too sprang, the hairs of my head catching stiff horror from
my fancies.

"Your name? Can you imagine me ignorant of your name, or
anything concerning you? Mérimée! Why, did you not sit yesterday and read of me in a letter of Cosmo's?"

"Ah-h . . .," hysteria bursting high in sob and laughter from my
arid lips— "Ah! ha! ha! Xélucha! My memory grows palsied and
grey, Xélucha! pity me—my walk is in the very valley of shadow!—
senile and sere!—observe my hair, Xélucha, its grizzled growth—
trepidant, Xélucha, clouded—I am not the man you knew, Xélucha,
in the palaces—of Cosmo! You are Xélucha!"

"You rave, poor worm!" she cried, her face contorted by a species of malicious contempt. "Xélucha died of cholera ten years ago
at Antioch. I wiped the froth from her lips. Her nose underwent a
green decay before burial. So far sunken into the brain was the left
eye—"

"You are—*you are Xélucha!*" I shrieked; "voices now of thunder howl it within my consciousness—and by the holy God, Xélucha,
though you blight me with the breath of the hell you are, I shall
clasp you, living or damned—"

I rushed toward her. The word "Madman!" hissed as by the
tongues of ten thousand serpents through the chamber, I heard; a
belch of pestilent corruption puffed poisonous upon the putrid
air; for a moment to my wildered eyes there seemed to rear itself,
swelling high to the roof, a formless tower of ragged cloud, and
before my projected arms had closed upon the very emptiness of

insanity, I was tossed by the operation of some Behemoth potency far-circling backward to the utmost circumference of the oval, where, my head colliding, I fell, shocked, into insensibility.

When the sun was low toward night, I lay awake, and listlessly observed the grimy roof, and the sordid chair, and the candlestick of tin, and the bottle of which I had drunk. The table was small, filthy, of common deal, uncovered. All bore the appearance of having stood there for years. But for them, the room was void, the vision of luxury thinned to air. Sudden memory flashed upon me. I scrambled to my feet, and plunged and tottered, bawling, through the twilight into the street.

THE BRIDE

"He shall not see the rivers, the floods, the brooks
of honey and butter"— *Job*.

They met at Krupp and Mason's, musical-instrument-makers,
of Little Britain, E.C., where Walter had been employed two years,
and then came Annie to typewrite, and be serviceable.

They began to "go out" together after six o'clock; and when Mrs.
Evans, Annie's mamma, lost her lodger, Annie mentioned it, and
Walter went to live with them at No. 13 Culford Road, N.; by which
time Annie and Walter might almost be said to have been engaged.
His salary, however, was only thirty shillings a week.

He was the thorough Cockney, Walter; a well-set-up person of
thirty, strong-shouldered, with a square brow, a moustache, and
black acne-specks in his nose and pale face.

It was on the night of his arrival at No. 13, that he for the first
time saw Rachel, Annie's younger sister. Both girls, in fact, were
named "Rachel"—after a much-mourned mother of Mrs. Evans';
but Annie Rachel was called "Annie," and Mary Rachel was called
"Rachel." Rachel helped Walter at the handle of his box to the top-
back room, and here, in the lamplight he was able to see that she
was a tallish girl, with hair almost black, and with a sprinkling of
freckles on her very white, thin nose, on the tip of which stood
collected, usually, some little sweats. She was thin-faced, and her
top teeth projected a little so that her lips only closed with effort,

she not so pretty as pink-and-white little Annie, though one could guess, at a glance, that she was a person more to be respected.

"What do you think of him?" said Annie, meeting Rachel as she came down.

"He seems a nice fellow," Rachel said: "rather good-looking. And strong in the back, you bet."

Walter spent that evening with them in the area front-room, smoking a foul bulldog pipe, which slushed and gurgled to his suction; and at once Mrs. Evans, a dark old lady without waist, all sighs and lack of breath, decided that he was "a gentlemanly, decent fellow." When bed-time came he made the proposal to lead them in prayer; and to this they submitted, Annie having forewarned them that he was "a Christian." As he climbed to his room, the devoted girl found an excuse to slip out after him, and in the passage of the first floor there was a little kiss.

"Only one," she said, with an uplifted finger.

"And what about his little brother, then?" he chuckled—a chuckle with which all his jokes were accompanied: a kind of guttural chuckle, which seemed to descend or stick straining in the throat, instead of rising to the lips.

"You go on," she said playfully, tapped his cheek, and ran down. So Walter slept for the first night at Mrs. Evans'.

On the whole, as time passed, he had a good deal of the society of the women: for the theatre was a thing abominable to him, and in the evenings he stayed in the underground parlour, sharing the bread-and-cheese supper, and growing familiar with the sighs of Mrs. Evans over her once estate in the world. Rachel, the silent, sewed; Annie, whose relation with Walter was still unannounced, though perhaps guessed, could play hymn-tunes on the old piano, and she played. Last of all, Walter laid down the inveterate wet pipe, led them in prayer, and went to bed. Most mornings he and Annie set out together for Little Britain.

There came a day when he confided to her his intention to ask for a rise of "screw," and when this was actually promised by His Terror, the Boss, there was joy in heaven, and radiance in futurity, and secret talks of rings, a wedding, "a Home." Annie felt herself not far from the kingdom of Hymen, and rejoiced. But nothing, as yet, was said at No. 13: for to Mrs. Evans' past grandeurs thirty shillings a week was felt to be inappropriate.

The next Sunday, however, soon after dinner, this strangeness occurred: Rachel, the silent, disappeared. Mrs. Evans called for her, Annie called, but it was found that she was not in the house, though the putting away of the dinner-things, her usual task, was only half accomplished.

Not till tea-time did Rachel return. She was then cold, and somewhat sullen, and somewhat pale, her lips closing firmly over her projecting teeth. When timidly questioned—for her resentment was greatly feared—she replied that she had just been looking in upon Alice Soulsby, a few squares away, for a little chat: and this was the truth.

It was not, however, the whole truth; she had also looked in at the Church Lane Sunday School on her way: and this fact she guiltily concealed. For half an hour she had sat darkly at the end of the building in a corner, listening to the "address." This address was delivered by Walter. To this school every Sunday, after dinner, he put down the beloved pipe to go. He was in fact, its "superintendent."

After this, the tone and temper of the little household rapidly changed, and a true element of hell was introduced into its platitude. It became, first of all, a question whether or not Rachel could be "experiencing religion," a thing which her mother and Annie had never dreamt of expecting of her. Praying people, and the Salvationist, had always been the contempt of her strong and callous mind. But on Sunday nights she was now observed to go out alone, and "chapel" was the explanation which she coolly gave. Which chapel she did not specify: but in reality it was the Newton Street Hall, at which Walter frequently exhorted and "prayed." In the Church Lane schoolroom there was prayer-meeting on Thursday evenings; and twice within one month Rachel sallied forth on Thursday evening—soon after Walter. The secret disease which preyed upon the poor girl could hardly now be concealed. At first she suffered bitter, solitary shame; sobbed in a hundred paroxysms; hoped to draw a veil over her infirmity. But her gash was too glaring. In the long Sabbath evenings of summer he preached at Street corners, and sometimes secretly, sometimes openly, Rachel would attend these meetings, singing meekly with the rest the undivine hymns of the modern evangelist. In his presence, in the parlour, on other nights, she quietly sewed, hardly speaking. When, at 7 p.m., she heard his key in the front door her heart darted toward its master; when in the morning he flew away to business her universe was cinders.

"It's a wonder to me what's coming to our Rachel lately," said Annie in the train, coming home; "you're doing her soul good, or something, aren't you?"

He chuckled, with slushy suction-sounds about the back of the tongue and molars.

"Oh, that be jiggered for a tale!" he said: "*she's* all right."

"I know her better than you, you see. She's quite changed—since you've come. Looks to me as if she's having a touch of the blues, or something."

"Poor thing! She wants looking after, don't she?"

Annie laughed, too: but less brutally, more uneasily.

Walter said: "But she *oughtn't* to have the blues, if she's giving her heart to the Lord! People seem to think a Christian must be this and that. A Christian, if it comes to that, ought to be the jolliest fellow going!"

This was on a Thursday, the night of the Church Lane prayer-meeting, and Walter had only time to rush in at No. 13, wash his face, snatch his Bible, and be off. Rachel, for her part, must verily now have been badly bitten with the rabies of love, or she would have felt that to follow to-night, for the third time lately, could not fail to incur remark. But this consideration never even entered a mind now completely blinded and entranced by the personality of Walter.

Through the day her work about the house had been rushed forward with this very object, and at the moment when he banged the door after him she was before her glass, dressing in blanched, intense and trembling flurry, and casting as she bent to give the last touches to her fringe, a look of bitterest hate at the projection of her lip above the teeth.

This night, for the first time, she waited in the chapel till the end of the service, and walked slowly homeward on the way which she knew that Walter would take; and he came striding presently, that morocco Bible in his hand, nearly every passage in which was neatly under-ruled in black and red inks.

"What, is that you?" he said, taking into his a hand cold with sweat.

"It is," she answered, in a hard, formal tone.

"You don't mean to say you've been to the meeting?"

"I do."

"Why, where were my eyes? I didn't see you."

"It isn't likely that you would want to, Mr. Teeger."

"Go on—drop that! What do you take me for? I'm only too glad! And I tell you what it is, Miss Rachel, I say to you as the Lord Jesus said to the young man: 'Thou art not far from the kingdom of heaven.'"

She was *in* it!—near him, alone, in a darkling square, yet suffering, too, in the flames of a passion such as perhaps consumes only the strongest natures.

She caught for support at his unoffered arm; and when he bent his steps straight homeward, she said trembling violently: "I don't wish to go home as yet. I wish to have a little walk. Do you mind, Mr. Teeger?"

"Mind, no. Come along, then," and they went walking among an intricacy of streets and squares, he talking of "the Work," and of common subjects. After half an hour, she was saying:

"I often wish I was a man. A man can say and do what he likes; but with a girl it's different. There's you, now, Mr. Teeger, always out and about, having people listening to you, and that. I often wish I was only a man."

"Oh, well, it all depends how you look at it," he said. "And, look here, you may as well call me Walter and be done."

"Oh, I shouldn't think of *that*," she replied. "Not till—"

Her hand trembled on his arm.

"Well, out with it, why don't you?"

"Till—till we know something more definite about you—and Annie."

He chuckled slushily, she now leading him fleetly round and round a square.

"Ah, you girls again!" he cried, "been blabbing again like all the girls! It takes a bright man to hide much from them, don't it?"

"But there isn't much to hide in this case, as far as I can see—*is* there?"

Always Walter laughed, straining deep in the throat. He said: "Oh, come—that would be telling, wouldn't it?"

After a minute's stillness, this treacherous phrase came from Rachel: "Annie doesn't care for anyone, Mr. Teeger."

"Oh, come—that's rather a tall order, *any* one. *She's* all right."

"But she *doesn't*. Of course, most girls are silly, and that, and like to get married—"

"Well, that's only nature, ain't it?"

This was a joke; and downward the laugh strained in his throat, like struggling phlegm.

"Yes, but they don't understand what love is," said Rachel. "They haven't an idea. They like to be married women, and have a husband, and that. But they don't know what love is—believe me! The men don't either."

How she trembled!—her body, her dying voice—she pressing heavily upon him, while the moon triumphed now through cloud glaring a moment white on the lunacy of her ghostly face.

"Well, I don't know—I think *I* understand, lass, what it is," he said.

"You don't, Mr. Teeger!"

"How's that, then?"

"Because, when it takes you, it makes you—"

"Well, let's have it. You seem to know all about it."

Now Rachel commenced to tell him what "it" was—in frenzied definitions, and a power of expression strange for her. *It* was a lunacy, its name was Legion, it was possession by the furies; it was a spasm in the throat, and a sickness of the limbs, and a yearning of the eye-whites, and a fire in the marrow; it was catalepsy, trance, apocalypse; it was high as the galaxy, it was addicted to the gutter; it was Vesuvius, borealis, the sunset; it was the rainbow in a cesspool, St. John plus Heliogabalus, Beatrice plus Messalina; it was a transfiguration, and a leprosy, and a metempsychosis, and a neurosis; it was the dance of the mænads, and the bite of the tarantula, and baptism in a sun: out poured the wild definition in simple words, but with the strife of one fighting for life. And she had not half done when he understood her fully; and he had no sooner understood her, than he was subdued, and succumbed.

"You don't mean to say—" he faltered.

"Ah, Mr. Teeger," she answered, "there's none so blind as those who will not see."

His arm stole round her shuddering body.

Everyone is said to have his failing; and this man, Walter, in no respect a man of strong mind, was certainly on his amatory side, most sudden, promiscuous, and infirm. And this tendency was, if anything, heightened by the quite sincere strain of his mind in the direction of "spiritual things": for, under sudden temptation, back rushed his being, with the greater rigour, into its natural channel. On the whole, had he not been a Puritan, he would have been a Don Juan.

In an instant Rachel's weight was hanging upon his neck, he kissing her with passion.

After this she said to him: "But you are only doing this out of pity, Walter. Tell the truth, you are in love with Annie?"

He, like Peter, tumbled at once into a fib. "That's what *you* say!"

"You are," she insisted, filled with the bliss of the fib.

"Bah! I'm not. Never was. You are the girl for me."

When they went home, they entered the house at different times, she first, he waiting twenty minutes in the street.

The house was small, so the sisters slept together in the second-floor front room; Walter in the second-floor back; Mrs. Evans in the first-floor back, the first-floor front being "the drawing-room." The girls, therefore, generally went to bed together: and that night, as they undressed, there was a row.

First, a long silence. Then Rachel, to say something, pointed to some new gloves of Annie's, asking: "How much did you give for those?"

"Money and kind words," replied Annie.

This was the beginning.

"Well, there's no need to be rude about it," said Rachel. She was happy, in paradise, despised Annie that night.

"Still," said Annie, after a silence of ten minutes before the glass, "still, I should never run after a man like that. I'd die first."

"I haven't the least idea what you're talking about," replied Rachel.

"You have. I should be *ashamed* of myself, if I were you."

"Talk away. You're a little fool."

"It's *you*. Throwing yourself at the head of a man who doesn't care for you. What *can* you call yourself?"

Rachel laughed—happily, yet dangerously.

"Don't bother yourself, my girl," she said.

"Think of going out every night to meet a man in that way: look here, it's too disgusting of you, girl!"

"Is it?"

"You can't deny that you were with Mr. Teeger to-night?"

"That I wasn't."

"It's false! Anyone can see it by the joy in your face."

"Well, suppose I was, what about it?"

"But a woman should be decent, I think; a woman should be able to command her feelings, and not expose herself like that. Believe me, it gives me the creeps all over to think of."

"Never mind, don't be jealous, my girl."

The gentle Annie flamed!

"Jealous! of you!"

"There isn't any need, you know—not *yet*."

"But I'm *not*! There never *will* be need! Do you take Mr. Teeger for a raving lunatic? I should go and have some false teeth put in first if I were you!"

Thus did Annie drop to the rock-bed of vulgarity; but she knew it to be necessary in order to touch Rachel, as with a white-hot wire, on her very nerve of anguish, and, in fact, at these words Rachel's face resembled white iron, while she cried out, "Never mind my teeth! It isn't the teeth a man looks at! A man knows a finely built woman when he sees her—not like a little dumpy podge!"

"Thank you. You are very polite," replied Annie, browbeaten by an intensity fiercer than her own. "But still, it's nonsense, Rachel, to talk of my being jealous of you. I knew Mr. Teeger six months before you. And you won't know him much longer either, for I don't want to have mother disgraced here, and this is no fit place for him to lodge in. I can easily make him leave it soon—"

At this thing Rachel flew, with minatory palm over Annie's cheek, ready to strike. "You *dare* do anything to make him go away! I'll tear your little—"

Annie winked, flinched, uttered a sob, no more fight left in her.

So for two weeks the situation lasted. Only, after that night, so intense grew the bitterness between the sisters, that Annie moved down to the first-floor back, sleeping now with Mrs. Evans who dimly wondered. As for Walter, meanwhile, his heart was divided within him. He loved Annie; he was fascinated and mesmerised by Rachel. In another age and country he would have married both. Every day he came to a different resolve, not knowing what to do. One thing was evident—a wedding-ring would be necessary, and he purchased one, uncertain for which of the girls.

"Look here, lass," he said to Annie in the train, coming home, "let us put a stop to this. The boss doesn't seem to be in a hurry about that rise of screw, so suppose we get spliced, and be done?"

"Privately?"

"Rather. Your ma and sister mustn't know,—not just yet a while."

"And you will still keep on living at the house?"

"Well, of course, for the time being."

She looked up into his face and smiled. It was settled. But two nights afterwards he met Rachel on his way home from prayer-meeting; at first was honest and distant; but then committed the incredible weakness of going with her for a walk among the squares, and ended by winning from her an easily granted promise of marriage, on the same terms as those arranged within Annie.

When, the next day at lunch-time, he put his foot on the threshold of the Registrar's office to give notice, he was still in a state of agonized indecision as to the name which he should couple with his own.

When the official said, "Now the name of the other party?" Walter hesitated, shuffled with his feet, then answered:

"Rachel Evans."

Not till he was again in the street did he remember that Rachel was the name of both the girls, and that liberty of choice between them still remained to him.

Now, from the day of "notice" to the day of wedlock, an interval of twenty-one clear days must by law, elapse, and Walter, though weak enough to inform both the sisters of the step he had taken, was careful to give them only a vague idea of the date fixed. His once clear conscience, meanwhile, was grievously troubled, his feet in a net; he feared to speak to God; and went drifting like flotsam on the river of chance.

And chance alone it was which at last cast him upon the land. The fifth day before the marriage was a Bank Holiday, and he had arranged with Rachel to go out with her that day to Hyde Park, she to wait for him at an arranged spot at two o'clock. At two, then, at a street-corner, stood Rachel waiting, twirling her parasol, walking a little, returning. Walter, however, did not appear, and what could have happened was beyond her divination. Had he misunderstood or missed her? Though incredible, it was the only thing to think. To Hyde Park, at any rate, she went alone, feeling desolate and *ennuyée*, in the vague hope of there meeting him.

What had happened was this: Walter had been half-way toward the rendezvous with Rachel, when he was met in the street by Annie, who had gone to spend the day with a married friend at Stroud Green, but had returned, owing to the husband's illness. Seeing Walter, her face lit up with smiles.

"Harry's down with the influenza," she said, "so I couldn't stay and bore poor Ethel. Where are you going?"

For the first time since his "conversion" twelve years before, Walter, with a high flush, now consciously lied.

"Only to the schoolroom," he said, "to hunt for something."

"Well, I am open to be taken out, if any kind friend will be so kind," she said fondly.

Now he had that morning vowed to himself to wed Rachel; and by this vow he now again vowed to be bound. All the more reason why, for the last time, he should "take out" Annie.

"Come along, then, old girl," he gaily said: "where shall we go?"

"Let us go to Hyde Park," said Annie. And to Hyde Park they went, Walter, ever and anon, stabbed by the bitter memory of waiting Rachel.

At five o'clock the two were walking along the north bank of the Serpentine westward toward a two-arched bridge, which is also pierced by a third narrow arch over the bank: to this narrow arch, since it was drizzling, they were making for shelter, when Rachel, a person of the keenest vision, sighted them from the south bank. She was frantic at once. Annie, who was supposed to be at Stroud Green! *What treachery!* This, then, was why . . . She ran panting along the bank, toward the bridge, then over it, northward, and now heard the two under the arch, who stood there talking—of the wedding. Unfortunately, just here is a block of masonry, which prevented Rachel from leaning directly over the arch to listen. Yet the necessity to hear was absolute: so she ran back clear of the masonry, and bent far over the parapet, outwards and sideways toward the arch, straining neck, body, ears, and anyone looking into those staring eyes *then* would have comprehended the doctrine of the Ferine Soul. But she was at a disadvantage, heard only murmurs, and—was that a kiss? Further and further forth she strained. And now suddenly, within a cry, she is in the water, where it is shallow near the bank. In the fall her head struck upon a stone in the mud.

For three days she screamed continuously the name of Walter, filling the street with it, calling him hers only. On the third night, in the midst of a frightful crisis of cries, she suddenly died.

"Oh, Rachel, don't say you are dead!" cried Annie over her.

The death occurred two days before the marriage-day, and on the next, Walter, well wounded, said to Annie: "This knocks our little affair on the head, of course."

Annie was silent. Then, with a pout, she said: "I don't see why. After all, it was her own fault, entirely. Why should we suffer?"

For the feud between the sisters had become cruel as death; and it outlasted death: Annie, on the subject of Rachel and Walter, being no longer a gentle girl, but marble, without respect or pity.

And so, in spite of the trepidations and hesitancy of Walter, the marriage took place, even while Rachel lay stretched on the bed in the second-floor front of No. 13.

The ceremony did not, however transpire without hitch and omen. It was necessary, first of all, for Walter to forewarn Annie that he had given notice of her to the Registrar by her second name of "Rachel"—a mad-looking proceeding that was almost the cause of a rupture which nothing but Walter's most ardent pleadings could steer him clear of. At any rate it was to "Rachel," and not to "Annie" that he was, as a matter of fact, after all married.

After the ceremony, performed in their lunch-time, they returned to business together in Little Britain.

At ten o'clock the same night, as he was going up to bed, she ran after him, and in the passage there was a long, furtive kiss— their last on earth.

"Twelve o'clock?" he whispered intensely.

She held up her forefinger. "One!"

"Oh, say twelve!"

She did not answer, but drew her palm playfully, across his cheek, meaning consent, for Mrs. Evans was an inveterately heavy sleeper. He went up. And, careful to leave his door a little ajar, he extinguished his candle, and went to bed. In the apartment nearby lay stark in the dark—with learned, eternal eyelids and drowsy brow—the dead.

Walter could not but think of this presence close at hand. "Well, poor girl!" he sighed. "Poor Rachel! Well, well. His way is in the sea, after all, and His path in the Great Deep, and His footsteps are not known." Then he thought of Annie—the little wife! But

instead of Annie, there was Rachel. The two women fought vehemently for his thought—and ever the dead was stronger than the
living. . . . Instead of Annie there was Rachel—and again Rachel.

At last he could hear twelve strike from a steeple, and sat up in
bed, listening eagerly for the door to open, or a footfall on the floor.

A little American clock ticked in the room; and in the flue of
the chimney was a sough and chaunt just audible.

Suddenly she was intensely with him, filling the chamber—from
nowhere. He had heard no footstep, no opening of the door: yet
certainly, she was with him *now*, all suddenly, close to him, over
him, talking breathlessly to him.

His first sensation was a shuddering which strongly shook him
from head to foot, like the shuddering of Russian cold. She held
him down by the shoulders; was stretched at length on the bed,
over him; and the room seemed full of a rustling and rushing, very
strange, like starched muslins rushing out in stormy agitation. She
was speaking, too, to him in *breathless haste*, whimpering a secret
gibberish which whimpered like a pup for passion—about love and
its definition, and about the soul, and the worm, and Eternity, and
the passion of death, and the nuptials of the tomb, and the lust
and hollowness of the void. And he, too, was speaking, whispering
through his pattering teeth, saying: "Sh-h-h, Rachel—Annie, I
mean—sh-h-h, my girl—your ma will hear! Rachel, don't—sh-h-h,
now!" But even while he kept up this "sh-h-h dear—sh-h-h, now,"
he was conscious of the invasion of a strange rage, of such a
strength as if energy was being vehemently pumped into him from
some behemoth omnipotence. The form above him he could hardly
discern, the room was so dark, but he felt that her garment was
flowing forth from her neck in a continuous flutter, with the rustling of the starch of a thousand shrouds, like the outflow of a pen-
nant in wind; and the quivering gauze seemed now to swell and fill
the chamber, and now to sink again to the size of woman. And ever
the rhapsody of love and death went on, mixed with the chattered
"Sh-h-h, Rachel—Annie, I mean," of Walter; till, suddenly, he was
involved in an embrace so horrible, felt himself encompassed by a
might so intolerable, that his soul fainted within him. He sank back;

thought span and failed in darkness beneath the spell of that lullaby; he muttered, "Receive my spirit. . . ."

After two days Walter, still unconscious, died. His disfigured body they placed in a grave not far from Rachel's.

A SHOT AT THE SUN

I tell you something which I have seen with my own eyes; you believe it or not, as you like.

I am an old fellow now at this date of writing, and what I tell of happened forty years ago, in the old slavery days, down South.

Charles K. Brownrigg at that time was the owner of two hundred and forty-five niggers, not to mention fifteen hundred acres of cotton plantation. And I take it upon me to state that he was the worst-shunned and the worst-feared man in the Southern States of America.

He was a big, red man, with hard, hairless jaws and a goat-beard, and continually went about with a gun on his shoulder. His estate house, a rambling place, lay a little outside of Cliftonville (in South Carolina), and looked directly upon his plantations. That gun which he carried had shot, at one time or another, five separate niggers—nobody had the least doubt of it in Cliftonville—yet by some strange power which was in him, or about him, Brownrigg had escaped justice.

One day—it was in "the hot" of the year '59—a maroon rushed into the shed where Brownrigg was overseeing the reaping, with the words:

"Massa, massa, Brams and Jess done gone run 'way!"

Brams was a negro youth of twenty, and Jess a mulatto girl, shapely as Venus, both slaves of Brownrigg. Brams and Jess, from the first mutual glance some months before had loved; and now, by concert, had taken to the woods and wilds in some mad hope of finding free happiness.

Brownrigg's Panama hat was low on his forehead that morning, and his face even before this announcement had worn a scowl, for he was in money difficulties; he had had two bad years with the cotton, and as the news of the flight passed the lips of the maroon Brownrigg sent the long lash of a short-handled cowhide coiling about the man's legs with the crack of a Maxim gun, while the slave skipped in a dance of pain.

There was something very queer about Brownrigg—he was no ordinary slave-owner. Now, for instance, when he threw down the whip, and the slave lay writhing in the "long-grass," it was natural to expect that he would have rushed instantly away, hurried together dogs and horses, and set out after the fugitives. But he did nothing of the sort.

What he did do was to put his hand into his waistcoat-pocket, draw out three little black stones, deposit them in his left palm, and stare at them for some three minutes. They were obiah-stones.

Brownrigg, standing with his knickered bowlegs apart, put a finger-tip to his lips, touched each of the stones with spittle, and rattled them in his left hand. Then he opened the hand, put the middle stone back into his pocket, and with two fingers of the right hand struck down smartly upon the two remaining stones. They started away from his palm in divergent directions; Brownrigg noted the directions and picked them up.

Only then did he set out. He hurried to the estate house, blowing a whistle. In ten minutes two pursuing parties had started in the directions which the stones had indicated, and in less than an hour Brams and Jess were safely lodged in the estate ward-house. It may have been only chance, or it may have been Brownrigg's obiah-stones, that caught them; of course, I do not know—I merely state facts.

Brams and Jess were to be pitied that day, if ever two poor mortals were to be pitied. I say that day, meaning that day above all other days whatsoever; for on that day Brownrigg had in him the humour of ten demons. I am going to tell you why. Perhaps

you are aware that there are three special days (sometimes it is
four, or even five, but usually it is three) when, during the cotton-
reap, it is of the greatest importance that the sun shine strongly
and steadily, without rain or even cloud. Cloud means loss, rain
disaster, the reason being that the new-plucked fruit needs just at
that time the swelter of the sun for what is called its "fibring." Now
this particular day when Brams and Jess ran away and were captured was the second of the three critical days in that year, and the
sun was not shining too well, and Brownrigg was angry with it.

You may imagine perhaps that the sun did not care so very much
about Brownrigg's anger, but this was the very point which was in
doubt all through Cliftonville that day; and it is no exaggeration
to say that positively hundreds of bets were being made in the
saloons, in the Exchange, at the store doors, as to whether the sun
would shine, and, if not, as to whether Brownrigg would command
it to shine, and, in that case, as to whether or not it would obey
Brownrigg.

The fact is that during the previous year's reap, one afternoon,
when the sun had gone behind a cloud, Brownrigg had been clearly
seen to do an extraordinary thing. Standing in midfield he had
hurriedly loaded his gun; he had then cocked the hammer ready
for shooting; then he had taken his massive silver watch in his left
hand, and three niggers near had heard him say, with a nod of the
sun, these strange words:

"I give you five minutes!"

And one minute, two, three minutes passed, and the sun had
remained hidden; and four minutes had passed, and it had remained hidden; and as the five minutes ended it had walked out
into open sky with clear, blistering face.

Now Cliftonville was not a bit more superstitious than anywhere
else, and in another man such conduct would have seemed to it
simply silly. But in Brownrigg it somehow did not seem silly. He
was felt to be a genuinely diabolical and dreadful man. It was
known for a certainty that with blackened face he had attended
the rites and midnight orgies of the negro obiah-men in the depths
of the forest. All Cliftonville knew it. And at the top of his estate

house was some sort of cupola in which at night his light was seen
to shine, no one knowing in the least what Brownrigg was doing
there—whether he was star-gazing, or whether he was holding
intercourse with who can say what or whom.

And therefore, I say, the bets in Cliftonville were many that
day, and a thrill of excitement filled the town; and when, about
two in the afternoon, the sun went definitely behind a spread of
cloud, looking as if it meant to stay there and casting a shade over
the land, all the lanes leading to Brownrigg's plantation were covered with groups of twos and threes, of fives and tens, slouching
out innocently that way to see what there was to see.

At that hour Brownrigg was with the two runaways in a foul
hole of the estate ward-house—he and they were alone. He had tied
them together with many whorls of rope which entered the flesh,
and he had laid them so upon the mud floor, with outstretched
arms. At his feet were two pails of boiling water, whose surface
still bubbled, and in his hand his gun.

"Now, you two young niggers!" was all he said.

Upon the two forms he tossed in three spurts the contents of
one pail, the tied mass on the floor filling the cell with yells and
flinging itself about in wriggling spasms. Then he put down the pail,
took from his waistcoat-pocket one of the little obiah-stones, spat
on it, dropped it into the other pail, and said these words aloud:

"I give the lives of these two young niggers for a good reap.
The moment that water cools, let 'em die, Bam, let 'em die, O Bam."

Then Brownrigg put his gun to his shoulder and took aim. He
had not the least intention of killing, for slave justice, though crude,
was yet an existent fact, and he had been too often suspected of
murder already. But he took aim; he was a good shot, and though
the den was dark he could see. He sighted the fleshy parts of the
now quietly-groaning mass.

He pierced the shoulder of Brams; a minute, then *ping!*—he
pierced the thigh of Jess; another minute, then *ping!*—he pierced
he knew not what, for at this third shot the gun gave such a jarring
kick at his shoulder that he staggered backward. The shock was
very unexpected. He frowned.

"Why, what's matter with the old gun?" he muttered.

He cast a glance at the pail containing the stone, shouldered his gun, and ascended. As he mounted the light shone on a hideous face distorted with passions.

The first thing he saw now was that the sun was not shining as it should.

He at once went down the back-lane toward the plantation, around he cast his lurid eyes, and must have observed that every path and niche of foliage was thronged with people from Cliftonville. But he took no interest in them. All along the cotton overseer and nigger were at work—but in shadow—the sun was behind a cloud.

Every minute Brownrigg was losing seventy-five dollars.

All eyes were fixed upon Brownrigg. All about him was a murmur of tongues. Bets ran high. Brownrigg seemed unconscious of it all.

Suddenly, with a jerk, he moved. He put his left hand to his waistcoat-pocket.

This was a signal for a general crowding round him; through field and path they came, everyone, however, keeping a respectable distance.

There was a rock near to Brownrigg, and on the top of this he put his watch, together with the leather strap which attached it to his waistcoat. Face upward he settled it, just under his eye; and he put his gun to his shoulder, and with a face of diabolical wickedness he pointed it at the sun.

As he did so he said these words:

"Three minutes—I give you three."

The words were heard by an overseer who at that moment had happened to approach Brownrigg. And the overseer, holding down his little finger with his thumb, lifted on high three fingers behind Brownrigg's back to show the crowd how the matter stood.

At once hundreds of watches were snatched from hundreds of pockets, and held in hundreds of palms. A minute passed. Not a sound now but the soft rush of the breeze in the cotton leafage, every man feeling his heart beat thickly in his bosom.

The second minute is gone. The sun remains clouded, and steadily points Brownrigg's muzzle at it. Every five or six seconds he gives a downward glance at his watch. In all that crowd of on-lookers there is hardly now a single face not pallid with excitement.

Suddenly there is a stirring—there is the wildest sensation! The sun is re-adjusting itself—there is a working, a movement yonder on high—the clouds are giving way, as when a crowd opens for the passage of Royalty! He has won his way—he shines triumphantly—the world is sweltering in his blaze.

From the fields and lanes there went up a shout. Brownrigg was seen to nod, as if to say, "Ah, so much the better for you!" There were still fifteen seconds lacking to the completion of his three minutes.

During the next five minutes there ensued an agitated scene among the crowd; bets were being settled, comments made; on the outskirts there was a tendency toward departure for Cliftonville. It seemed probable that the saloons would do a brisk trade that day, for considerable sums had changed hands.

Brownrigg had again put on his watch. He was talking to the overseer who had approached him. In the midst of his talk he was seen to snatch up his cow-skin "cart-whip," and crack it round the bare legs of a negro who had happened to pass too near.

All at once those who had sauntered from the outskirts of the crowd to return to the town stopped, and ran back with cries to their former stations. With a strange suddenness the sun had buried itself into cloud, involving the land in shadow.

Expectation now stood more wildly on tiptoe than ever. The betting instinct at this fresh impetus was on the point of manifesting itself with tenfold vigour; but, as a matter of fact, not a single bet was made, for Brownrigg left them no time. With a gesture of horrible rage he snatched away his watch, placed it on the stone, snatched up his gun, and pointed it upward.

The overseer, still near him, drew away, and, holding down his third and fourth fingers with his thumb, lifted on high his first two behind Brownrigg's back for the information of the crowd. Brownrigg had said:

"Two minutes—I give you two."

And once more the hundreds of watches lay flat in the hundreds of palms. And in silence a minute passed.

It must have been about this time, as the Cliftonville folk said afterwards, that the negro Brams drew himself along the mud floor of his cell, wounded as he was, dragging with him his companion in misery. He had heard the curse pronounced against him, and seen the obiah-stone dropped into the hot water. With a push he upset the pail, and took out the stone. That is what he afterwards asserted.

But whatever truth is to be credited to the statement of the black, the fact remains that Brownrigg stood with gun pointed at the sun; and a minute passed and the sun remained hidden.

Obstinately this time. A minute and a half—and no one dared to breathe; a sense of the awful oppressed the heart; the waiting air seemed crowded with something momentous. The breeze died away, as if holding its breath to watch that blasphemy.

Then—at last—with a shock of fear everyone knew that the two minutes were over, and the sun remained a mere blotch.

Bang! Brownrigg fired.

He vanished. He perished. Never could one have conceived such a thing. To say that the gun burst and sent him into eternity is to put it very feebly: *he disappeared*. Gun and Brownrigg and watch were wiped out. The folk at Cliftonville used to tell that not a single trace was left of him—that he was clean eaten up and swallowed by the wrath of heaven. That is an exaggeration—but not much of one; some traces were found—but *wonderfully* few. I state facts.

THE BELL OF ST. SʹPULCRE

It was during my tramp through Provence three summers ago that I came one evening to Lebrun-les-Bruyères, a hamlet near the bottom of the Bezons valley. Here I found the inn so poor, that I resolved to tramp on to Cargnac, four miles off.

"But," said an old vigneron, whom I asked to put me on the path through the forest, "you should go round about by the road."

"Why?" I asked him— "that means another kilomètre?"

"We of these parts hardly use the path now," was his answer: "don't you go that way"—with a certain earnestness and admonition . . .

"What, wolves about here?" I asked him.

He lowered his voice to say: "You may see someone named La Mère Gouvion"—as if to say "you may see Beelzebub."

I supposed that he meant a ghost, and, as I knew something of Southern superstitiousness, and was in a hurry, I handed him a franc, and went on by the forest-path.

I found it in some parts choked with bush—myrtle, kermes-oak—which I had to part before me; and by the moonshine above the bush I saw in that short distance two of those mounds named barrows, placed there by "the fairies"; then, when I had tramped three kilomètres through a rather intolerable solitude, the shock came: three mètres to my left within a sort of clearing I saw the woman . . .

She was seated on a fragment of one of those rocks that they call "menhirs."

I had the impression in the hazy moonshine that she was moving her shoulders slowly from side to side, her hand supporting her jaw, some grace in the fall of her rags suggesting a statue set on a pedestal. Her stature, I could see, was gigantic—her great arms like clubs, her great bosom and spread of shoulder, her mouth open in a cavern of darkness that looked oblong, her hair black-and-grey, a tangle of snakes; and, as I walked past, her eyes followed me with that kind of gaze with which an ox stops cropping to gaze after a passer.

The image of this woman filled my mind until I got to Cargnac, near nine; and that same night, while sitting in an inn-garden with swings, nine-pins, arbours, I was told by my host the story of "La Mère Gouvion."

"She came," he told me, "of a well-to-do family who owned land on the far side of Lebrun-les-Bruyères, her father being a mighty big man, known as a hard bargainer as far as Avignon and Orange, and in Lebrun everybody feared him, even the curé, for it was said that he did not believe in the good God, he drank half a litre of cognac every night, so that one could hear him marching up and down his verandah to a late hour, quarrelling with nobody, and carrying on; terrible he was when the drink had him, like a man mad with sun-stroke.

"And one summer, when the phylloxera had rotted his vine-leaves, and things were looking bad for harvest, on an awful night long remembered he raised his hand, defied the heavens to do their worst, and challenged the bell of St. Sépulcre to ring in his hearing—for the bell was said to be a little audible from his yard.

"His wife ran to hide under a bed, dreading the bell-toll, his daughter Maude herself trembled. Some had it to say that the bell did ring in his hearing; however that was, he perished shortly afterwards in convulsions, and was buried without the blessing of the Church.

"Soon after him his good woman also passed away: and Maude Gouvion was left mistress of all.

"And now things began to look alive indeed. If the patch of yellowish moss appeared on all the vineleaves of the parish, Maude Gouvion's trellises were still green."

Maude's spray and pruning-scissors should, no doubt, have accounted for this prosperity, but there were those who thought of black magic when the mulberry-disease and the failure of the madder-crop, which were the cry all round, seemed to keep clear of her fields.

"The truth was that her man toiled for her with the consciousness of her hard eyes behind them, for she was more masterful than any man; and, moreover, she covered her land with a newfangled sort of sandy stuff from Marseilles, so that, the next vintage, sixty barrels of light wine rolled off in her cart to Avignon, as against le père Gouvion's maximum of fifty-three.

"Meanwhile, no one could stand the sight of her passions, if anything went wrong, as when she threw big Huguénin, the blacksmith, down some stairs for laming a mule in shoeing. In Lebrun-les-Bruyères the curé called 'Silence!' at anyone who mentioned her name. She had not once been inside the church door since her father's death."

But one Sunday morning, she being then thirty-five, Maude, to everyone's astonishment, turned up in the little church in the valley. "Never," said my landlord, "was seen such finery, rings and ribbons, though Maude was ordinarily slatternly in dress; and she carried her head high, as though the church was not good enough for her feet, while the curé stammered and changed colour.

"And why do you think she did this? It was as a preliminary to coming out as a married woman, for she was about to marry the little Tombarel, the shoemaker, as was soon known. And there was a great whispering and excitement then, for everyone knew that no one would have wished to marry Maude, rich as she was, a woman whose own father, as report said, had heard the bell: so that Maude must have fixed upon the little Tombarel for her own reasons, and done her own wooing."

"But which bell is it," I asked, "that you keep speaking of?"

He looked astonished. "Well, I should have thought that even a stranger . . . I mean—do I not?—the bell of St. Sépulcre."

"What does this bell do?" I asked him.

"It is a sound which one should not hear," he answered, with a frown. "It is believed to bring—well, I could not tell you—evil upon those who hear it."

He was silent. Then: "But talking of this poor little Tombarel, everyone pitied him. It is said that, on his taking a pair of sabots to the presbytère, the priest admonished him to trust to the saints for protection from the Evil One; and, in saying this, he was supposed to throw a stone at Maude Gouvion. A week before the civil marriage Tombarel ran away to Cazalès, but Maude followed him, and, it was said, knocked him down with a box; so they came back together, and were married.

"Soon afterwards Maude gave birth to her son Pierre. As for the poor Tombarel, he did not survive his marriage three months.

"This Pierre grew up a sickly, pale lad; but the uglier everybody thought him, the prouder his mother was of him. He was everything to her—she went foolish with love only to look at him.

"He was a cripple, with disease of the hip-joint, and three times a week for years his mother took him over to La Risolette to be seen to. When the doctor told her that the child could not possibly live, she only laughed, and said the man was a fool who did not know his business. And live it did.

"But Pierre had a mental disease as well—his crazy craving for blood: for to sling a pebble from a catapult into the eye of a pig was his delight. At thirteen he was the death of a little girl, and later on was discovered with a cut that he had made in his own neck. His mother slung him to her shoulder that day, with that square opening of the mouth which was her way in her agitations, and ran to La Risolette with the dead weight, not waiting for a cart. It was the feat of a horse."

Such, then, was Pierre. The children shrank from contact with him, and it got to be a prophecy in the village that the day would come when the bell of St. Sépulcre would sound upon the ears of Maude Gouvion's son.

"But," said mine host, in a *patois* whose quaintness I despair of quite conveying, "whatever he did, if he stuck a calf, or half killed a child, or lay down all day fuddled by the roadside, his mother still laughed and petted him: this only made her love him the more proudly and the more loudly. She was foolish with her love."

"Pierre," he went on, "was sweet on Rosalie Tissot, granddaughter of Tissot, the schoolmaster, the prettiest golden-haired fairy that ever was, engaged to be married to Martin Dejoie, who was a carpenter at La Risolette. Pierre lay in wait for her everywhere, with a patience which was strange for him; but she laughed at his shrunken form, with a derision in which there was ever more terror than laughter, knowing how cruelly he loved her, hardly knowing perhaps what a peril lay in her laughter.

"When the date of her marriage with Martin Dejoie came near, Pierre went and threw himself at his mother's knees in a room where she sat shelling peas, saying to her: 'Mother, I shall go and kill myself, for I am the laughing-stock of the place because I am not like others, and, if I do not have Rosalie, they will laugh at me the more.' Now, his mother's heart was like a harp to him, he knew that to tell her of the folks' laughing was to lash her into a scratching cat, and 'Wait, Pierre,' says she now over her pease, quite quietly: 'wait, my son; you shall marry this girl.'

"That same night when the village was asleep Mother Gouvion wrapped her head up, and came down upon Tissot's cottage near the church, Tissot nearly dropping dead with fright when he hobbled from bed in his red-wool nightcap and saw her standing there, so big that she had to bend her body to get in. Well, she offered everything for Rosalie—eight thousand francs in the Credit at Avignon, the olives, the two presses, the stock and plant—all should be Pierre's and Rosalie's: and meantime the old Tissot sat shivering, hands on knees, not knowing what to say.

"At last he stammers that Rosalie would not consent, since her marriage with Martin Dejoie was a marriage of love. 'Rosalie is only a child,' says la Mère Gouvion; 'leave her to me.' 'Well, well,' says Tissot.

"So Mother Gouvion returned home satisfied. If only matters had rested there! But she had hardly gone when Tissot woke up his grandson, and sent him with a note to tell Martin Dejoie to be sure to come over to Lebrun the next morning. So Martin Dejoie came; but, on coming, he put his head in at the school-door, the children saw him, and two hours later Mother Gouvion knew all about that meeting. The two men had a confabulation together, Tissot declaring that the only way was for Martin to carry off Rosalie secretly to Avignon the night before the ten days' notice was up, and marry her there. But it was no secret in the village that three of the days were already gone, and the silly old man did not stop to consider that Mother Gouvion would surely know when the ten days would expire. As a matter of fact, she had no sooner heard of that interview between Tissot and Dejoie than she knew perfectly well what had been settled. It is said in Lebrun-les-Bruyères that she sent a message that same evening to Dejoie, asking him to come and talk the matter over with her, but that Dejoie would not even receive the message. If this is true, it was the last attempt made by la Mère Gouvion to change Dejoie's mind in his scheme to outwit her."

At eleven, then, in the night preceding that tenth day of notice, Martin Dejoie, a tall active chap, was crossing the moor between La Risolette and Lebrun-les-Bruyères, the moor on which stands St. Sépulcre. He was coming to meet Rosalie, who, with Tissot's old *gouvernante*, was waiting for him in a cart behind the presbytère-wood, to be off with him to Avignon; and he was taking the shortest road to her, though people coming from La Risolette to Lebrun usually make a detour to avoid the moor, so desolate is its barren expanse, on which grows only vine-stumps and some lavender-shrubs, with here or there a miasmatic *clair* (pool), or a cypress standing out blighted against the sky, or a gang of those black rocks, having hollows, that the Provencals call *cagnards*. Over all north-west winds draw along volumes of a white dust, wide-winged, there being often mistral over the moor when the valleys lie tranquil.

At one part of this Dead Sea Border of Provence stands, where it has stood since the time of the Franks, the ruins of St. Sépulcre, choked now with brambles, hiding behind a strange rankness of vegetation. But the belfry remains unbroken, and, they say, the bell-rope, and the bell.

I will not delay to tell you the ancient tale of bale which gave to this bell its awesomeness among all those glens: but for the poor wretch who hears its tone life is practically over, heart fails and brain—this throughout a district of sceptical France extending from beyond Lebrun-les-Bruyères quite on, I believe, to Hudin: the hearer of the bell is accursed; what he sets about shall fail, and shall rebound with tribulation upon his head; if he be not instantly struck down, his life will still be poisoned; the air will hurt him; water will burn him; his blessedness will be in death.

On the night when Martin Dejoie started out for Rosalie from La Risolette the mist on the moor was luminous with moonlight, and only a little wind moved: so that Mother Gouvion could see some distance from the church-step, where she stood hidden within the mass of sarsaparilla and kermes-oaks that choked the church-portal. "For many years no foot had ventured so near St. Sépulcre as hers this night, and she drank brandy from a vial to keep her defiance bright in her brain—all that I am telling you now being only what la Mère Gouvion herself revealed long afterwards, and every word's true. She had groped to see if the bell-rope was still there, intending, if not, to drag herself up like a cat to get at the bell; but the rope was there, still pretty strong, though rotted—she could see a little by the rays of moonlight that came through the ruins; and now she stood peering between the bushes at the foot-path over the moor, waiting for Martin Dejoie to appear: for she understood that, with such a business in hand, he would not make a detour round St. Pierre, but would come over the moor.

"At last, near eleven, a sound of someone whistling reached her, for Martin did not like to be passing so near the bell, so was whis-tling to himself for company; and at once Mother Gouvion set to work, first plugging up her ears with cotton-wool, and over this a

bandage, her plan being to make the bell clang, yet not hear it herself. Her only trouble was the doubt whether the man coming was
Martin. Suppose it was Pierre himself? Pierre sometimes crossed
the moor at night; Pierre whistled. But it was all right—it was Martin—she saw that, when he had got opposite. He stopped his whis-
tling then, bent his head, crossed his breast—in the vigour of his
life—a young man just going to be married—suddenly clang, clang,
clang for him . . .

"On her face she lay watching him where he had dropped
against one of the *cagnards*; then she stole away home, elated,
thinking in herself, 'I didn't hear the bell-sound! I didn't hear it!'

"Well, Rosalie and Tissot waited in vain for Martin Dejoie that
night; it was not till five days later that his body was found at the
bottom of that ravine north of the moor that is called 'Le Dé du
Diablo.' Whether he tumbled down there in his distraction, or
dashed himself down in his despair, is not known, but he was believed to have heard the bell; and it was years before anyone supposed that his death was not owing to an act of God.

"And so la Mère Gouvion kept her word; and Rosalie in a few
months was married to Pierre.

"But," said my host, in his Doric *patois*, "it was never a good
thing for la Mère Gouvion that she did what she had done. Rosalie
was the worst wife that Pierre could have had, for she was so winning and sweet, and he loved her so much, that for months at a
time he was a changed lad: and the result was this, that there would
ensue reactions, during which the white face of that little lame man
became a fright in the valley, he going about like a dog with the
hydrophobia, his eyes alight. Once he stabbed his mother in the
arm, and sometimes had to be watched lest he should stab himself. And so it went on near five years.

"And they had misfortunes in the vineyard, too. There came
three bad years, when even L'Hermitage and La Nerte and the big
vintages of Provence came to nothing; and the fourth year la
Mère Gouvion's madder-yield was a gone hope before May; and
she had to sign a paper with the agent at Cargnac which almost

compromised the shelter over her head. So she was not very happy in her mischief-doing, after all.

"But she adored her 'petit,' her 'little one,' never less, gloried in secret over the deed she had done for him; and when he made himself a terror she hugged herself, preferring terror to laughing-stock. 'They won't grin with their ugly gums at my petit, my little one, now,' she'd say.

"And one bitter winter's night all came to an end . . .

"Pierre had broken loose again; screams reached even to the village from the Gouvion vineyard; and presently a girl came run-ning down to the presbytère, saying that Rosalie would be killed. Heaven knows what really happened, for Rosalie was never seen again, so it is supposed that Pierre must have killed her, and that la Mère Gouvion did away with her body somehow; but no body was ever discovered, so that all that part of the business remains a mystery. Mother Gouvion, who raved out a great deal of what I am saying now during her brief imprisonment afterwards, never said anything about this matter.

"However, when the curé hears this, he begins to pray, than saddles his mule, and gallops off through the gale for Avignon. Before midnight a body of *sergents* arrive at the vineyard; they search for Pierre; Pierre cannot be found. La Mère Gouvion, sew-ing, with her mouth opened square, tells them that she does not know where he has gone to."

A wild night—I have seen three such in Provence—lightnings that terrify, a very deluge of water, tempest from the north calling to whirlwind from the west: a Southern storm . . . Mother Gouvion dashed out into it the moment she found herself free of the *sergents*—forgot her uncovered head, but remembered to take every sou she possessed. She had arranged to meet Pierre out on the moor, the only safe meeting-place, intending, it seems, to take, or send, him to the coast, to get him aboard a ship—nothing would be impossible to her. The officers, it was true, were scouring the valley on horseback with lanterns; but they were nothing; she would outwit them . . .

But when, on reaching the moor, she ran to the agreed *cagnard*, Pierre was not in it; to the next—Pierre not there; and with distracted runs she dashed from *cagnard* to *cagnard*. Her heart misgave her now, her glance questioned the heavens—they were black enough; and, stumbling about within a tempest of hair, a pillar of seaweed that stumbles, she lifted her voice: *"Pierre!"*—wayward boy of her heart: where, then, was he?

And another terror struck her—the bell. . . it was believed to bleat some midnights when storms were abroad on the moor . . . "But not to-night!"—and, as she said this, a vaster tantrum of the tempest terrorized her. She stumbled and was down in the mud; a prayer broke from her.

A night of climaxes of wind: and in the midst of each the woman beseeching, coaxing: "Any other night, not to-night; it would not be right; would be hard on a poor mother's heart"—for hours, till the gale began to abate, and the danger ended.

It was only toward morning, when, though the darkness was as black as ever, the storm had lulled and her dreads of the bell were at rest, it was then that, all at once—she heard it. Not a clamorous clang, clang, this time, as when she had rung it for Martin Dejoie, but one toll only, floating out doleful on the breast of the trembling air.

It was over, then? No hope? Suddenly the woman threw up her head, gnashed, shook her fist, as her father before her had done, at the bell, at the heavens. "Blast away bell . . . !" Bells were nothing: she would discover her little one as soon as there was a little light—would tear him from the clutch of the *sergents*: it would be all right yet.

"On setting out once more to search, she found herself just in front of the church, and, as some sheet-lightning was playing then, she chanced to observe the mark of a man's foot before the church-portal. At this she started, chilled to the marrow by a sense of the supernatural: for it was not to be believed that any living being would have come so near the bell on a night so wild. Under her breath she uttered 'Martin Dejoie?' . . . for what power had rung the bell in her hearing? it had not been the wind!

"Just then a tramp of horses' hoofs reached her ears—the *sergents* still ransacking the countryside for Pierre; and she ran into the bush at the church-door, lest they might spy her in the play of the lightning. Five years before she had stood just there— and done a thing. And now her flesh shivered to see the sarsaparilla freshly trampled, the branches parted: someone had entered St. Sépulcre that night! and at the thought of the vengeance of the murdered dead her heart turned faint."

But some fascination led her steps over the threshold, and she stood in the still thicker gloom within, hearing the rasping of her own throat, hearing the gallop of a heart thumping out the whole gamut of fright, pride, desperation; till, all at once, a blaze of lightning searched the church, and by it was revealed to her the reason why the bell had rung: it was because someone had tied the bell-rope round his throat, kicked away a stone, and hanged himself there. He hung still now: and eye to eye they looked—mother and son.

They found her the next morning wandering on the moor, harmless and listless, with a slanting smile; and they took her to the asylum at Avignon where, after many weeks, something resembling reason returned to her. When they had gathered her story from her mutterings, they let her out again; but she would not go home, took up her abode in woods, etc., sleeping in *cagnards*, living on olives, nuts, fruits. Her favourite haunt (if she still lives) is the "menhir" by the abandoned path between Lebrun-les-Bruyères and Cargnac.

THE GREAT KING

"Belphegor was no ordinary devil:"—*Machiavelli*

"You never," said my Uncle Quintus, "heard the story of the Great King? Well, that, perhaps, goes without saying, for you are unable to read cuneiform writing, and I only, and one other learned man, have as yet deciphered the history."

My Uncle Quintus—the indefatigable man—had but lately returned from digging and delving among the ruin-heaps of Nimroud and Khosabad, and where the village of Hillah stands today, where Babylon was. It was a wild night, rags of gusts tormented the tapestries, the flicker only of the fire lighted us. We made it the centre of a mumping semicircle while my Uncle Quintus puffed from a petty pipette the smoke of some preparation of *cannabis*, which had followed him from the East.

"What you have already heard about the King," he said, "is that he went mad with pride; but even then you have no notion of the man's intensities—Nero, Sardanapalus, were innocents. And with all this he was a coward, too."

The queen was Nicotris from Ionia, her Western name Moira, she having the straight nose, the bulging chin, of the daughters of the Greeks. Intercourse between East and West was not yet very close, and it is not known by what providence she was drawn to Babylon, but the King saw, and in his greed for the novel, loved her. And now was seen a spectacle: the Ionic woman was observed

to acquire an altogether singular power over the mind of Nebuchadnezzar—a Chaldean king—the embodied majesty—the
splendour of the heavens revealed in garments of flesh. And when
Nicotris, from being loved, grew to be *feared*, all marvelled. Yet
she was the mildest of women: the mighty men called her "the
suave" Queen Nicotris.

A wasting malady fell upon this lady. She lay as dead—cold in
the black-stone coffin—and her maidens, with dole and plaint,
anointed her lips with oil, and through the nights wailed round
her their wild *nenia* for the soul flown from life, thrumming the
dulcimer and ten-stringed psaltery to chaunts starry, strange,
lamenting in melody many days. But when the wardens of the
necropolis, followed in procession by the horned archpriests of
Astarté, came to bear her from the palace to the tomb, Nicotris,
starting from catalepsy, opened her blue eyes, and awoke once
more to life. The like was not known before, this dual habiting of
earth and the land of shadows. From that day the King ceased to
love his queen.

The great stature of Nicotris, her emaciation, the pallor of her
face, wrought strongly on the fancy of the King. She would pass
lightly as a shadow, the diadem on her head, through the banquet-
ing-chamber, where the King, bright with wine, sat at midnight
with his ministers; and as she so passed, she would hold up, mildly
smiling, a thin, forewarning finger. Then the silence of a minute,
and a frown on the King's brow.

The mystery of her "awaking from the dead" freed her from all
compulsion. None could tell what dark secrets she hid within her
brain, brought back from those deep, pale kingdoms into which
her venturesome spirit had strayed, on what sights of terror her
wide eyes had rested in all the trance of that far travel! Was she,
indeed, a woman amongst women, or a true visitant from the grave?
The King no longer companied with her: nard and cassia and musk
could not overcome that odour of the tomb which, in his fantasy,
she bore about with her; he shunned the calm of her smile; he fled
the embrace of her fleshless breast; first awe, then hate, filled the
heart of the King for the suave Queen Nicotris.

Yet Nicotris loved the King, though, knowing all his weak-
nesses, his pride, she constantly sought to curb him. Often she
would draw him, in spite of himself from the revelry of wine to the
moon-lit garden-paradise of the palace, they forming then a great
contrast, she tall a head above him, the King obese, swart, with
thick lips, and flowing beard. Often, too, she would constrain him
to follow her to the top of that tremendous temple of Bel—pyrami-
dal, seven-terraced, to symbolise the planets—where stood the
observatory of the astrologers. And here, on this height, when in
the dark morning Pleiades sloped steeply in the skies, the Queen
would wax ecstatic, and with her scarlet-robed arm, would sweep
from azimuth to azimuth the starry deeps, prophesying with author-
ity of one Highest of All—asking who caused the horned horse of
Astarté to haunt the earth, and whose hand hurled "the crooked
serpent" across the vault. From all this the King would turn with
loathing.

But her will was law in the Court. When, for instance, the rem-
nants of Nineveh rebelled, and it was decided that they should all
be slain, the Queen walked calmly into the council-hall, and with
warning, with persuasiveness, prayed for their preservation;
whereupon the King dashed his sceptre down, and stalked from
the hall; the Ministers passed out in silence after him: while
Nicotris, left alone, bending to the big black baboon from the crags
of Ararat, which ever accompanied her steps, said with her placid
smile: "You see, Pul, my friend, how these men receive the admo-
nitions of wisdom!" Yet that day the irresistibleness of her will
prevailed, and the conquered were spared.

The King was returning from hunting the lion on the plain of
Dura, and passing slowly in his chariot through the labyrinth of
Babylon when suddenly at a corner he saw a maiden whose beauty
overcame his soul. She was daintily shod in badger's skin, and
shimmered like a daughter of shahs in fine linen, and silk, and
broidered work—blue and purple and vermilion—an emerald ray-
ing merrily from her forehead. Her veil being lifted, for a moment
the King saw fully the vision, and then the damsel span and vanished down a shadowy alley. The King ordered two of his lords to

follow, who thought they saw her enter a house, and into this they ran—the dwellings being all constructed pyramid-wise, with a terrace on the flat roof of each story, on which grew the palms, and cedars, and vines of the famed pleasure-gardens. In a nook, perhaps, of one of these the maiden hid; the people of the house did not know her; the officers tremulously sought her everywhere; but she had vanished. They questioned themselves: was this, then, a creature of air sent by destiny to trouble the brain of the King—a warning from the gods? The nervosity of Nebuchadnezzar, his terror of death, of the sight of death, of the world of spirits, had infected all his Court.

When the King reached the steps of the palace, "Where is Nicotris, the Queen?" he asked of the cup-bearer, who presented to him, while yet in the street, a goblet of spiced wine.

"She lies ill in the forecourt of the women's quarter," answered Vajezatha.

Many times that day did the King inquire of the state of Nicotris. An impatience possessed him as to whether she would fall again into the unnatural death-life—the hateful death without its decay, the unholy life without its pulse—perhaps to wake again? The thing, he thought, must end—he would end it. And he remembered the vision of brightness and grace in the street of the city.

He visited her in person at dawn, a fiendish intent born in his brain, the harem being a series of chambers grouped round one of the courts of the palace, and the palace itself a low structure, placed on the top of an immense platform of glazed bricks. The King passed through the gloom of a vault, guarded on each hand by winged cherubim, which formed the entrance to the harem and found Nicotris reclining on an ivory couch in one of the "galleries," her only guard the old ape, the faithful Pul, garrulous by her side. The King gazed long at her, a paleness on his face; he had sworn to end it—with his own secret hand. But though Nicotris could not speak, as if she divined the evil of his thoughts, as if she had heard of the meeting in the street, she lifted up a thin finger. Nebuchadnezzar turned away.

Late that same day a message came to the King declaring that Queen Nicotris had, to all appearance, entered the state of death.

She was carried by her damsels in an uncovered coffin of black marble to a corner of the paradise, if haply the breezes from the plain might again revive her, the paradise occupying a court at a corner of the platform on which the palace stood, abutting the city walls, and enclosed on two sides by the alabaster parapet of the platform, and on the other two by columns connected by curtains of silk. Here many a fountain plashed on crocus and daphne and ixia; gourd, melon, and fig; the love-apple and the henna-tree; and at one end stood a pigmy ebon temple to the God Nisroch, guarded by winged bulls. Before the steps of this the Queen was laid:

The King stepped from the banquet at midnight and walked in the garden, his brain brave with the bright wine of Iran, exultation filling him that he was free at last—forever—from the awesome Nicotris. She should be promptly entombed, he said; no re-awaking this time! He did not dream how near the queen's body lay.

All suddenly—before the temple steps—he saw. Marble she slumbered below the moon. The King sprang backwards, groaning in pain. Panic seized him, then tumultuous rage. How came she here? It was a fate's mockery, and with the eyeballs of the striped hyena of Shinar shining in his head, like the ounce before it springs he crouched, and just so sinuously crept toward the coffin, drawing with horrid furtiveness a pigmy scimitar from his girdle. He struck. Only *once* has the hand of a man committed an infamy so mephitic. The gash slashed the integuments which ligament the hinges of the jaw together—the mouth howled agape. The King saw the redness—and saw no more.

As he ran, a sob in his throat, two eyes, questioning, upbraiding, from behind a pillar, met his own. He knew the eyes of Pul, the ape, and dashed forward to fell the beast with a stroke, but Pul vanished.

The manner of the Assyrians was to sepulchre in caves without a city, cut out of the rock, or built of painted bricks, each coffin being placed within a rock-chamber of its own, the coffin itself of stone, and the lid of a vitreous material, similar to the modern glass. In such fashion, followed by the mourning Pul, was the good Queen Nicotris, on being found mysteriously disfigured—and *now* at least supposed to be really dead—borne to her rest on the following day, the seventh of the month Adar.

Thus had the King cast off from him the coils of Nicotris. But as he passed at night-fall of that day to the halls of the harem through the now vacant bedchamber of the Queen, a new wretchedness befell him. It was dark; the curtains of the galleries were drawn; he was alone. In the obscurity—a sighing. Peering, he was aware of a something—an outline. The King turned and fled.

The distemper of the restless mind possessed the King in those days. He would leap from sleep with distraught eye and drenched hair, like a man haunted. A night-sound, the human shape of a drapery, had power to dismay him. He hated solitude. No longer did the banquet of wine work its magic of forgetfulness.

He sent in secret for the chief of the soothsayer-priestesses, who served day and night in the temple of Astarté, and she, coming in the darkest hour before the day, had conference with the King in an inner gallery of the palace, the King sitting on the edge of his couch in disarray, she doddering before him, bent with age, dry of face, with tiny bright eyes full of knowing.

"Two things," he said, "you shall do, or die: you shall lay the spirit that infests me; and you shall tell me the name and abode of a maiden whom, on the first of Adar, I saw in the streets of Babylon."

"I can do even more—I can *show* the King the maiden," answered the hag.

"How?"

"In vision first. If the King will come to an appointed spot tomorrow at midnight, alone—I will show the King this thing."

"I will come."

When the sibyl descended the stairway in the wall, the King rose and walked to and fro in the gallery. He looked over the endlessness of Babylon, on which the moon shone, on the pyramids, temples, the three days' journey of the city walls. From that station he could see on the plain the colossal golden image which he himself had set up. And he stamped with his foot; he brandished his arm, challenging. The thought swelled within him: "Is not this great Babylon . . . ?"

And while the King was so thinking, arms from behind involved him, and the touch of a hand lay on his throat. He fell faint . . .

All the next day he wandered from court to court, unkinglike, with ragged head, with foam-flecked beard, and the flight of a dagger from his hand ended in the breast of a cup-bearer who approached with wine.

As night fell his brow grew gloomier, he sitting on the throne of the audience-hall, his head drooping to his knees, the majesty all gone. At midnight he dismissed all; and, looking this way and that, crouched secretly down the great stairway to the south-west gate over against the palace.

Here Zeresh, the sorceress, awaited him. They passed together over the plain, the wind soughing across the desert; and there was a threatening of thunder. But the moon shone bright.

The King stalked, Zeresh struggling to keep by him. Presently he stopped.

"Whither would you lead me?"

"To the city of tombs, O King."

"The what?"

"It is there only that I have power to show the King the vision."

The King moved onward more slowly.

"I will tell you something," he said, abruptly, "and let your science unravel it. The Queen Nicotris is dead: yet, as I passed through her apartment by night, a form seemed to stand before me."

Zeresh smiled.

"I know not," she answered, "but if the form was of nothing human, might it not have been that of the favoured Pul, which doubtless still haunts his mistress's chambers?"

"Yet I had ordered that the ape should be hunted from the palace. But what say you to hands, cold like the hands of Nicotris; laid on my flesh in the morning watch?"

Zeresh showed a tooth.

"Without doubt the hands of the playful Pul, oh, King, returned from banishment by climbing the palace platform."

They had come to the ruins of Hur, where the brool of the lion, the whine of the wild cat, stalking amid the fallen walls, caught the ear. On the right the Euphrates; piled round, "whatsoe'er of strange sculptured on alabaster obelisk, or jasper tomb, or mutilated sphinx," outlived the wreck of the erections of the world's first cities. The desolation here was complete.

"Tell me," the King said, "what is the nature of the vision which waits for me."

"The King will first enter the anti-chamber of a tomb."

Nebuchadnezzar shuddered.

"Here heaven will descend to wanton with the nostrils of my lord."

The sibyl had, in fact, commanded two damsels to be in waiting in the darkness, with censers exhaling vapours.

"The King," she continued, "will now advance, draw aside a tapestry, descend three steps, and enter the second hall of the dead; immediately a swarm of spheres will wawl sweetness to his ear."

She had similarly secreted to this room cunning lutists with flute and dulcimer.

"Once more the King will advance, draw aside a curtain and now, before him, he shall see—"

"*Her?*"

"In a nimbus."

She had stationed in this third hall the most lovely of her acolytes, robed in cloth of silver; directly in front of whom a cauldron over a fire, containing a combination of natron, bitumen and sulphur, was to send up a smoke, through the obscure of which the vision should loom: and the King's' eye having rested upon her, the young priestess was to vanish into one of the side-chambers.

The wind had risen, and splashes of rain began to fall accompanied by thunderclaps.

An eagle flew low athwart their way.

"That," Zeresh said, in the strain of the animistic anthropomorphism of the East, "is the Eagle. He gazes into the sun's heart.

How strong his wing! See him preen for flight! He is the emblem
of pride."

The King glanced distrustfully at her.

They came to a tarn, by which, on one leg, stood a bittern, in
the hurricane which now swept the plain.

"See," said Zeresh, "the bittern: he broods by the lonesome
pool; gloomy he is: the emblem of the sullen mood, ever ungrate-
ful, never content."

The King frowned at this.

They had nearly reached the outermost bounds of the city of
the dead, when a bison bounded bellowing across their way.

"Look!" Zeresh cried, "the wild ox! He eats the grass of the
earth, yet spurns the earth with his foot. Who can tame him? He
tosses his head in his strength. He is the emblem of the unbridled
spirit—what they of Ionia call 'atasthalia,' the undisciplined soul."

"Cease, hag!" the King cried.

Zeresh covered her mouth with her hand.

They had now come to the entrance to the tombs, when all at
once both stopped as if struck to stone, the gold of the hag's face
growing a ghastlier hue, a new terror weakening the King's knees. A
darkness had fallen upon the earth. The moon brooded a lurid ruby.

"Astarté' veils her face!" rattled Zeresh's throat: "there is
wrath!"

But when the earth's shadow began to journey from the girdle
of the satellite, the hag asked, "Will the King advance?"

The King was leaning on a rock. His lips quivered, but could
not speak.

"Let us proceed," urged the witch, "or the King's chance of seeing the vision may pass." With effort he raised himself, to walk
now with steps all inconsequent through rows of mausoleums, till
Zeresh stopped before an open portal.

"If my lord has courage to enter; the revelation will not fail; all
will be as I said—the odours, the music, the vision."

"But the tomb is black as doom; I dare not pass through it!"

"The gloom is necessary," Zeresh answered; "there is nothing
for my lord to dread."

The King trembled through the portal into a passage, at the end of which, pushing aside a curtain, he entered the first chamber, lost in the darkness, hearing behind him, down the corridor, the coronachs of the breezes sighing. He waited stationary, that the promised fragrances might gratify him: his nostrils were assailed by the smell of death exhaled by the sarcophagi.

Uttering a grunt of disgust, he groped onward, and drawing aside a tapestry, descended three long steps to the second apartment.

Instantly he was aware of another presence in the apartment, a being rushing like the wind from end to end, which presently in brushing briskly past, touched him. A spirit riving in his pangs! So, too, had thought the maidens secreted there by Zeresh, who had fled with shrieks from the cave before the spectre, not knowing that Pul, since he had followed his mistress to the tombs, had become a denizen of their solitudes.

But the music! With all of sense that remained to him—with a despairing *hope*—the King listened, straining every dazed faculty to catch the strains, while to and fro swept the breath of Pul. And now, indeed, there came a sound—but loud, heart-madding—a sound of clash and clangour, like the crackling of glass, like the battering apart by the dead of the bars of the prison house of death.

The King's flesh crept, and with all sense of direction lost, casting up his arms, he ran. Thus he came to the third drapery, which parted before his flight.

And now at last there was light. The cauldron of Zeresh burning over a pan containing embers, sent up its pharos of vapour, in the midst of which the King's eye lighted on a form at whose horror his brain tottered: a form tall, wrapped from head to foot in the cerements of the grave, her arms outspread, her brow bound about with a napkin. He saw the straight nose—the bulging chin—the risen Nicotris! And, as he looked, the face-cloth, knotted loosely above the poll, slowly unravelled itself, and dropped; the gashed jaws, held together by a single ligament, dropped agape.

. . . From her throat there broke an outcry . . .

King Nebuchadnezzar stood with his eyes staring before him—the muscles of his face rigid—his thick lips parted. So passed a full minute. Then he drew his fingers across his forehead with a look of lunacy; but this, too, soon passed; and now he was calm, as his mouth sidled and settled into the smile of idiotcy.

And he was driven from men; and his dwelling was with the beasts of the field; and his hairs were grown like bird's feathers, as the eagle's; and his nails like bird's claws, as the bittern's; and he did eat grass as the wild ox.

And his body was wet with the dew of heaven.

THE PALE APE

"A big thing of a pig."—*Aristophanes*.

Yesterday again I stood and looked at Hargen Hall from the lake; and it is this that has brought me to write of my life in it. Wintry winds were whistling through the withered bracken and the branches, whirling withered birch-leaves about the south quadrangle; and no birds sang.

When I first entered it I was a girl, one might say—gay enough; but now I have known what one never forgets; and the days and the hairs grow grey together.

Five titled names among my friends gained me an entrance to Hargen in the fall of the year '08. I arrived on the evening of 10th November; and shall never forget the strangeness of the impression made on my mind that night: for even ere I rounded into sight of the house, the sound of the waters far off filled me with a feeling of the eerily dreary—the house being almost surrounded with mountain and cliff, down which a series of cascades shower; and that night I had some difficulty in catching quite everything that was said to me, though in two or three days, maybe, my ear became used to the tumult.

It was four days before I met Sir Philip Lister himself—Davenport, the old butler, told me that his master was "indisposed"—but Sir Philip sent me a polite missive inviting me to take things carelessly a little: so I spent the first days in learning my pupil's moods, and in roaming over the place, from "Queen Elizabeth's Room"—

behind the bed still hung a velvet shield broidered with the royal arms in white wire—to the apes and the cascades. A sense of forlornness pervaded it all, for scarcely ten of us were in all the desert of that place, with an occasional glimpse of two or three gardeners, or a groom. The kitchen was now a paneled hall like a chapel, with windows of painted glass containing the six coats-of-arms of the Lister-Lynns, a hall in whose vastness the cook and her assistant looked awfully forlorn and small; and hardly even a housemaid ever now entered all that part of the east wing which had been singed by a fire fifty-five years since.

It was on the fourth forenoon, a day of "the Indian summer," that my pupil took me to see the apes. There were three of them—two chimpanzees, one gibbon—in three rooms of wire-netting close to the east line of cliffs, i e., about six hundred yards from the house. There, chuckling and chattering in the shadow of chestnuts, they lived their lives, anon speculating like philosophers upon their knots, or hearkening to the waters which chanted near in their ears. And there was a *fourth* room of netting in the row, but empty; as to which my pupil said to me:

"The one that used to be in this fourth room was huge, Miss Newnes, and had a pale face. He died some time before I came to Hargen: but his ghost walks when the moon is at the full."

"Now Esmé," I muttered. (Her name was Esmé Martagon, daughter of the Marquis de Martagon and of Margaret Lister, Sir Philip's sister; the child being at this time twelve years of age, and an orphan—a rather pretty elf with ebon curls, but as changeable as the shapes of mercury, now bursting with alacrity, and now cursed with black turns of sadness.)

"But if I have seen it?" she gravely replied, gazing up at me with her great eyes.

"The ghost of an ape, Esmé," I muttered.

For answer, flying off into vivacity, she cried to me:

"Come, you shall hear it!"—and she led the way northward through the park, until we walked down a dark path tremulous with spray, where one of the smaller waterfalls came down. By stepping on the tops of rocks in its froth, one could get, in the rear of the torrent, into a grot, where the greenery grew very vigorous and gay from the perpetual spray; and when I had followed Esmé's career into this hollow in the rock, she hollaed into my ear in opposition to the tons of thunder sounding down: "Now, listen a little: this one is named 'The Ape.'"

For some minutes—three to six—I heard nothing but the burden of the cascade's murmur, and was now about to say something sceptical, when there sounded what I am bound to say affected me in a rather startling way—a sound very sharp and energetic—the *chuckle, chuckle* of a monkey—most pressing, most imperative, in its summons to the attention. It was over in a moment; but presently came again: and in the course of half an hour's listening it came altogether five times, not quite at regular intervals, but still with a kind of periodicity: and I concluded that some small cause, perhaps only a condition of the wind, acted ever and anon to modify the cataract's tract, and produce this curious cackling.

My pupil hollaed to me: "And if you kept on waiting to hear, and listening to it, do you know what would happen to you, Miss Newnes?"—and when I asked what, she called: "You would go stark mad!"

"Not I," I said.

One of the shadows darkened the child's face; and presently she remarked: "I should, I know. Three of the ladies of the Listers, and one of the Lynns, have—among them my mother's mother. It is in the blood, I think."

I started!—for I now suddenly believed her. Indeed, to my consciousness, there was something ironic in the torrent's chuckle, and at once, taking the child's hand, I said: "Come."

Late in the day when we were together in what is called "the Great Hall," Esmé, ever sage beyond her age, again spoke of the chuckling cascade, begging me not to mention, or show it to her Cousin Huggins when he came: for a young man of this name, who had hardly been at Hargen since he was six, was coming from India in some months, and was expected to spend a month with us.

It was that night that, for the first time, I saw Sir Philip Lister: for he dined with Esmé and Mrs. Wiseman and me in the main

building dining-room, the old Davenport waiting upon us in state
with his silent footsteps, we five making a pretty insignificant group
in that great room, whose array of windows have a south aspect
upon the south quadrangle. It has (or had) tapestry all round, and
rows of Jacobean carving-tables, which give the room an air of very
gloomy state; and a wood-fire bickered on the iron-work fire-back,
under whose oak over-mantel Sir Philip sat with Esmé and me ten
minutes, then took himself away into his own sequestered nook of
the house.

Two days after this he again had dinner with us, and again the
day after that; but that third time the child, in one of her chatterbox
fits, chanced to observe that "Uncle Philip is lending his presence
since Miss Newnes has come"—and like a bird that shies Sir Philip
showed himself no more to us for many days.

I regretted this, for his presence interested me, his manners
were in such a high degree grave, dignified, and gracious. He was
big, and, if not handsome, interesting to the eye—quaint, one might
say—his face smooth like an actor's, his hair longer than usual,
with great owl-eyes, whose glowering underlook was thronged, to
my thinking, with mysteries of sorrow—something shifting, though,
uncandidly shy, in them. His age I guessed to be about forty-five.

He was engaged in the writing of what I heard was "a great
work," six volumes long, on "The Old Kingdom" (fourth of sixth
dynasty of Egyptian Kings), and lived a life of such privacy, that it
was three weeks ere I met him afresh. Meantime, Esmé and I entered upon the course of our adventurous studies— "adventurous,"
for never for two hours together was my pupil the same girl. Esmé
had fits of headache; and she had fits of reading, when she feasted
upon volumes with a hungry vulture's greed; and she had fits of
indolence, dormouse torpors, fits of crying, dark-minded lamen-
tations, fits of flightiness, of crazy dissipation, of craving for—wine.
As for her knowledge, it was astonishing in such a child, and she
anon plied me with queries to which I could find no reply.

On a forenoon in the fourth week, when she was feeling out of
sorts, we were sauntering in the park, when, for once, I saw Sir
Philip out of doors. We came upon him with his face against the

ape-house netting, gazing in at the gibbon—so eagerly, that we were
near him ere he seemed to hear us. When he suddenly saw us, he
stood struck into a posture as of suspense, but presently was very
affable in his reserved manner, and conversed with me some minutes about the apes and their various traits. They had the names
of Egyptian kings, the chimpanzees being Pepy II. and Khety, and
the gibbon Sety I.; and at the gibbon Sir Philip shook his finger,
saying with a playful solemnity: "*That fellow! That fellow!*"—I had
no idea what he meant.

Suddenly, in the midst of our talk, he—with a certain awkward-
ness of his lids—proposed a picnic-luncheon out of doors to which
Esmé and I readily assented. But three minutes afterwards he
started, furtively murmuring the words: "I must be getting back to
work," and was gone—to my astonishment!

After this he again made himself very scarce for three weeks.
Esmé and I, meantime, got into the habit of spending our hours of
labour in the great hall, sitting on a day-bed that lay in the solar-
room gallery there—the gallery from which of old one gazed down
upon the retainers at table below; and those days of my life, that I
whiled away in that place, are to me at present days touched with
much strangeness and a tone of Utopia. But the great place was
quite plain and empty—a plain ceiling, plain white walls, oak-pan-
elled half-way up: only, as it was lighted by fourteen great windows with shields of painted glass, when the sun glowed through
them, it transfigured that old room into glory-land. . . . But it is
gone from me now like a dream, and I shall not see it again.

It was on the Thursday afternoon of my thirteenth week at
Hargen that I received from Sir Philip Lister a singular missive:
he had injured his thumb, he said, and wished to know if I would
"kindly write from his dictation." But what, then, I asked myself,
was to become of Esmé meantime? I did not wish to leave the child!
However, I could not say no: and so entered that day the sacred
den. He, with his fingers in a sling, instantly jumped up with a
gush of apologies, showering upon me a thousand thanks that were
at once gushing and shy, till the shyness triumphed, and he was
suddenly silent and done. Then, I sitting at an old abbey-table, he

on an old farm-house settle, he dictated to me with his eyes closed, in a low tone, all about Khufu, and Khafra, and the things of "the Pyramid Age," until I had the impression that he was himself something Egyptian and most ancient, and I with him, and in which age of the world we were I was not at some moments certain. In the midst of the dictating he all at once pressed his left palm upon his forehead, as if tired or muddled, his eyes tight shut; and, jumping up, he muttered to me, "thank you! thank you!" offering me his hand. Some of his actions had a wonderful swiftness and suddenness; and that hand of his which I touched was as chill as snow: so that I made haste from him.

That night I retired, as usual, soon after eleven to my room, which was in a rather remote and lonely region of the house; and was soon asleep. Two hours later I awoke terrified—I could not quite tell why—but so terrified, that I found myself sitting up in bed—with a singular sound, or the memory or dream of a singular sound, lingering about my ears: and I was trembling, my brow was wet with sweat. Through my two windows, which stood open, shone the full moon's light, lying over the floor, lighting the stamp-work tapestry on my right; and I could hear the night-breeze breathing drearily through the leaves of the cedar, some of whose branches, held up with chains, brushed my panes. For some minutes I sat so, hearing my heart beating in my ears, the breezes shivering through the tree, the streams showering, the soundlessness of the house and hour, and as conscious of some living spirit hovering round me as though I saw it. If it had lasted long, I must have lost consciousness, or else cast off the oppression of it with a shriek: but presently something reached my ear—a chuckle, a little giggle of glee, just distinct enough to convince me that it was due to no lunacy of my ear: and immediately, with a creeping in my hair, but a species of rage and desperation elevating me, I was out of bed, and at one of the windows: for just after the chuckle a sharp rush through the leafage of the cedar seemed to reach me, and I rushed to see.

What I saw made me faint—whether instantly or after some seconds I cannot say: I know that when I came to my senses I was seated on the floor with my forehead leaning on my old oak chair, and the tower-clock was now sounding the hour of three. But however soon I may have swooned after seeing it, it was not so instantly that I could have the slightest doubt as to the actualness of what my eyes saw. For though the moonlight left the interior regions of the tree's leafage in some obscurity, I was sure that some brute of the ape species with a pale face was hanging there in the cedar— hanging head-downward among the network of chains and branches in such a way as to see into my chamber; and I have an impression of hearing—either before I fell, or through my swoon afterwards—a succession of chucklings; and then a voice somewhere remonstrating, pleading, commanding, in a secret species of shout; and then a strangled outcry of horror, of anguish, somewhere, all mingled with a dream of the chuckle of the chuckling stream.

But the strongest of my impressions was undoubtedly that drowning outcry of horror—an impression so strong, that I could hardly believe it to be a dream, or all a dream. This cry was somehow connected in my mind from the first with old Davenport; and this feeling was confirmed in me when Davenport was nowhere to be seen the next day, nor for four days after. Mrs. Wiseman, the housekeeper, who for days was pale, and occasionally fell into a vacant staring, told me that Davenport was "suffering." She asked me no questions as to the night, but I twice caught her eye piercingly bent upon me with a meaning of inquiry, of anxiety, in it; and the same thing was true of Sir Philip when, three days later, he appeared towards evening: for he took my hand with a tender solicitude, and a lingering look of question in his gaze. As for Davenport, when I next saw him it was under a tree in the park, where he sat like a convalescent, in his flesh that pathetic pallor of the flesh of aged people who have passed through an illness; and the wrappings round his neck could not wholly hide from my eyes that his throat had been most brutally bruised.

During those days it was as if a blow had fallen upon Hargen. Esmé no longer laughed, and a lower tone of talk overtook us all. It was obvious that each held the consciousness of a secret which none dared breathe to another; and in vain I consumed days of musing in seeking to see into the meaning of these things. For my part, I was ailing, nor could quite hide it. I had the thought of moving out of my room, which I now shrank from entering even in the day-time, but did not care to show so openly that I was afraid. Through the nights I burned a light, but slept with my nerves awake. Not that I was ever of a very nervous temperament, I think: but terror infected me like a sickness in those days; the stare of eyes of affright in the night was ever present in my imagination; and Hargen soon grew to be to my haunted heart the very home of gloom. Then one day, on a sudden, all this trouble of mind rushed away from me like a shadow; and my being galloped into a mood of gladness in which gloom was abolished, and I forgot to be appalled in the dark.

I will tell of it very briefly. It happened that one afternoon when Esmé and I were sitting listlessly in that solar-room gallery, an open grammar lying idle between us, suddenly behind us, there rose out of the floor, as it seemed, a young man who clapped his fingers over Esmé's eyes, smiling with me the while. "Cousin Huggins!" the child cried out—much surprised, for Huggins Lister was not expected at Hargen for some days yet. He caught her up in his big arms, and bussed her like a gun, for he was a being made all of ardours and horse-play: and then he looked into my eyes, and I looked into his eyes.

It was as if I had always known him—long before I was born; and what hurried me more into the sort of maelstrom in which I was now caught was the circumstance, that on the day after that first day Esmé took a chill, remained in bed, and I was all alone with Huggins Lister in that wilderness of Hargen. The young man was, or pretended to be, interested in old things, and would have me show him all the cassone and old needlework, the Spanish glasses giving their glints of gold, the old girandoles with their amorini. He dined with me, we two alone, and Mrs. Wiseman: for Sir Philip more than ever kept himself to himself. Only, on the fourth evening when Huggins Lister and I were walking in the park, Sir Philip suddenly appeared before us, walking with precipitate steps the other way; did not pause, nor utter a sound, as he passed by us with a bowed brow, his hat raised; but when he had gone some way beyond us, he stopped, and—shook his finger at us! was going, too, I am sure, to venture to say something, but failed; and suddenly was gone on his way again. I remember being very offended at the moment: but a moment more, God forgive me, had forgotten that Sir Philip Lister lived.

I showed the young man the apes, and the Queen's Room, and the cascades, save one, and the ivory inlay of the two Spanish chests, and the Tudor fireplaces, and what was in "the long gallery"; and still he wished to see things. And just under the window that lights the great staircase, there stands on the landing a sedan-chair painted with glaring variegations, the window-glass casting the gauds of the six coats-of-arms of the Lister-Lynns upon the already gaudy chair: in which chair he got me to sit—it was high noon, on the open stair, but we were as solitary there as if night veiled us in a monastery; and, indeed, all that waste of Hargen seemed but made to beguile and mislead our feet to our fate—he got me to sit in it, I say, and then, having me well in his bondage in the sedan-chair, began to sob to me with passion; and when I hid away my face for pity of him there in his passion on his knees, and dashed one wild tear from my eyes, the young man ravished my lips with his lips, there in the chair on the stair that day. I could not help it, for in respect of me Huggins Lister came, and saw, and conquered! and I was as one drugged with honey-dew, and danc-ing drugged, in Huggins Lister's hands.

Also, the young man persuaded like a hurricane! and hurried me as madly into marriage as those sand-forms of the sand-storm which madly waltz into oneness. Within six months, he said, he would arrange everything so as to proclaim the marriage; but meantime it must be secret, and must be immediate! Against this tyranny I made a feint of resistance; but half-heartedly; and it availed me nothing: indeed, he was dear to me, and near, and had me all in the hollow of his hand and heart. And so one forenoon I stole out of Hargen gates, and met him at a house in St. Arvens townlet, the place of our marriage; but, as we were passing out, married, from the door of the house, my heart bounded into my mouth to see Sir Philip Lister walking hardly ten yards away. Yes, he who never left home was there before my eyes in the broad light in St. Arvens street with his oak-stick—walking away from us, indeed, seeming unaware of our presence: yet I have an impression, too, of his head half-turned toward us a moment, of a face ashen with agitation: and my heart, for all its warmth, shivered as with a mortal chill in me.

My reeling feet led me back to Hargen in a kind of dream, a wedded wife, as wild with thoughts as with wine that day, for I was my beloved's, and he was mine: and in what way I spent that day I could not say, since I was new in heaven, and can but remember my fruitless efforts to hide from Esmé's eyes the state of my mind: for she had lately risen from her ailment, and I made a pretence of study with her, and I was severe with my dear, denying him my presence until the evening; and even then retired betimes, leaving him sighing.

My chamber-door I barricaded with a chair—a bridal childishness, since, to secure the room, I should have locked it. And I lay awake for a long hour, looking at the luminosity of the full moon, until, wearied out by the reel of my day's dream, I fell into a brief sleep.

From this a roar awoke me: and may a sound like that sound never more come to me to summon me with its trump. I understood that some soul was in *extremis*, and out of the deeps of grief and horror was horridly appealing to his God; and, finding myself on the ground, I knelt one wild second, crying aloud: "Almighty God, guard my love from harm in this house of horror." A moment more I had thrown a gown round me, and was gone out of the door.

As I ran along the corridor, trying to strike a light to the candle that I carried, there seemed to reach my ear from somewhere a chuckle very hushed and low, like the jackal chattering over its carrion; and my fingers were so shaken by this thing, that they failed to bring the match into relation with the candle's wick. When the heat reached my hand I dashed down the match. Still running, I lit another—or half lit it: for in the instant when the match fused

at the scratch, saw— or in some manner knew—that some mad and
monstrous animal was with me; at the same moment the match
went out, or was puffed out; and a thing most chilly cold touched
my skin. I felt pain then, the pain of the awe of the darkness; and I
stood palsied. But within some seconds, I think, I was rushing
afresh toward the corridor-end, without the candlestick now, which
had dropped from me; so that I could not see that the portal at the
end, which I expected to be open as usual, was shut; and I rushed
with a shock upon it. It was not only shut, but locked!—finding
which, I, standing there, piled the passion of my whole soul into
cry on cry, crying "Huggins! Sir Philip! Davenport! Huggins!" then
I stood, hearing the streams murmuring as through eternity in the
silence of the night, and the strong knocking of my heart against
my side—but no reply to my calls.

This was not very astonishing, as my room was in such a
solitary part of the mansion: and I stood imprisoned, suffering,
expecting every second the coming upon me of that which would
strike me dead with fright. The stillness lasted half a minute, perhaps, and then I became aware of a sound outside the door, a bumping going down the stairs in a regular way, like something massive
being dragged down, with bump, bump, bump: and such was the
solemnity and mystery of this thing to me in my solitude there in
that gruesome gloom, that to linger any longer there in my
pain soon grew to be impossible to me; and before I knew what I
was doing I was out of a window, moving along a ledge fifty feet
aloft toward the next window. The ledge was scarcely more than a
foot wide, I think, and how I dared it, and why I did not fall, I
can't now say. With my nose close to the wall—conscious all the
time of drizzle tossed by high winds, conscious of the night full of
a wild light, though the moon was quite hidden—I stepped
flutteringly along over thin snow in dizzy suspense, keeping
my sob until I should reach the next window: and there, as I leapt,
I gave it vent, and fainted at my safety. I did not cease to hear,
though, the bumping sound going down; and when it got to the
bottom, something in me gave me the dauntlessness of heart to go
after it.

Down I crept, haltingly, crouching, stair by stair. Halfway down I seemed to hear something being dragged over the floor below. I went on down. The sound had now gone out through a doorway, and I knew which doorway; but as I followed that way, my bare toes struck upon something cold, and I dropped upon my hands over it. I moaned then for pity of myself, because it was dark, and because I did so suffer. But I was conscious, as I dropped, of a rattle of matches, for I still had the match-box in my hand, without knowing that I had it: and the desire took me to strike a light. It was some time, though, before I would, or could, and when I eventually ventured, I saw the sight of the body of the old butler in his night-attire lying wildly before me on the floor: and I knew by a look that was in his eyes that they were for ever sightless.

At the same moment I was aware of the slamming of a door some way off; and again I knew which door—the little side-portal by the kitchen-entrance, leading out northward into the park— and again something gave vigour to my knees, and lifted my feet, to go to see. I made my way to the little portal; opened it slowly; my soles were out on the snow. And before me on the short gravel-path going north into the park I distinctly saw the pale ape, bearing a body against his breast. A moment later he laid down his heavy load, and bent over it; and when I saw him horribly muttering over it, something in me stooped, took up a stone, and threw it at the brute.

It went straight to his head.

After some seconds the creature raised himself slowly, and raced with reeling feet into the darkness of the park.

I staggered then to the body, and saw that it was Huggins Lister strangled; and on the body of my beloved my senses left me.

It was ten in the day before I knew anything more; and then I lay on a bed, on one side of it Esmé, on the other side Mrs. Wiseman.

The latter had a fixed stare; and from the manner in which Esmé was smiling, with her face held sideward, while she persistently counted on her fingers, I could make out that the child was now insane.

I lay still, I said nothing; little I cared.

Presently a girl named Bertha entered to murmur the words: "He isn't found yet"; and from some words murmured in reply by Mrs. Wiseman, I gathered that Sir Philip Lister had disappeared.

Little I cared, I lay still and sullen, with closed lids.

Near noon again came the news that the men seeking for Sir Philip Lister could even yet discover no trace of him; but at about five in the evening he was found dying in the hollow of the rock that lies behind the cascade that they call "The Ape," and was brought to the Hall.

Very soon afterwards Mrs. Wiseman, who had then left my side, flew in again to me with crying eyes, imploring me to try and go for a moment to the dying man, who was hungering to have one sight of me; and I let her throw some clothes over me, and was led by her to the death-bed.

By this time I knew—for Mrs. Wiseman during the day had revealed it to me in a flood of tears—that Sir Philip Lister's mother had too much listened to the chuckling cascade, and so had borne him the being he was—a being capable at any agitation of shedding his human nature to resume the nature of the brute, and hurling away human raiment with his human nature in the murderous turbulence of his nocturnal revels—he who in my eyes had been so perfect in gentleness, so shy, so staid! But none the less I shuddered to the soul when he touched my hand to pant at me through the death-ruckle rolling in his throat: "I have loved you well"—a shudder which perhaps saved me from death or from madness, for I had lapsed that day into a mad apathy. It was nearly night then, and the light in there was very dreary; but I could still see that the hair which overgrew the ogre's frame was considerably more than an inch deep—greenish, and gross as the gorilla's. It clasped him round the throat and round the wrists in lines perfectly defined, like a perfect coat of fur that he wore; and it did not thin, but continued no less thick where it abruptly ended than everywhere else.

But he had "loved me well," and I him now—for if he had been perniciously jealous, it was for love of me that he had been jealous; and in dying he looked into my eyes with human eyes, kindly, mildly, looking "I have loved you well"; and when with his last strength he pointed to where the pebble I had flung had sunk into his skull, then I lifted my voice and wept to God because of him, and myself, and Hargen Hall and all, not caring any longer if my face was buried in the horror of his hairy breast. And so he died, and Huggins Lister, and I was left alive.

DARK LOT OF ONE SAUL

What I relate, ladies, is from a document found in a Cowling Library chest of records, written in a very odd hand on fifteen strips of a material resembling papyrus, yet hardly papyrus, and on two squares of parchment, which Prof. Stannistreet recognises as "trunkfish" skin; the seventeen pages being gummed together at top by a material like tar or pitch. A Note at the end in a different hand and ink, signed "E. G.," says that the document was got out of a portugal (a large variety of cask) by the Spanish galleass *Capitana* between the Bermudas and the Island of St. Thomas; and out of knowledge that at this point a valley in the sea-bottom goes down to a depth of four thousand fathoms affords, as will be noticed, a rather startling confirmation of the statements made in the document. The narrator, one Saul, was born sixteen to twenty years before the accession of Queen Elizabeth, and wrote about 1601, at the age of sixty, or so; and the correspondence of his statements with our modern knowledge is the more arresting, since, of course, a sailor of that period could only know anything of submarine facts by actual experience. I modify a few of his archaic expressions, guessing at some words where his ink ran.

* * *

This pressing paucity of air hath brought me to the writing of that which befel, to the end that I may send forth the writing from the cave in the portugal for the eye of who may find it, my pen being a splinter broken from the elephant's bones, mine ink pitch from the lake, and my paper the bulrush-pith. Beginning therefore with my birth, I say that my name in the world was James Dowdy Saul, I being the third child of Percy Dowdy Saul and of Martha his wife, born at Upland Mead, a farm in the freehold of my father, near the borough of Bideford, in Devon: in what year born I know not, knowing only this, that I was a well-grown stripling upon the coming of Her Grace to the throne.

I was early sent to be schooled by Dominie John Fisher in the borough, and had made good progress in the Latin Grammar (for my father would have me to be a clerk), when, at the age of fifteen, as I conjecture, I ran away, upon a fight with Martin Lutter, that was my eldest brother, to the end that I might adopt the sea as my calling. Thereupon for two years I was with the shipmaster, Edwin Occhines, in the balinger, *Dane*, trading with Channel ports; and at his demise took ship at Penzance with the notorious Master Thomas Stukely, who, like many another Devon gentleman, went apirating 'twixt Scilly and the Irish creeks. He set up a powerful intimacy with the Ulster gallant, Master Shan O'Neil, who many a time has patted me upon my back; but, after getting at loggerheads with Her Grace, he turned Papist, and set out with Don Sebastian of Portugal upon an African expedition, from which I felt constrained to withdraw myself.

Thereupon for a year, perhaps two, I was plying lawful traffic in the hoy, *Harry Mondroit*, 'twixt the Thames' mouth and Antwerp; till, on a day, I fell in at "The Bell" in Greenwich with Master Francis Drake, a youth of twenty-five years, who was then gathering together mariners to go on his brigantine, the *Judith*, his purpose being to take part in Master John Hawkins' third expedition to the settlements in Espaniola.

Master Hawkins sailed from Plymouth in the *Jesus*, with four consorts, in October of the year 1567. After being mauled by an equinox storm in Biscay Bay, we refitted at the Canaries, and, having taken four hundred blacks on the Guinea coast, sailed for the West Indies, where we gained no little gold by our business. We then proceeded to Carthagena and Rio de la Hacha; but it should now be very well known how the *Jesus* lost her rudder; how, the ships' bottoms being fouled, we had perforce to run for San Juan de Ulloa in the Gulf of Mexico; and how, thirteen Spanish galleons and frigates having surprised us there, the Admiral de Bacan made with us a treaty the which he treacherously broke at high noon-day, putting upon us the loss of three ships and our treasure, the *Minion* and the *Judith* alone escaping: this I need not particularly relate.

The *Judith*, being of fifty tons portage only, and the *Minion* of less than one hundred, both were now crowded, with but little water aboard, and the store-chests empty. After lying three days outside the sand-ridge, we set sail on Saturday, the 25th September, having heard tell of a certain place on the east reaches of the Gulf where provisions might be got. This we reached on the 8th October, only to meet there little or nothing to our purpose; whereupon a council was called before Master Hawkins in the *Minion*, where one hundred of us proffered ourselves to land, to the intent that so the rest might make their way again to England on short rations.

The haps of us who landed I will not particularise, though they were various, God wot, remaining in my head as a grievous dream, but a vague one, blotted out, alas, by that great thing which Almighty God hath ordained for a poor man like me. We wandered within the forests, anon shot at by Indians, our food being roots and berries, and within three weeks reached a Spanish station, whence we were sent captives into Mexico. There we were Christianly behaved to, fed, clothed, and then distributed among the plantations—a thing amazing to us, who were not ignorant of the pains put upon English sailors in Spain; but in those days no Holy Office was in Mexico, and on this count were we spared, some of us being bound over to be overseers, some to be handicraftsmen in the towns, etc. As for me, after an absence from it of seven months, I once more found myself in the township of San Juan de Ulloa, where, having ever a handy knack in carpentry, I had soon set myself up for a wright.

No one asked me aught as to my faith; I came and went as I thought good; nor was it long but I had got some knowledge of the

Spanish tongue, stablished myself in the place, and taken to wife Lina, a wench of good liking, daughter of Señora Gomez of the *confiteria*, or sweetmeat-store; and out of her were born unto me Morales and Salvadora, two of the goodliest babes that ever I have beheld.

I abode in San Juan de Ulloa two years and eleven months: and these be the two years of quietness and happiness that I have had in this my life.

On the 13th afternoon of the month of February in the year 1571 I was wending homeward over the *prado* that separated my carpentry from the *confiteria* of my mother-in-law, when I saw four men approaching me, as to whom I straightway understood that men of San Juan they were not: one was a Black Friar, so hooded and cowled, that of his countenance nothing was discovered, save the light of his eyes; another was bearded—of the Order of Jesus; another wore the broad chapeau of a notary, and the fourth had the aspect of an alguazil, grasping a bâton in his hand. And, on seeing them, I seemed to give up heart and hope together: for a frigate hulk had cast anchor that morning beyond the sandridge, and I conjectured that these men were of her, were ministers of the Holy Office, and had heard of me while I was awork.

I have mentioned that no Inquisition was in Mexico afore 1571: but within the last months it had been bruited in San Juan that King Phillip, being timorous of English meddling in the gold-trade, and of the spread of English heresy, was pondering the setting up of the Holy Office over Espaniola. And so said, so done, in *my* case, at any rate, who, being the sole heretic in that place, was waylaid on the *prado* in the afternoon's glooming, and heard from the alguazil that word of the familiars: "follow on"; to be then led down the little *callejon* that runneth down from the *prado* to the coast, where a cockboat lay in waiting.

To the moment when they pushed me into the boat, I had not so much as implored one more embrace of my poor mate and babes, so dumb was I at the sudden woe: but in the boat I tumbled prone, although too tongue-tied to utter prayer, whereupon an oarsman put paw upon me, with what I took to be a consoling movement: a gesture which set me belching forth into lamenting. But with no long dallying they put out, having me by my arms; and beyond the sandridge I was took upon the poop's ladder into the frigate, led away to the far end of the forecastle's vault, and there left with a rosca loaf, four onions, and a stoup of water in the sprit room, a very strait place cumbered by the bulk of the bow-sprit's end, and by the ends of a couple of culverins.

I know not yet whither it was the will of my captors to carry me, whether to Europe, or to some port of the Spanish Main; but this I know that the next noon when I was led apoop, no land was visible, and the sea had that hard aspect of the med-sea.

Our ship, the which was called the *San Matteo*, was a hulk of some four hundred tons portage, high afore, and high stuck up apoop, her fore castle having two tiers, and her poop's castle three, with culverins in their ports. Her topsides were so tumbled home, that her breadth at the water may have been double her breadth at her wales, and she had not the new-fangled fore-and-abafts of Master Fletcher, such as the *Judith* wore to sail on a wind. But she was costly built, her squaresails being every one of the seven of heavy florence, broidered in the belly, and her fifty guns of good brass fabric. She was at this time driving free afore the wind under full spread, but with a rolling so restless as to be jeopardous, I judged. In fact, I took her for a crank pot, with such a tophamper and mass of upper-works, that she could scarce fail to dip her tier of falcons, if the sea should lash.

I was brought up to the master's room, the which was being used as an audience-chamber, and there at a table beheld five men in file. He in the centre, who proved to be both my accuser and judge, presently gave me to know that the evidence against me had been laid before the Qualifiers of the Office—which Qualifiers I understood to be none other than themselves there present—and been approved by the said Qualifiers; and when I had given replies to a catalogue of interrogatories as to my way of life in San Juan, I was then straightway put to the question. My breast, God wot, was rent with terrors, but my bearing, I trust, was distinguished by Christian courage. The interview was but brief: I

demurred to kiss the cross; whereupon the President addressed
me—he being the Dominic that I saw on the *prado*, a man whose
mass of wrinkles, although he was yet young, and his wry smile
within a nest of wrinkles, I carry still in my mind. My rudeness, he
said, would prove to be but puny: for that during the day I should
be put to a second audience in order to move me to a confession,
and after to the screws.

For that second audience I waited, but it came not: for, huddled
up in a corner 'twixt the sprit's end and a culverin's end, I became
more and more aware that the *San Matteo* was labouring in the
sea, and by evening mine ears were crowded with the sounds of
winds, so that I could no more hear the little sounds of the cook's
house, the which was not in the hold, as with English vessels, but
in a part of the fore castle abaft my cell. No food was brought me
all that day, and I understood that all had enough to trouble them
other than my unblest self.

I fell into a deep sleep, nor, I believe, awaked until near the
next noon, though between noon and midnight was but little dif-
ference in my prison. I now anew knew, as before, of a tumult of
winds, and understood by the ship's motion that she was now flee-
ing afore the gale, with a swinging downhill gait. Toward night,
being anhungered, I got to thumping in desperate wise upon my
prison, but no signal was given me that any heard me, and doubtless I was unheard in that turmoil of sounds.

And again I fell into forgetfulness, and again about midday, as
I conjecture, bounded awake, being now through the door, the
which a stripling had just opened. He tumbled toward me with a
bowl of tum-tum and pork, and, having shot it upon my lap, put
mouth to mine ear with the shout: "Eat, Englishman! Thou art
doomed for the ship!"

He then fell out, leaving me in a maze. But I think that I had
not ended the meal when the meaning of his words was but little
uncertain to me, who was versed in the manners of the sea, and of
Spanish seamen in especial; and I said within myself "the *San
Matteo* is now doubtless near her end; the sun hath gone out of

the sky; the course peradventure lost: and I, the heretic, am condemned to be thrown away, as Jonah, to assuage the tempest."

The rest of that day, therefore, I lay upon my face, recommending my spirit, my wife, and my children to my Creator, until, toward night, three sailors came in, laid hands on me, and hauled me forth; and I was hardly hauled to the castle's portal, when my old samite coif leapt off my head, and was swept away.

Surely never mortal wretch had bleaker last look at the scheme of being than I that night. There remained some sort of disastrous glimmering in the air, but it was a glimmer that was itself but a mood of gloom. A rust on the nigh horizon that was the sun was shining on high above the working of the billows, then hurling itself below, with an alternate circular working, as it were a dissolute or sea-sick thing. The skies were, as it were, tinted with inks, and appeared to be no higher beyond the sea than the mizzen-top, where sea and sky were mixed. I saw that the poop's mast was gone, and the *San Matteo* under two sails only, the mizzen-top sail and the sprit sail: yet with these she was careering in desperate wise like a capon in a scare from the face of the tempest, taking in water with an alternate process over her port and starboard wales, and whirled to her top-castles in sprays: so that she was as much within the sea as on it. Our trip from my prison to the poop's castle must have occupied, with his halts, no less than twenty minutes of time, so swung were our feet between deep and high: and in that time a multitude of sounds the most drear and forlorn seemed borne from out the bowels of the darkness to mine ears, as screams of craziness, a ding-dong of sea-bells, or cadences of sirens crying, or one sole toll of a funeral-knell. I was as one adream with awe: for I understood that into all that war of waters I was about to go down, alone.

Lashed to the starboard turret of the poop's castle by a cord within the ring at its paunch was a portugal, such as be employed to store pork on big voyages; and, sprawling on the deck, with his paws clutching within a window-sill of the turret, was the Jesuit, his robes all blown into disarray, with him being the ship's master, having a hammer's handle sticking out of his pouch, and four others, the particulars of whose persons mine eyes, as though I had scores of eyes that night, observed of their own act.

As I staggered near the lax keeping of my guardians, the portugal was cast aslant to his lashing, and I could then descry within it one of those 30-inch masses of iron ballast, such as be named dradoes; by the which I understood that I should not be tossed forth coffinless, as Jonah, but in the portugal: inasmuch as the corpse of many a Jonah hath been known to "chase i' the wake," as mariners relate, to the disaster of them in the ship; and the coffining of such in ballasted casks has long been a plan of the Spanish in especial.

On my coming to the turret, he whom I took to be the master put hand upon me, uttering somewhat which the hurricane drowned in his mouth, though I guessed that he egged me to go into the portugal: and indeed I was speedily heeled up and hustled in. Resistance would have been but little difficult to me, had I willed, but could have resulted only in the rolling overboard of others with me: nor had I a spirit of resistance, nay, probably lost my consciousness upon entering, for nothing can I remember more, till the top was covered in, save only one segment of it, through which I on my face glimpsed three struggling shapes, and understood that the Jesuit, now upheld 'twixt two of the shipmen, was shouting over me some litany or committal. In the next moment I lay choked in blackness, and had in my consciousness a hammer's banging.

Whether awake or adream, I seemed to recognise the moment when the portugal's mass splashed the ocean; I was aware of the drado's bulk tumbling about the sides, and of a double bump of the iron, the one upon my breast, the other upon my right thigh.

Now, this was hardly owing to the water's roughness, for my last glance abroad before going into the portugal had shewn me a singular condition of the sea: the ship appeared to have driven into a piece of water comparatively calm, and pallid, a basin perhaps half-a-mile in breadth, on a level rather below the rest of the ocean that darkly rolled round its edge; and the whole seemed to me to move with a slow wheeling: for I had noted it well, with that ten-eyed unwittingness wherewith I noted everything that night, as the mariners' apparel, or the four-square cap of the Jesuit crushed over his nose, or the porky stench of the portugal . . .

Down, swiftly down, and still profounder down, I ripped toward the foundry of things, to where the mountains and downs of the mid-sea drowse. I had soon lost all sense of motion: still, I divined—I knew—with what a swiftness I slid, profoundly drowned, mile on mile, and still down, from the home of life, and hope, and light, and time. I was standing on the drado, no less steadily than if on land, for the drado's weight held the portugal straight on end, the portugal's top being perhaps one inch above my head—for my hands touched it, paddling for some moments as though I was actually adrown, like the paddling pattes of a hound in his drowning. But I stood with no gasping for a good span, the portugal was so roomy; and it proved as good-made as roomy, though soon enough some ominous creakings gave me to know that the sea's weight was crushing upon his every square inch with a pressure of tons; moreover, both my palms being pressed forth against the portugal's side, all at once the right palm was pierced to the quick by some nail, driven inward by the squeezing of the sea's weight; and quickly thereupon I felt a drop of water fall upon my top, and presently a drop, and a drop, bringing upon me a deliberate drip, drip: and I understood that the sea, having forced a crack, was oozing through atop.

No shock, no stir was there: yet all my heart was conscious of the hurry of my dropping from the world. I understood—I knew—when I had fared quite out of hue and shape, measure and relation, down among the dregs of creation, where no ray may roam, nor a hope grow up; and within my head were going on giddy divinations of my descent from depth to depth of deader nothingness, and dark after dark.

Groan could I not, nor sigh, nor cry to my God, but stood petrified by the greatness of my perishing, for I felt myself banished from His hand and the scope of His compassion, and ranging every moment to a more strange remoteness from the territories of His reign.

Yet, as my sense was toward whirling unto death, certain words were on a sudden with me, that for many a month, I think had never visited my head: for it was as if I was now aware of a chorus of sound quiring in some outermost remoteness of the heaven of heavens, whence the shout of ten thousand times ten thousand mouths reached to me as a dream of mine ear: and this was their shout and the passion of their chanting: "If I ascend up into Heaven, He is there; if I make my bed in Hell, behold, He is there; if I take the wings of the morning, and dwell in the uttermost parts of the sea, even there shall His hand lead me, His right hand shall hold me."

But the lack of air, that in some minutes had become the main fact of my predicament, by this time was such, that I had come to be nothing but a skull and throat crowded with blood that would bound from me, but could not; yet I think that in the very crux of my death-struggle a curiosity as to the grave, and the nature of death—a curiosity as frivolous as the frolics of a trickster—delayed my failing; for I seemed to desire to see myself die.

Still upon my top, with a quickening drip, drip, dropped the leak, and this in my extremest smart I ceased not to mark.

But there came a moment when all my sentience was swallowed in an amazing consciousness of motion. First I was urgently jerked against the portugal, the which was tugged sidewards by some might: some moments more, and the portugal bumped upon something. By a happy instinct, I had stiffened myself, my feet on the drado, my head pressed against the top piece; and immediately I was aware of precipitous rage, haste the most rash, for a quick succession of shocks, upon rocks, as I imagine, quick as you may say one, two, three, knocked me breathless who was already breathless, racking the cask's frame, and battering me back, so to say, out of my death into sense. And or ever I could lend half a thought to this mystery of motion-on-the-horizontal down by the ocean's bottom, I was hounded on to a mystery still more astounding—a

sound in the realm of muteness—a roar—that very soon grew to a
most great tumult. During which growth of tumult I got the consciousness of being rushed through some tunnel, for the concus-
sions of the cask on every side came fast and more frightfully faster;
and I now made out, how I cannot tell, that the direction of my
race was half horizontal, and half downward, toward the source of
that sounding. How long the trip lasted my spirit, spinning in that
thundering dark, could hardly sum up: it might have been a minute
or live, a mile or twenty: but there came a moment when I felt
the portugal lifted up, and tossed; it was spinning through space;
and it dropped upon rock with a crash which ravished me from
my consciousness.

So intemperate was this mauling, that upon returning to myself after what may have been many hours, I had no doubt but that
I was dead; and within myself I breathed the words: "The soul is
an ear; and Eternity is a roar."

For I appeared at present to be a creature created with but one
single sense, since, on placing my fingers an inch afore my face, in
vain I strained my vision to trace them; my body, in so far as I was
any longer cognizant thereof, was, as it were, lost to me, and blotted out; so that I seemed to be naught but an ear, formed to hear
unceasingly that tumult that seemed the universe: and anew and
anew I mused indolently within me: "well, the soul is an ear; and
Eternity is a roar."

Thus many minutes I lay, histing with interest to the tone of
the roar, the which hath with it a shell's echoing that calleth,
making a chaunting vastly far in the void, like an angel's voice far
noising. What proved to me that I was disembodied was the apparent fact that I was no longer in the portugal, since I at present
breathed free; nevertheless, upon becoming conscious in the course
of time of a stench of sea-brine, and presently of the mingling therewith of the portugal's stink of pork, I straight-way felt myself to be
living flesh; and, on reaching out my fingers, felt the sufficient reason of my breathing, to wit, that the portugal's bottom had been
breached in, and a hoop there started by his fall, for the staves'
ends at that part at present spread all asprawl. I was prostrate upon

my back, and the drado and broken portugal's bottom lay over my legs, so that the portugal must have toppled over on his side after striking on his end.

The next circumstance that I now observed was a trembling of the ground on which I lay, the which trembled greatly, as with a very grave ague.

I set myself then to talk with myself, recalling, not without an effort of my memory, the certain facts of my predicament: to wit, firstly, that I had been cast in a cask from a bark called the *San Matteo*, not less than a century agone, I thought; I had then beyond doubt gone down toward the bottom of the sea; here some sea-river had undoubtedly seized and reeled me through some tunnel beneath the sea's base: and the under-tow of this sea-river's suction it was which must have occasioned that basin-like appearance of the sea's surface with a circular working, observed by me some moments before my going in the portugal. This salt torrent, having caught my cask, must have hurtled me through the tunnel to a hollow hall or vault in the bowels of the earth at the tunnel's mouth, and had then hurled the portugal from the tunnel's mouth down upon some rock in the grotto, and so broken the portugal's bottom. The cave must contain the air which it had shut in in the age of the convulsion of nature which had made it a cave, peradventure ere the sea was there, thus permitting me to breathe. And the roar that was roaring should be the thundering of the ocean tumbling down the walls of the hall from out the tunnel's mouth, the preponderousness of which thundering's dropping down occasioned that ague of the ground which was shaking me.

So much I could well sum up; also, from that echo's humming, whose vast psalmodying haunts the waterfall's thunder, I judged that the hollowness of the hall must be large beyond thought. More than this I understood not; but, this being understood, I covered my face, and gave myself to lamenting: for, ever and again, together with the thunder and his echo, worked certain burstings and crashes of the cataract, brief belchings breaching on a sudden, troubling the echo with yet huger rumours, madding sad to hearken to; and my hand could I not descry, stared I never so crazily nigh;

and the ague of the ground was, as it were, a shivering at the shout
of God-omnipotent's mouth: so that sobs gobbled forth of my bosom, when I understood the pathos of this place.

On throwing my hands over my eyes to cry, I felt on them a
slime crass with granules, perhaps splashed upon me through the
open end of the portugal on his tumble, the which when I had
brushed away, with much anguish I got my head round to where
my feet had been. No doubt had I but I should of necessity perish
of thirst and the dearth of food; but that I might come to my doom
at liberty, I crept forth of my prison, as a chick from the rupture of
his shell.

A tinder-box was in my pouch, but, in the swound of my comprehension, I did not then remember it, but moved in darkness
over a slime with my arms outstretched, drenched ever with a
drizzle, the source of which I did not know. Slow I moved, for I
discovered my right thigh to be crushed, and all my body much
mauled; and, or ever I had moved ten steps, my shoe stepped into
emptiness, and down with a shout I sped, spinning, to the depth.

My falling was stopped by a splash into a water that was warm,
into which I sank far; and I rose through it bearing up with me
some putrid brute that drew the rheum of his mucus over my face.
I then struck out to swim back to the island from whose cliff I had
tumbled: for I saw that the cavern's bottom was occupied by a sea,
or salt pond, and that upon some island in this sea the cask must
have been cast. But my effort to get again to the island availed not,
for a current which seized me carried me still quicker, increasing
at the last to such a careering that I could no more keep me up
over the waves; whereupon an abandonment of myself came upon
me, and I began now to drown, yet ever grasping out, as the drowning do; and afore I swooned I was thrown against a shore, where,
having clutched something like a gracile trunk, I dragged my frame
up on a shore covered over with that same grainy slush, and
tumbled to a slumber which dured, I dare say, two days.

I started awake with those waters in mine ear whose immortal
harmony, I question it not, I will for ever hear in my heart; and I
sat still, listing, afeared to budge, lest I should afresh blunder into

trouble, while mine eyeballs, bereft of light, braved the raylessness
with their staring. My feet lay at a sea's edge, for I could feel the
upwashing of the waves, the which wash obliquely upon the shore,
being driven by a current: but near as they were, I could hear ne'er
a splash, nor anything could hear, except the cataract's crashing,
joined with the voice of his own echoing, whose music tuneth with
the thundering a euphony like that of lute-strings with drum
ahumming, and anon the racket of those added crashings, when
masses more ponderous of the cataract drop; and I did ever find
myself listing with mine ear reached sideward, drawn to the
darksome chaunting, forgetting my hunger, and the coming of
death: listing I wot not how long, perhaps hours, perhaps night-
longs: for here in this hall is no Time, but all is blotted out but the
siren's sorrow that haunts it: and a hundred years is as one hour,
and one hour as a hundred years.

I remarked, however, immediately, that the waves which
washed my feet were not warm like that part of the water where I
had fallen into the lake; so that I understood that the lake is a cauldron of different temperatures at different parts, the waters which
roll in from the ocean being cold, but the lake warmed by flames
beneath the cave: indeed, each region of the cave, so far as my feet
ever reached in it, is always warm to the hand, and the atmosphere
warm, though thick, and sick with stinks of the sea.

After a long while I found the tinder-box within my pouch,
wherein also I found a chisel which I was bringing to my house to
sharpen on the night of my capture, and also a small gar or gimlet.
So I struck a flash that cut mine eyes like a gash, and I kindled a
rag, the which glowed a rich gore-colour upon an agitated water
rushing past the shore; and although only a small region of the
dark was lit up, I could see sufficient of the shore's sweep to understand that I was standing on a mainland made of granite, but not
altogether without marl on the ground, nigh behind me being a
grove of well-formed growths resembling elms, all gnarled and
venerable, yet no taller than my belly, although some do come to
my neck. Their leaves be milk-white, and even of a quite round
shape, and they do for ever shake themselves with the ground that

shakes, and produce a globose fruit, the which is blanched, too, and their boles pallid. I saw long afterwards another dwarf of just the same shape, only his fruit oozeth a juice like soap's water, that maketh a lather. On the lake also I have lately seen by the torch's light near the island a weed with leaves over two yards long, the which be caused to float on the water by small bladders attached to it; and also the marshy spot by the promontory is the forest of bulrushes, that show a tuft, or plume, at their summit, and they do shake themselves, their stem being about three feet high, and they shoot out a single root that groweth visible over the ground seven feet or more in his length, besides which, I observed none other shrubs, save a pale purple fungus, well-nigh white, growing on these rocks where I write, and in the corridor which is on this side of the pond of pitch.

But in that minute's glimmering, while my rag's light was dancing on the waves, I knew what super-abundance of food lay for me in this place, to be had by only putting forth of my hand: for in that paltry area of the water I saw pale creatures like snakes seven or eight feet long, tangled together in a knot, and some more alone, and four globose white beings, so that I could see that the lake is alive with life; and they lay there quite unaware of the light that pried on their whiteness, so that I decided that they be wights deprived of eyes. A very long time later on, probably many years, I came upon the stream to the lake's left, by the promontory, the which is thronged with oysters, with many sorts of pearl, and conch shells: but at the first I saw it not.

To have the creatures of the lake, I take stand to my knees in the water's margin (for farther I may not enter for the strength of the current), lean forward with the torch, and abide the coming of the creature of my liking, the which resembles the creatures called a trunk-fish in the tropics, being of triangular form, with freckles. The species of the creatures of the lake be few, though their number great; and, as all the plants be very pigmy, so all the animals be of great bigness, save one thing resembling a lizard, a finger in his length, that I have seen on the reefs, and his tail is formed in the shape of a leaf, and engorgeth itself grossly, and it gazeth through great globose eyeballs that glare lidless, but they be blind eyeballs; and one only wight of the lake has eyes, but they do hang by a twine out of his eye-sockets, and dangle about his countenance, and be blind. As to their catching, this I managed at starting without so much as a torch, but by the touch alone; nor do their sluggish natures struggle against my grabbing, but by their motions I understand the wonder that they have what creature he might be who removeth them from their secret home. The flesh of one and all is soft and watery, yet cruel tough, and crude to the tongue. My repasts at starting were ate raw; but afterwards I made fires with the tree-trunks, the which being dry-timbered, I could chop down with the chisel and a rock for my hammer. Later on when I did find out the rock-hall, I laid my fire there: but almost all the rags of my garments, except my jerkin, had been burned up for tinder, before I unearthed the marsh of bulrushes, whose pith served me from thenceforth both for tinder and food, and at present also for parchment: for, boiled in the hot rivulet in the rock-hall, the pith and fish together giveth an excellent good food, when, being voided of moisture, and pounded, they become a powder or flour; so that when I had once come at the bulrushes, where, too, are the oysters, being put upon the plan of boiling, I no more roasted my food as before.

For what appeared a long period, as it were long weeks, I mollified my thirst by soaking my body on the shore's verge, where the waves break; but thirst became a rage in my throat, like that lust of light in mine eyes, so that sometimes, pronouncing a shout, I did desperately drench my bowels, drinking my fill of the bitterness, the which, I am convinced, is more bitterer than the bitterness of the outer sea. By this time I had roamed exploring far around that part of the shore on which I was cast up, and had found about me a boundless house of caves, chambers, corridors, with dwarf forests, and stretches of sponges of stone, boulders, and tracts of basalt columns, a fantastic mass to me of rock and darkness, all racked, and like the aspen dancing, to the farthest point of my wandering, all inhabited by the noise of the waters' voice, and stinking of the sea with so raw a breath, that in several spots the nostrils scarce can bear it. There be shells of many shapes and dimensions upon the land, many enamelled with gems and pearl, sea-urchins also, star-fish, sea-cucumbers, and other sea-beasts with spines, mussels nigh to the promontory on the lake's left, corals, and many kinds of sponges, many monstrous huge and having a putrid stench, some, as it were, sponges of stones, others soft, and others of lucid glass, painted gallant with hues of the rainbow, and very gracious shaped, as hand-baskets, or ropes of glass, but crude of odour. Till I had set up my hearth in the rock-hall, I rambled about without any torch, for the cause that I knew not yet well the inflammable mood of the wood, nor had yet tumbled upon the sulphur, nor the pitch, with which to lard the torches; and, walking dark, with just a flash anon, I did often count my footsteps, it might be to a thousand, or two, till tired out. But spite of my ramblings, my body had knobs like leprosy, and was lacerated with my scratching, and racked with the rushing through me of the salt draughts which I drank, afore ever I chanced upon fresh water. That day I descended by three great steps that are made as by men's hands, and that lie peradventure half a mile from the lake, into a basalt hall, vastly capacious, so that forty chariots could race abreast therein; and the walls be as straight as the walls of masons, the roof low, only some twenty foot aloft, flat and smooth and black, and at the remote end of it a forest of basalt columns stands. There I marked that the air was even warmer than the warm air near the lake, and it was not long ere I had advanced into a hot steaming, with a sulphur stench, the which I had no sooner perceived than I fell upon my hands over a heap which proved, when I had struck a flash, to be slushy sulphur. I also saw a canal cut through the floor across the rock-hall's breadth, as regular as if graved there, this being two feet deep, as I discovered, and two feet across, through which canal babbled a black brook, bubbling hot, the floor on each bank of the canal being heaped with sulphur. I had soon scooped up some of the fluid with the tinder-box, and upon his cooling somewhat, I discovered it to be fresh, though sulphurous, and also tarry, in his taste; and thenceforth I had it always cooling in rows of conch shells by the rock-hall's left wall.

And during all the years of my tarrying in this tomb, the rock-hall hath become, in some manner, my home. There, in a corner nigh the three steps, I made up a fire; I put round it stones, and over the stones a slab, and plaiting my beard into my hair behind me, I there broiled my meat, until the time when I took to boiling the mixed trunk-fish and bulrush in the canal's boiling brook; and for a long while I kept the fire ever fed with wood from the tiny forests: for that I loved his light.

But, as to light, I have nineteen times beheld it in this dark from other causes than mine own fires, seventeen times the light being lightning: for lightning I must call it, the land lightning like the sky: and this I understand not at all. But I was standing by the water's margin, bent upon catching my white blindings, when the cavern became far and wide as it were an eye that wildly opened, winked five million to the minute, and as suddenly closed; and after a minute of thick darkness as afore, it opened once more, quick quivered, and closed. And there all ghast I stayed, in my heart's heart the ghast thought: "Thou, God, Seest Me." But though mine eyes staggered at the glare, I fancy that in fact it was but faint, and the ghost only of a glare, for of the cave's secrets little was thereby revealed unto me: and sixteen times in like wise his wings have quivered, and the wildness of his eye hath stared at me like the visitations of an archangel: and twice, besides, I have beheld the cave lighted by the volcano.

But it was long before ever the volcano came that I fell in with the mescal: for it was no long time after that surprise of lightning that, in pacing once to the shore to take up some trunk-fish which I had thrown in the slush there—I think eight or twelve years may then have gone over me—I happened to bruise in my fingers one of the pigmy globose fruit, and there oozed out of it a milk that I put to my lips. It was bitter, but I did swallow some drops unawares, the result whereof was wondrous: for even ere I reached the beach, an apathy enwrapped my being; I let myself drop down by the breakers' brim; my brow and body collapsed in a lassitude; and my lips let out the whisper: "pour on: but as for me, I will know rest." I was thereupon lapped in trances the most halcyon and

happy; the roaring rolled for me into such oratorios as my mouth
may not pronounce, though I appeared, so to speak, to *see*, more
than to hear, that music; and in the mean time mine eyes, fast
closed, had afore them a universe of hues in slow movement and
communion, hues glowing, and hues ghostly and gnomelike, some
of them new hues to me, so that I knew not at all how to call them,
with cataracts of pomegranate grains pattering, waves of parrot
green, wheels of raspberry reeling, dapplings of apple and pansy,
pallid eyeballs of bile and daffodil, pellucid tulips, brooks of
rubies, auroras, roses, all awork in a world earnester than Earth,
that it were empty to attempt to tell of.

I had heard tell at San Juan of the shrub which they do name
"the mescal button," chewed by the Mexicans to produce upon them
such revelations of hues; and I have concluded that this shrub of
the cave must be of nature akin. But though the gift of it transfigured that stink-pit beneath the sea into a region of the genii for
me, I was aware that to munch thereof was presumptuous, for the
troubles that his rancour bringeth upon the body of men were
quickly obvious upon me. But I made never an attempt to abandon
his happiness, for it wheeleth through the brain to so sweet a strain,
and talketh such gossip to the organs of the consciousness, as I do
not suppose to be true of the very lotus, nor of that pleasant root
that is known as nepenthe.

I have spent years on years, nay, as it seems to me, eras on
eras, in one dreaming by the sea's rim, while my soul, so to speak,
passed into the cataract's inmost roar, and became as one therewith. I lay there naked, for at first I had preserved my jerkin and
shirt to serve for tinder, until I tumbled upon the discovery of the
bulrush-pith, whereupon I employed the jerkin and shirt to contain the pith and fish for their boiling; so after the last of my
trouser's rags had shredded from around my legs, and my shoes,
too, from my feet, through great periods of time I have lain there
naked, though enveloped to my belly in my hair and beard, idly
dreaming, finding it too dreary a trial to seethe my food, and often
eating raw, having long agone let the fire in the rock-hall go out.
In the end I have shirked even the burden of bending in the sea's

surf, or of journeying to the mussel stream, to get at my grub, and will spend considerable periods with never a hit other drink or meat than that bittersweet milk of the mescal.

From this life of sloth twice only have I been disturbed by fright, the first time when the volcano came, the second time when I observed the increasing dearth of air to breathe; and on each occasion I was spurred to take torch and search further afield than e'er before what the vault holds—in both searches meeting with what turned out serviceable to my needs: for in the first search I butted on the bulrush bush, which I believe I butted on years ere I observed this increasing dearth of air; and it was the increasing dearth of air which sent me peering further a second time, and then I saw the pond of pitch. This latter is beyond the forest of basalt columns at the far end of the rock-hall; and it was in passing to it through those columns that I saw the beast's bones, that be bigger, I believe, than several elephants together, although the beast resembles an elephant, having straight tusks, exceeding long; and his jaw hath six huge teeth, very strange, every several tooth being made of littler ones, the which cling about it like nipples; and there among those pillars his ribs may have rested for many a century, some of them being now brittle and embrowned; and beyond the pillars is a passage, perfectly curved, having a purplish fungus growing upon his rock; and beyond the passage is a cavern than whose threshold I could no farther advance, for the bed thereof is a bitumen sea, which is half-warm and thick at the brink, but, I think, liquid hot in the middle; and all over his face broods a universe of rainbows, dingy and fat, which be from the fat vapours of the pitch bringing forth rainbows, not rainbows of heaven, but, so to say, fallen angels, grown gross and sluggish. But years ere this, I think, I had seen the bulrushes: for, soon after the volcano came, in roaming over the left shore of the cataract's sea—the which left shore is flat and widespread, and hath no high walls like the right side—I walked upon a freshet of fresh warm water, and after following it upward, saw all round a marsh's swamp, and the bush of bulrushes. This is where the oysters be so crass, and they be pearl oysters, for all that soil be crass with nacreous matter of every sort, with barrok pearls, mother-of-pearl, and in most of the oysters which I opened pearls, with a lot of conch shells that have within them pink pearls, and there be also the black pearl, such as they have in Mexico and the West Indies, with the yellow and likewise the white, which last be shaped like the pear, and large, and his pallor hath a blank brightness, very price less, and, so to say, bridal. As to the bulrush his trunk is triangular (like the trunk-fish), some five inches wide at the bottom, and giveth a white pith good for food. I came, moreover, upon the discovery after a long time that, since this pith lieth in layers, these, being steeped in water, and afterwards dried, do shrink to a parchment, quite white and soft, but tending to be yellow and brittle in time.

But for these two adventures, first to the bulrushes, and then to the pond or sea of pitch, I cannot remember that that long trance I had by the shore was broken by any excursion. But I had a rough enough rousing in that hour when, upon opening mine eyes, I beheld, not the old darkness, but all the hall disclosed in scarlet, and felt the cavern in movement, not with that proper trembling that I knew, due to the pre ponderousness of the cataract's mass over the earth's fabric, but racked with an earthquake's racking: and when mine eyes, now shyer than the night-bird's, recovered their courage, I observed the sea's whole surface heaved up like sand-heaps, dandled up with the earthquake's dancing. Now also for the first time I saw aloft to my right the tunnel's monstrous mouth, out of which the cataract's mass tumbleth down, the mouth's top rim being rounded, like the top lip of a man's mouth crying aloud. I saw also the cataract rolling hoary across his whole breast's breadth, woolly with flocks and beards of froth, as it were Moses' beard, except at the centre, where it gallops glassy smooth and more massy, for there the sea cometh out from the tunnel's inwards to stretch itself out in that mouth that shouteth aloud. I saw also the roof like a rufous sky of rock, and right before mine eyes lay an island, long and narrow, upon the which I had been cast at the first, for there yet lay the portugal on the right end of the island, that right end lying quite nigh the cataract, and the island's left end some twenty yards from the lake's left end. And I saw the

lake in his entirety by spying over the island's centre, where the
land lies low, the lake having an egg's form, perhaps two miles in
his length, I being at the egg's small end. I saw also that the cave's
right side, where the wall rises sheer, is washed directly by the
lake's wheeling career; and since the cataract there crashes down,
along that right side I cannot advance; nor along the cave's left
side can I advance so much as a mile, for there a headland juts out
into the lake, dividing that side of the cave into two great rooms. I
saw also nigh the far shore of the lake four more small islands of
rock, and I was shewn, from the lake's ocean-like aspect, that his
waters be vastly profound, his bottom being doubtless housed far
down in the planet's bowels. All was lit up, and some distance beyond the lake's far boundaries I saw the mouth of some cave,
through which came up a haze of radiance sparkling, and vaulting
stones, and therewith some tongues of flame, which now showed,
and now withdrew their rouge.

I gathered that some volcanic action was going on under the
cavern, and as I there stayed, agape at it, I saw arise out of the
lake in the remote distance, and come toward me, a thing, with the
which I so long had lived, and known it not. His body lay soft in
curves on the billows nigh a furlong behind his uplifted head, and
I could not fly, nor turn mine eyes from the pitifulness of his appearing in the light. His head and face be of the dimension of a
cottage, having a shameful likeness to a death's-head, being bony,
skinny, and very tight-skinned, and of a mucky white colour, with
freckles. It hath a forehead and nose-ridge, but, where eyes should
be, stands blank skin only; and it drew nigh me with the toothless
house of his mouth wide open in a scream of fear, distrusting Him
that made it: for the air was waxing still hotter, and it may have
had an instinct of calamity, peradventure from some experience
of the volcano's fierceness a century since. It travelled nigh under
the island's right end through the cataract's foam, and then close
under me, nor could see me look at his discovered nudity, nor could
my rooted foot flee from it; and on it journeyed, circling the lake's
surface with the dirge of his lamentation. Immediately after I lost
my reason through the fierceness of the heat, and reeled; and when

I came back to myself the cave was as black as ever. And once again, long afterwards, I saw flames flutter in the cave beyond the lake, a grey dust rained over the lake's face, the great creature arose, and a grove of the trees at this end were seared with heat; but since then the event has never been seen.

But it was soon subsequent to this second convulsion that I made an observation: to wit, that unless I was well under the rule of the mescal fruit—when I do scarce seem to breathe—I became aware of an oppression of the chest. And this grew with me; so that I began to commune within me, saying: "Though the cavern be vast, the air that it containeth must be of limited volume, and I have inhaled it long: for whereas when I hither came I was a young thing, I am now old. My lungs have day by day consumed the wholesome air; and the day approacheth when I must surely perish."

At the commencement it was only when I lay me to rest that the trouble oppressed me, but, sat I up, it passed; then after, if I sat, it oppressed me; but, stood I up, it passed: so that I understood it to be so that a lake of noxious vapour lay at the bottom of the air of this place, a lake due to my breathing, that each year grew in depth and noxiousness, the longer I breathed: this vapour having a sleepy effect, not happy like the mescal's, but highly unhappy, making me nightmares and aches of my body. In the beginning I got relief by going to live in other regions than in the rockhall and on the beach: but in every direction my way hath now been blocked, for I have now inhabited in turn every cranny of the cavern whereto I am able to penetrate, and the vapour is in all, troubling also the shrubs of all sorts, the which let fall their heads, and shed their health. There remain some coigns among the rockeries, wherein, when I toil aloft to them, I may yet breathe with some freedom; but that my days are numbered I know. My God! my God! why hast Thou created me?

But soon after understanding the manner of my undoing, I began to argue in myself as regards the cavern and his architecture as never formerly, arguing that whereas so great volumes of water came in, and the vault was not filled, there must needs be some outlet for an equal volume to flow out. I was led to conjecture that the tunnel which admits the sea into the cavern is at some sea-mountain's summit; that the cavern must be in the mountain's bowels; and that the outflow out of the cavern must be down another much longer tunnel, leading down to the mountain's bottom into the sea. I therefore conceived the notion that, if I could reach the portugal, get it repaired, and, in it, introduce myself into the tunnel of outflow (the which I knew to be beyond the head land on the lake's left, where the lake's two wheeling currents meet), then I should be carried down and out into the bottom of the sea, should thereupon rise to the sea's surface—for the unweighted portugal would certainly float with me—and there I might bore a hole or two in the portugal's upper belly for air, and be picked up by a ship before my stores were done, and before my death from hunger or suffocation, I being well drugged with the mescal, and so but little breathing or eating. As to introducing myself into the tunnel of outflow, nothing more was necessary than to get the portugal to the headland's end, get myself into it, and roll myself in the portugal from the headland's end into the lake: where the currents would not fail to bear me toward the place of outflow, and I should be sucked down into the tunnel.

I meditated that the stupendousness of the attempt in no fashion lessened my chance: for that laws will act exactly on the immense scale as on the small. The portugal I could get to by going into the lake at the egg's-point of the lake, whence the current would carry me away along the left shore toward the inland, the left end whereof I might catch by continually swimming strong to the right; and lest I should be dashed to fragments in my grand journey through the tunnel, I determined to pad the portugal's inside with the bulrush pith; and moreover I devised a sliding-door in the portugal's side, the which when I should reach the sea's surface would be furnishing me with breathing: in the making whereof I did not doubt but that my former craft in carpentry would help me out. That I might be struck blind by the moon's brightness, and surely by the sun's, upon opening mine eyes up there above I reflected: but I price eyes as of but paltry value to a man, and should estimate it no hardship to dispense with mine, such as they are.

On the whole, I had no fear; and the reason of my fearlessness, as I at present perceive, lay in this: that in my heart I never at all intended to attempt the venture. It was a fond thought: for, granting that I got out, how could I live without the cataract? I should surely die. And what good were life to me there in the glare of day, without the mescal's joys, and without the secret presence of the voice, and the thing which it secretly shouteth? In such separation from the power of my life I should pass frailly away as a spectre at day-break: for by the power of the voice is my frail life sustained, and thereon I hang, and therein I have my being. And this in my soul I must have known: but in the futile mood that possessed me, I made three several attempts to gain the portugal, terrified the while at mine own temerity; and twice I failed to make the left end of the island, for the current carried me beyond—toward the tunnel of outflow, I doubted not; yet were my terrors not of that horror mainly, but of the monster in the lake's depth, the which stayeth there pale and pensive, meditating his meditations: for I knew that if my foot or hand just touched his skin, I must assuredly reel and sink, shrieking mad, since I swam dark, but having an unlighted torch in my hand, the tinder-box being tied within my beard; and the first twice I was hurled to land upon the headland, but the third time upon the island's left end, and the rock of which I clambered up with my hands lacerated by shells. And after lighting the torch, I wrought my steps toward the island's right end; and there lay the portugal even as I had left it twenty, forty, years ago, the slime on his side yet wet from the water-fall's aura that haunts the island. And in that spot I saw, not the portugal alone, but moreover a sword's hilt, a human skull, and a clock's racket, thither tossed by the cataract. The portugal was still good, for the pitch which is on it: and having cast out the drado by an effort of all my strength, I struck out four of the nails from the three bottom pieces that had been sprung, nailed the three pieces, and the broken hoop of wood, too, to the side of the portugal, and so consigned the portugal to the waters, the which, I was assured, would bear it to the small end of the lake's egg-shape, as they had borne me upon mine ancient fall from the island.

But I had myself no sooner been spued again upon the mainland, more dead than alive, and there found the portugal stranded,
then I knew myself for a futile dreamer, wearying myself without
sincere motive: for that I should really abandon the cavern was a
thing not within the capability of nature. And there by the shore's
edge I left the portugal lying a good while, abiding for the most
part upon the crags of these rocks that be like gradients on the
right side of the hall, until that day when it was suggested to my
spirit how strangely had been given me both ink and paper in this
place, the knowledge moreover how to get the portugal forth of
the grot with a history of that thing which my God in song hath
murmured unto me, having furtively hid me with His hand, though
a seraph's pen could never express it; nor could I long resist the
pressure of that suggestion to write, and send forth the writing in
the portugal.

For the portugal's mending I had the gimlet, the chisel, mescal-
timber, and some of the nails from the sprung bottom, which could
be spared; nor was the job hard, since the one started hoop could
be nicely spliced. I rolled and got the portugal up to this level
ground in the rocks, surrounding myself, as I wrought, with tarred
torches, which I stuck in the rocks' cracks: for down below it is
reluctantly if a fire will now burn; and at this height also the torches
do burn with shy fires.

Or ever the portugal was repaired, I had got ready the pages
for writing, having divided fifteen of the bulrush piths into strips,
then wetted, and dried them; but there be spongy spots in them
where the lampblack that I have manufactured out of the pitch
runneth rather abroad under the spling of fish-bone that serves
for my pen, hurting the fairness of my writing. That I could write
at all I rather doubted, on the count that I have not for so long
handled pen nor spoken, and on the count moreover of the trembling: for not only the pen trembleth by reason of mine age, but
the parchment trembleth by reason of the vault's trembling; and
between these two tremblements, in a sick sheen which flickers
ever, these sheets have, letter by letter, been writ. The fifteen sheets

of pith, moreover, have proved too little, and I am writing now on the second of two sheets that are sections of a fish's skin.

But now it is finished: and I send it out, if so be a fellow in the regions above may read it, and know. My name, if I have not yet writ it down, was James Dowdy Saul; and I was born not far from the borough of Bideford in the county of Devon.

My God! My God! why hast Thou created me?

I ask it: for the question ariseth of itself to my mind because of the crass facts of my predicament; yet my heart knoweth it, Lord God, to be the grumble of an ingrate: for a hidden thing is, that is winninger than wife, or child, or the shining of any light, and is like unto treasure hid in a field, the which when a man findeth, he selleth all, and buyeth that field; and I thank, I do thank Thee, for Thy voice, and for my lot, and that it was Thy will to ravish me: for the charm of Thy secret is more than the rose, exceeding utterance.

THE PLACE OF PAIN

Though my theme is about the place of evil, and about how the Rev. Thomas Podd saw it, it is rather a case of evil in heaven: for I think British Columbia very like heaven, or like what I shall like my heaven to be, if ever I arrive so high—one mass of mountains, with mirrors of water mixed up with them, torrents and forests, and roaring Rhones.

It was at Small Forks that it happened, where I went to pass a fortnight—and stayed five years; and how the place changed and developed in that short time is really incredible, for at first Small Forks was the distributing center of only three mining-camps, and I am sure that not one quarter of the district's two million tons of ore of today was then thought of.

At the so-called Scatchereen Lode, three miles from the lake, there was one copper smelter, but not one silver-lead mine within fifty miles, and no brewery, no machine-shop, no brick plant. Nor had Harper Falls as yet been thought of as a source of power.

It was Harper Falls that proved to be the undoing of Pastor Thomas Podd, as you are to hear; and I alone have known that it was so, and why it was so.

I think I saw Podd in my very first week at Small Forks—one evening on the Embankment.

(You may know that Small Forks runs along the shore of an arm of Lake Sakoonay, embowered in bush at the foot of its mountains—really very like a nook in Paradise, to my mind.)

Podd that evening was walking with another parson on the Embankment, and the effect of him upon me was the raising of a smile, my eye at that time being unaccustomed to the sight of black men in parsons' collars and frocks. But Podd was rather brown than black—a meagre little man of fifty, with prominent cheek bones, hollow cheeks, a scraggy rag of beard, a cocky carriage, and a forehead really intellectual, though his eyes did strike me as rather wild and scatterbrained.

He was a man of established standing in all Small Forks, where a colony of some forty colored persons worked at the lumber-mills. To these Podd preached in a corrugated chapel at the top of Peel Street.

He held prayer-meetings on Monday nights, and one Monday night, when I had been in Small Forks a month or so, I stepped into his conventicle, on coming home from a tramp, and heard the praying—or, rather, the demanding, for those darkies banged the pew-backs and shook them irritably.

When it was over and I was going out, I felt a tap on my back, and it was the reverend gentleman, who had raced after the stranger. Out he pops his pompous paw, and then, with a smile, asked if I was "thinking of joining us." I was not doing that, but I said that I had been "interested," and left him.

Soon after this he called to see me, and twice in three months he had tea with me—in the hope of a convert, perhaps. He did not succeed in this, but he did succeed in interesting me.

The man had several sciences at his finger-ends; I discovered that he had a genuine passion for Nature; and I gathered—from himself, or from others, I can't now remember—that it was his habit ever and anon to cut himself off from humankind, so as to lose himself for a few days in that maze of mountains in which the Sakoonay district towers toward the moon.

No pressure of business, no consideration or care, could keep Podd tame and quiet in Small Forks when this call of the wild enticed him off. It seems to have been long a known thing about the town, this trick of his character, and to have been condoned and pardoned as part of the man. He had been born within forty miles of Small Forks, and seemed to me to know Columbia as a farmer knows his two-acre meadow.

Well, some two weeks after that second visit of his to me the news suddenly reached me that something had gone wrong in the Rev. Thomas Podd's head—could not help reaching me, for the thing was the gossip and laugh of the district far outside Small Forks.

It appears that late on the Saturday evening the reverend gentleman had come home from one of his vast tramps and truant interviews with Nature; then, on the Sunday morning, he had entered the meeting-house scandalously late, and had reeled with the feet of some moon-struck creature into the pulpit—without his coat! without his collar! his braces hanging down!—and then, leaning his two elbows on the pulpit Bible, he had looked steadily, mockingly, at his flock of black sheep, and had proceeded to jeer and sneer at them.

He had called them frankly a pack of apes, a band of black and babbling babies; said that he could pity them from his heart, they were so benighted, so lost in darkness; that what they knew in their woolly nuts was just nothing; that no one knew, save him, Podd; that he alone of men knew what he knew, and had seen what he had seen. . . .

Well, he had been so much respected for his intellectual parts, his eloquence, his apparent sincerity as a Christian man, that his congregation seem to have taken this gracelessness with a great deal of toleration, hoping perhaps that it might be only an aberration which would pass; but when the revered gentleman immediately afterwards took himself off anew into his mountains, to disappear for weeks—no one knew where—that was too much. So when he came back at last, it was to see another dark parson filling his place.

From that moment his social degeneration was rapid. He abandoned himself to poverty and tatters. His wife and two daughters shook the dust of him from off their shoes, and left Small Forks— to find a livelihood for themselves somewhere, I suppose. But Podd remained, or, at any rate, was often to be met in Small Forks, when he condescended to descend from his lofty walks.

Once I saw him intoxicated on the Embankment, his braces down, his hat in tatters—though I am certain that he never became a drunkard. Anyway, the thin veneer of respectability came off him like wet paint, and he slipped happily back into savagery. On what he lived I don't know.

I met him one afternoon by the new shipbuilding yard which the Canadian Pacific Railway was running up half a mile out of Small Forks. He sat there on a pile of axed pine-trunks lying by the roadside, his chest and one shin showing through his rags, his eyes gloating on the sky, in which a daylight moon was swooning; but, on catching sight of me, he showed his fine rows of teeth, crying out flippantly in French: "*Ah, monsieur, ça va bien?*"—in French, because Negroes are given to a species of frivolity in speech which expresses itself in that way.

I stopped to speak to him, asking "What has it been all about, Podd—the sudden collapse from sanctity to naughtiness?"

"Ah, now you are asking something!" he answered flippantly, with a wink at me.

I saw that he had become woefully emaciated and saffron, his cheek-bones seeming to be near appearing through their sere skin, and his eyes had in them the fire of a man living a life of some continual exaltation or excitement.

I wished, if I could, to help him; and I said, "Something must have gone wrong inside or out; better make a clean breast of it, and then something may be done."

On this he suddenly became fretful, saying, "Oh, you all think like a blame lot of silly little babies fumbling in the dark!"

"That is so," I answered; "but since you are wise, why not tell us the secret, and then we shall all be wise?"

"I tell you what"—shaking his head up and down, his lips turned down— "I doubt if some of them could stand the sight; turn their hairs white!"

"Which sight?" I asked.

"The sight of Hell!" he sighed, throwing up his hand a little.

After a little silence I said "Now, that's rot, Podd."

"Yes, sure to be, Sir, since you say so," he answered quietly in a dejected way. "That, of course, is what they said to Galileo when he told them that this globe moves."

With as grave a face as I could maintain, I looked at him, asking, "Have you seen Hell, Podd?"

"I may have," he answered; and he added "And so have you, by the way. You have probably seen it since you started out on this walk you are taking, and haven't known."

"Well, it can't be very terrible, can it," I said, "if one can see it and not know? But is Hell in Small Forks? For I'm straight from there."

At this he threw up his head with a rather bitter laugh saying "Yes, that's beautiful, that the ignorant should make game of those who know, and the worse be judges of the better! But, then, that's how it generally is." And now, all at once, whatever blood he had rushed into his face, and he pointed upward: "You see that world there?"

"The moon?" I said, looking up.

"The souls in that place live in pain," I heard him murmur, his chin suddenly sunken to his chest.

"So there are people on the moon, Podd?" I asked. "Surely you know that there is no air there? Or do you mean to imply that the moon is Hell?"

He looked up, smiling. "My, goodness, you'd give a lot to know, wouldn't you? Well, look here, I'll say this and it's the truth: that I've had a liking for you from the first, and I'll make you a business proposition, as it's you. You agree to give me three dollars a week so long as I live, and when I'm dying I'll tell you what I know, and how, teaching you the whole trick. Or I'll put it in writing in a sealed envelope, which you shall have on my death."

"Dear me," I said, "what a pity I can't afford it!"

"You can afford it well enough," was his answer, "but the truth is that you don't believe a word of what I say: you think I'm moonstruck. And so I am, a bit! By Heaven, that's true enough!"

He sighed and was silent some time, looking at the moon in a most abstracted manner, apparently forgetting my presence.

But presently he went on to say "Still, a spec., you might risk it. The payments wouldn't be for long, for I've developed consumption, I see—the curse of us colored folks—had a hemorrhage only yesterday. And then, as a charity, you might, for I'm mostly hungry—my own fault; but I couldn't keep on gassing to those poor fools, after seeing what I have seen. If you won't give me the three dollars a week, give me one."

Well, to this I consented—not, of course, in any expectation of ever hearing any "secret," but I saw that the man had become quite unworldly, unfit to earn his living, I considered him more or less insane—still consider so, though I am convinced now that he was not nearly so insane as I conceived: so I promised him that he might draw a weekly dollar from my bank while I was in Small Forks.

Sometimes Podd drew his dollar, but often he did not, though he was aware that arrears would not be paid, if he failed to present himself any week. And so it went on for over four years, during which he became more and more emaciated, and a savage.

Meantime, Small Forks and the Sakoonay district had ceased to laugh at the name of Podd, as at a stale joke, and the fact of his rags and degradation had become a local institution, like the Mounted Police or the sawdust mill—too familiar a thing in the eye to excite any kind of emotion in the mind.

But at the end of those four years Small Forks, like one man, rose against Podd.

It happened in this way: at that date the Sakoonay district was sending an annual cut of some four hundred million feet of lumber to the Prairie Provinces; the mining and smelter companies had increased to four—big concerns, treating three to four thousand tons of ore a day; in which consideration of things all through the district had arisen the cry: "Electricity! Electricity!"

Hence the appearance in Small Forks of the Provincial Mineralogist with a pondering and responsible forehead; hence his report to the Columbian Government that Harper Falls were capable of developing 97,000 horse-power; hence a simmering of interest through the district; and hence the decision of the Small Forks Town Council to inaugurate a municipal power-plant at Harper Falls.

But Podd objected!

He thought—this is what I found out afterwards—that Harper Falls were his; and he did not wish to have them messed with, or people coming anywhere near them.

However, he said nothing; the new works were commenced—so far as the accumulation of material was concerned; and the first hint of a hitch in the business was given one midnight of the beginning of May—a night I'll ever remember—when the mass of the municipality's material was burnt to cinders.

The blaze made a fine display five miles out of Small Forks, and I witnessed it in the thick of a great crowd of the townspeople.

It was assumed that the thing had been deliberately done by someone, since there was no other explanation. But the mystery as to who had done it!—for there was no one to suspect. And, like a spider whose web had been torn, the municipality started once more to collect materials for the plant.

Then, at the end of June, occurred the second blaze.

But this time there were night-watchmen with open eyes, and one of them deposed that he believed that he had seen Podd suspiciously near the scene of the mischief.

The town was very irritated about it, since the power-plant was expected to do great things for everybody.

At any rate, when Podd was captured and questioned, he did not exactly deny.

"It might have been I," was his answer; and "what if it was I?"

And this answer was a proof to me that he was innocent, for I took it to be actuated by vanity or insanity. The authorities must have thought so, too, for the man was dismissed as a ninny.

The town, however, was indignant at his dismissal; and three days later I came upon him in the midst of a crowd, from which I doubt that he could have come out alive, but for me, for he was now nothing but a bundle of bones, lighted up by two eyes. Indeed, my interference was rather plucky of me, for there present was a North-West policeman lending his countenance to the hustling of the poor outcast, a real-estate agent, the sawdust-mill manager, reeking of turpentine, and others, whose place it was to have interfered. Anyhow, I howled a little speech, pledging myself that the man was innocent; and my éclat as a Briton, perhaps, helped me to get him gasping out of their grasp.

When he found himself alone with me on the road outside the town, down he suddenly knelt, and, grasping my legs, began to sob to me in a paroxysm of gratitude.

"You have been everything to me—you, a stranger. God reward you—I have not long to live, but you shall know what I know, and see what I have seen."

"Podd," I said, "you have heard me pledge my word that you are innocent. Let me hear from you this instant that it was not you who committed those outrages."

With the coolest insolence he stood up, looked in my face, and said, "Of course I committed them. Who else?"

I had to laugh. But then I sternly observed, "Well, but you confess yourself a felon, that's all."

"Look here," he answered, "let's not quarrel. We see from different standpoints—let's not quarrel. What I say is, that during the few weeks or months I have to live no plant is going to be set up at Harper Falls—afterwards, yes. You don't know what I know about the Falls. They are the eye of this world; that's it—the eye of this world. But you shall know and see"—he looked up at the westering quarter-moon, thought a little, and continued: "Meet me here at nine on Friday night. You've done a lot for me."

The man's manner was so convincing, that I undertook to meet him, though some minutes afterwards I laughed at myself for being so impressed by his pratings.

Anyway, two nights thence, at nine, I met Podd, and we began a tramp and climb of some seven miles which I shall ever remember.

If I could but give some vaguest impression of that bewitched adventure, I should begin to think well of my power of expression; but the reality of it would still be far from pictured.

That little dying Podd had still the foot of a goat, and we climbed spots which, but for his aid, I could scarcely have negotiated—ghostly gullies, woods of spruce and dreary old cedar droning, the crags of Garroway Pass, where a throng of torrents awe one's ear, and tarns asleep in the dark of forests of larch, of hemlock, of white and yellow pine.

We were struggling upward through a gullock of Garroway Pass when Podd stopped short; and when I groped for him—for one could see nothing there—I discovered him with his forehead leant against the crag.

To my question, "Anything wrong?" he answered, "Wait a little—there's blood in my mouth."

And he added "I think I am going to have a hemorrhage."

"We had better go back," I said.

But he presently brightened up, saying, "It will be all right. Come."

We stumbled on.

Half an hour afterwards we came out upon a platform about eight hundred yards square, surrounded by cliffs of pine on three sides. A torrent dropped down the back cliff, ran over most of the platform in a rather broad river, lacerated by rocks, and dropped frothing in a cataract over the front of the platform.

"Here we are," Podd said, seating himself on a rock, dropping his forehead to his knees.

"Podd, you are in trouble," I said, standing over him.

He made no answer, but presently raised himself with an effort, to look at the moon with eyes that were themselves like moons—the satellite, about half-full, then waxing; and now in her setting quadrant.

"Now, look you," Podd said with pantings and tremblings, so that I had to bend down to hear him in that row of the waters, "I have brought you here because I love you a lot. You are about to see things that no mortal's eye but mine ever wept salt water at—"

As he uttered those words, I, for the first time, with a kind of shock, realized that I was really about to see something boundless for I could no longer doubt that those pantings had the accent of

truth; in fact, I suddenly knew that they were true, and my heart
began to beat faster.

"But how will you take the sight?" he went on. "Am I really doing you a service? You see the effect it has had on me—to think
that what made us—our own—should bring forth such bitterness!
No, you shan't see it all, not the worst bit; I'll stop the view there.
You see that fall rushing down at our feet? I have the power, by
placing a certain rock in a certain position in this river, to change
that mass of froth into a mass of glass—two masses of glass—immense lenses, double-convex. Discovered it by accident one night
five years since—night of my life. No, I am not well tonight. But
never mind. You go down the face of the rock at the side here—
easy going—till you come to the cave. Go into the cave; then climb
by the notches which you'll find in the wall, till you come to a ledge,
one edge of which is about two feet behind the inner eyepiece. The
moon should begin to come within your view within four minutes
from now; and I give you a five minutes' sight—no more. You'll see
her some three hundred yards from you tearing across your brain
like ten trillion trains. But never you tell any man what you see on
her. Go, go! Not very well tonight."

He stood up with an effort so painful, that I said to him "But
are you going into the river, Podd, and trembling like that already?
Why not show me how to place the rock for you?"

"No," he muttered, "you shan't know; you shan't! It's all right;
I'll manage; you go. Keep moving your eye at first till you get the
focus-length. There's a lot of prismatic and spherical aberration,
iridescent fringes, and the yellow line of the spectrum of sodium
bothers everywhere—the object-glass is so big and so thin, that it
hardly seems at all to decompose light. Never mind, you'll see
well—upside down, of course—dioptric-telescope images. Go, go;
don't waste time; I'll manage with the stone. And you must always
say—I paid you back—full measure—for all your love."

At every third word of all this his breast gave up a gasp, and
his eyes were most wild with excitement or the fever of disease.
He pushed and led me to the spot where I was to descend. And
"There she comes," his tongue stuttered, with a nod at the moon,

as he flew from me, while I went feeling my way with my feet, the cataract at my right, down a cliff-side that was nearly perpendicular, but so rugged and shrub-grown, that the descent was easy.

When I was six feet down I lifted my chin to the ledge, and saw Podd stooping within some bush at the foot of the platform-cliff to my left, where he had evidently hidden the talisman-rock; and I saw him lift the rock, and go tottering under its weight toward the river.

But the thought came to me that it was hardly quite fair to spy upon him, and when he was still some yards from the river I went on down—a long way—until I came to the floor of the cave in the cliff face, a pretty roomy cavern, fretted with spray from the cataract in front of it.

I went in and climbed to the ledge, as he had said; and there in the dark I lay waiting, wet through, and, I must confess, trembling, hearing my heart knocking upon my ribs through that solemn oratory of the torrent dropping in froth in front of me. And presently through the froth I thought I saw a luminous something that must have been the moon, moving by me.

But the transformation of the froth into the lenses which I awaited did not come.

At last I lifted my voice to howl, "Hurry up, Podd!"—though I doubted if he could hear.

Anyway, no answer reached my ear, and I waited on.

It must have been twenty minutes before I decided to climb down; I then scrambled out, clambered up again, disgusted and angry, though I don't think that I ever believed that Podd had wilfully made a fool of me. I thought that he had somehow failed to place the rock.

But when I got to the top I saw that the poor man was dead.

He lay with his feet in the river, his body on the bank, his rock clasped in his arms. The weight had proved too much for him: on the rock was blood from his lungs.

Two days later I buried him up there with my own hands by his river's brink, within the noise of the song of his waterfall, his stupendous telescope—his "eye of this world."

And then for three months, day after day, I was endeavouring in that solitude up there so to place the rock in the river as to transform the froths of the waterfall into frothless water. But I never managed. The secret is buried with the one man whom destiny intended, maybe for centuries to come, to know what paths are trodden, and what tapestries are wrought, on another orb.

COACHWHIP PUBLICATIONS

COACHWHIPBOOKS.COM

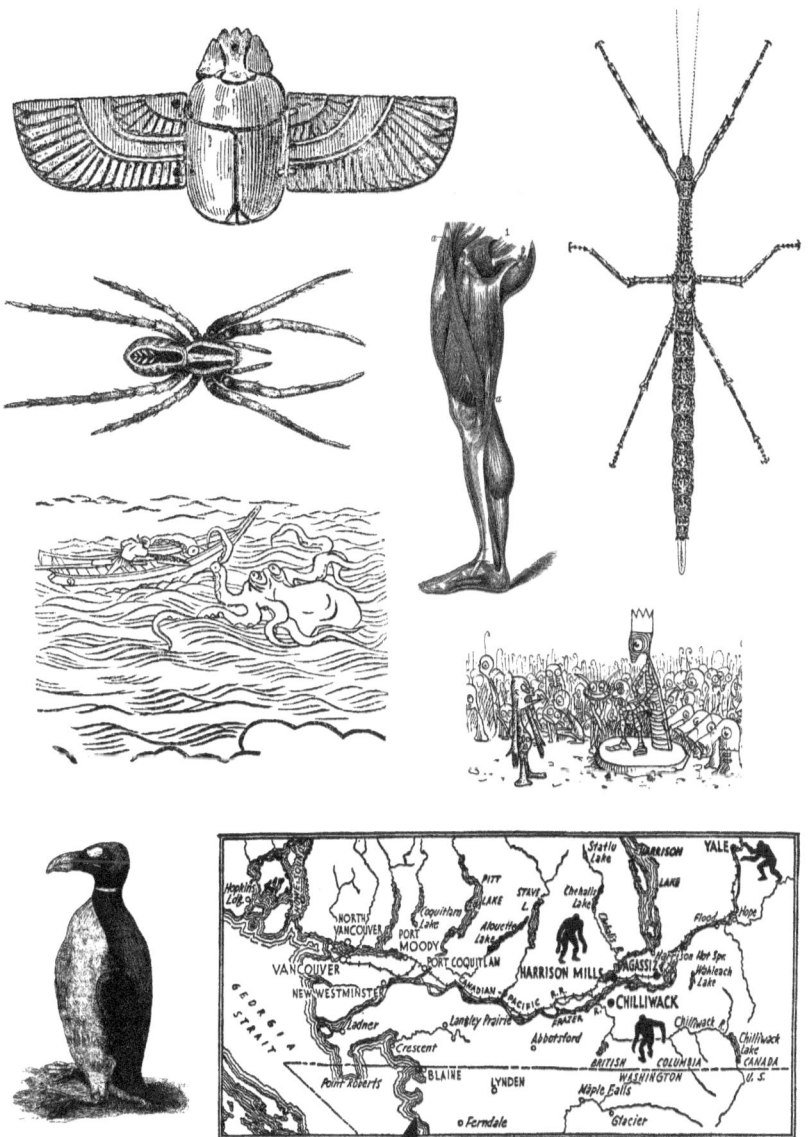

Ancient Haunts:
Stoneground Ghost Tales / Tedious Brief Tales
ISBN 1-61646-005-9

COACHWHIP PUBLICATIONS

COACHWHIPBOOKS.COM

BLACK SPIRITS
AND WHITE
RALPH ADAMS CRAM

TALES OF THE
SUPERNATURAL
JAMES PLATT

SHADOWS GOTHIC
AND GROTESQUE

Shadows Gothic and Grotesque
ISBN 1-61646-059-8

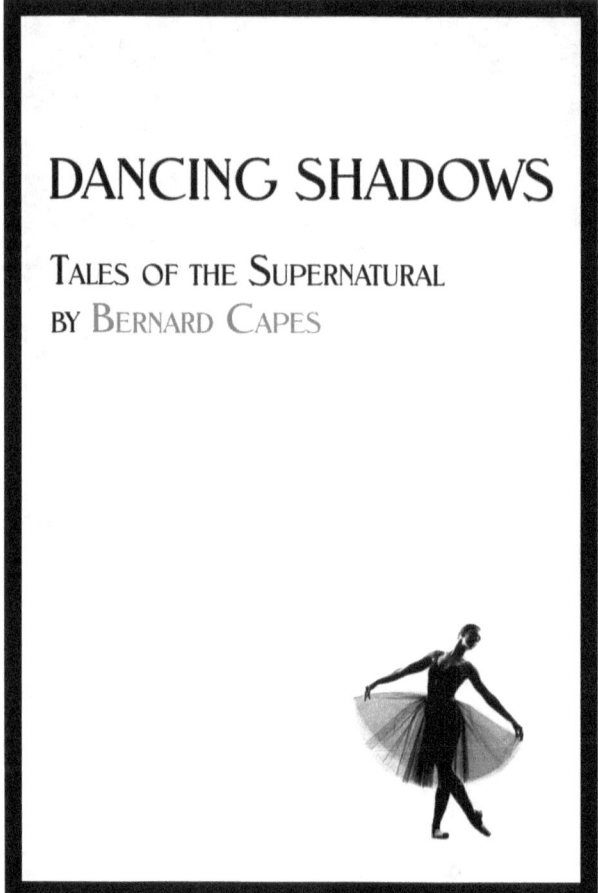

DANCING SHADOWS

TALES OF THE SUPERNATURAL
BY BERNARD CAPES

Dancing Shadows:
Tales of the Supernatural by Bernard Capes
ISBN 1-61646-093-8

Coachwhip Publications

CoachwhipBooks.com

Days of Doom:
Apocalyptic Visions & Unearthly Nightmares
ISBN 1-61646-110-1

www.ingramcontent.com/pod-product-compliance
Lightning Source LLC
Chambersburg PA
CBHW051255250626
47155CB00009B/3300